NOT MY BOWL OF RICE

By

B. R. Escober

ISBN: 1-4033-8882-2 (e-book)
ISBN: 1-4033-8883-0 (Paperback)
ISBN: 1-4033-8884-9 (Dustjacket)

Library of Congress Control Number: 2002095394

This book is printed on acid free paper.

Printed in the United States of America
Bloomington, IN

1stBooks - rev. 11/22/02

ACKNOWLEDGEMENTS

MARAMING SALAMAT PO!

Many people helped shape and complete this novel. To all of them, many, many thanks! *Maraming, maraming salamat po!*

To my friends and relatives who read the manuscript at various stages and have been so kind, encouraging and insightful throughout.

To my wonderful editor, Robin Smith, who told me that she smiled a lot and cried a couple of times too while reading and editing my book, which she described as 'entertaining, touching, instructive and charming.'

To my mother, Caridad, who left me with priceless legacies including much information about Filipino customs and traditions and most of the recipes in this book. Wherever you are, I know in my heart of hearts, you are shining on me everyday.

To my friend and soulmate, Paul. I'm happy and grateful that you are a salient part of my life. Without you, I am incomplete.

And finally, to all the immigrants in America and around the world. This book is for all of us.

Maraming Salamat Po!

-"It's not really my bowl of rice."
                                        - Mother

"Why do you always say that? The correct thing to say is, It's not my cup of tea!" I told Mother one day, fed-up with her made-up idiom, also irritated that she didn't think she felt like going to an air-conditioned matinee on that sweltering Philippine summer afternoon.

"Oy," she pointed out. "Look around you. Do you see any cups of tea lying around?" she asked, gesturing at our lunch table filled with wondrous Filipino dishes: pork adobo, lumpia, chicken barbecue and rice, lots of rice. Reluctantly, I shook my head. No tea. The only tea I drank was Salabat, ginger tea, and only when I was sick during the cold season or as a holiday drink on Christmas morning.

"No, huh? But look, bowls of rice! Bowls and bowls of rice! So, I say, 'Not my bowl of rice.' It's better. It's correct. Di ba?" Am I right? She announced this with a triumphant grin.

How could I argue with her twisted logic after that? Rice, to us Filipinos, is more than just a staple food. It is an integral part of our culture. The rituals involved in the cycle of planting, maintaining, irrigating, harvesting and ingesting rice have enriched our lives far beyond what a single staple could ever do.

Rice—steamed, white, fragrant and mild—is the center of the Filipino meal. Everything else is eaten with it. It is a shaper of our tastes: the very salty, the very sour, the very sweet, and the very spicy are especially savory when eaten against the bland background taste of rice. Filipinos simply cannot live without rice. So English idioms be damned, 'Not my bowl of rice' has more flavor for us Filipinos than a cup of tepid tea.

"So now you get my meaning," Mother said, seeing my acquiescent face. "Now, we can go to the movies!"

"Really?" I shrieked happily. Wow! Life is such a bowl of cherries. As long as you agree with Mother.

PROLOGUE

"Please do not let them do it, Esteban," my sister Maria and I pleaded with our cousin Esteban. "They'll take the—ah, your—thing and smash it and smash it with a rock till the—the foreskin is off!"

We had heard many horror stories about the ritual of *Tuli*, circumcision, and were passing them on to our wide-eyed, ashen-faced twelve-year-old cousin, Esteban. He was about to undergo this barbaric rite of passage into manhood, which would require him to endure the slashing of his foreskin without the comfort of anesthetic—all to prove his manliness.

There are myths about why boys undergo *Tuli*. Some parents think that circumcising their sons will make them grow taller and stronger. Others think, strangely enough, that circumcision develops the testicles and increases the size of the penis. I have even heard from some older cousins that it is shameful to marry an uncircumcised man, though it is not clear why.

I'm sure none of these myths mattered to Esteban at that moment. He was whimpering and shaking his head as his father approached to take him to the stage for this visceral rite of passage: the beach.

Maria and I sneaked out of the house and followed Esteban, his father, and a bunch of other fathers and sons as they headed for the beach. We reached the beach and hid behind a huge rock where we got an eyeful of the boys and men who were about to partake in the ceremony. Maria and I agreed to do whatever it took to stop them from mutilating our dear cousin.

A *Manunuli* presided over this. He was a local person who had mastered the skill of circumcising adolescents. He summoned the first prey, which to our relief wasn't Esteban. It was actually a boy Maria and I both disliked: a pimply-faced bully named Danilo. He looked anything but intimidating as he fearfully approached the *Manunuli*.

The *Manunuli* gestured for Danilo to lower his pants and straddle a banana log into which a wooden plug had been inserted as an "anvil". The *Manunuli* examined Danilo's penis, pulled his foreskin forward and chopped it with a quick blow of the knife in his hand.

Maria fainted as Danilo, shrieking like a cat doused in boiling oil, was told to run into the cold salty ocean to cleanse the wound.

"Maria! Maria!" I whispered nervously as I shook her shoulder to revive her. It took awhile. She awoke surrounded by boys wearing nothing but their fathers' large T-shirts to cover their newly circumcised penises wrapped in guava leaves.

❧

My name is Ligaya. I recently underwent a rite of passage myself, but it was nothing like Esteban's and the other boys'. When I experienced the start of my menstrual flow, Mother performed a ritual called the *Lihi*. I was told to jump down from the third step of our stairs in order to limit the duration of my menstrual flows to three days. Then Mother poured three cans of water over my body. Petals of *Gumamela*—hibiscus flower—were then crushed and rubbed on my wet skin to give me a rosy complexion. Then an egg was rolled over my cheeks to give me smooth skin.

I was prohibited from taking a bath during my period and ordered to refrain from eating green mangoes or any sour food. I tried to complain about this, since sliced green mangoes dipped in shrimp paste were a favorite snack, but Mother only told me I should be thankful they no longer practice the Ritual of Isolation when at the onset of menstruation, a girl is isolated in her room for as long as seven days and seven nights and visited by an array of the village's elder women who instruct her in women's rites and traditions. The ritual is compared to that of a caterpillar who morphs into a butterfly after days of hibernating inside a cocoon. Like the butterfly, the girl emerges from her room to face the world as a more self-confident, beautiful person.

I don't know about that. The beautiful part I mean.

My name, *Ligaya*, means happy in English. Of course, like the caterpillar-turned-butterfly, I'd rather have a name like *Maganda*. That means beautiful. It is also the name of the first Filipina woman, like Eve. The first Filipino Adam is named *Malakas*, strong. There's a legend about *Maganda* and *Malakas* that tells of a mythical bird flying over a large expanse of water, looking for a tree on which to perch its tired legs. It spots a gigantic bamboo tree. Tired and hungry, it decides to peck on it hoping to find sustenance within. After continuous pecking, the bamboo splits into two equal halves. A golden- skinned man and a very beautiful woman emerge from it, *Malakas* and *Maganda,* the first man and woman in the Philippines. And the bird? It probably became the first tasty meal. Poor bird.

But I digress.

Looking back at my reflection in our antique bathroom mirror, I did not see *Maganda*. I did not see *Ligaya* either. What I saw was a frowning thirteen year-old girl with straight black hair, yellow skin pigmentation, small and slanted eyes, large protruding ears, a flat face with high cheekbones, and a broad nose with nostrils so dilated as if breathing itself was an effort. Not so bad actually, except my older sister Maria had a fairer complexion, more chiseled facial features, deeper-set eyes, and a higher and more desirably narrow nose bridge. They say I inherited my features from my father who had distinct Chinese-Malayan features and Maria's *mestiza* features were from our mother whose Daddy was pure Spanish.

Oh, please don't get me wrong. This was not a case of sibling rivalry. It was just one of those teenager's awkward insecurities. I was somehow okay with my facial features, though I have to admit, I did go through the torture once of putting a clothespin on my nose to make it more aquiline. It didn't work. It just created a lumpy mass of red and swollen nose tissue.

Kind of like the way my armpits were now swollen and red from repeated rounds of "flexing and squeezing" to make my thirteen year-old breasts bigger. Yep, if I was stuck with *Ligaya* and not *Maganda*, I figured I might as well be a *Dalaga*, a maiden, a full-blown woman. That is why I'd locked myself in our cramped bathroom in the sweltering Philippine summer of 1979 in the first place.

I originally got the idea from *Gorgeous*, an American women's magazine I filched from the beauty parlor where mother had her regular perm and dye job. The illustrated article showed, step-by-step, how to exercise to give your breasts the appearance of a lift. "Wow!" I thought, and immediately imagined myself in chest-flattering sundresses and tight-fitting tank tops that would spotlight my newly swollen mounds and catch the hungry attention of cute high-school boys.

So one day, while the beauty parlor proprietress was busy making *tsismis*—gossip—with her customers, I lifted the magazine. I'd been hiding it under my pillow ever since, the way pimply boys probably hide the latest women's wear catalogs under their beds.

Truth be told, the inspiration for my quest really started about two years earlier, way before giddy talks of high school and boys. The inspiration came in a box. My Auntie Soledad, who lived in America, had sent us a huge Christmas package. Inside, among the prized Hormel and Spam canned goods, the cherished Hershey chocolate bars and my aunt's used clothes, was this boxed Mattel doll called "Growing Up Skipper". On the box it said: "She's 2 dolls in one for twice as much fun! Make her grow from a young girl to a teenager in seconds." Our mother frowned instantly at these blurbs, mumbled a cuss word directed at our stateside Auntie, and harrumphed loudly as she reluctantly let go of the box that Maria and I had grasped as if it contained the secret to curing acne.

What a doll Skipper was! Maria and I and, for reasons I couldn't explain then, our male cousin Esteban, spent endless hours playing with her. When you twisted her arm, she grew taller and developed breasts. Soon Maria, who was two years older than I, grew tired of the doll as her own breasts grew bigger. Esteban simply got bored with it, but I remained fascinated, secretly wishing I could twist my own arms to hasten my impending pubescence.

Then I saw that article in that American magazine, *Gorgeous*. I couldn't believe some of the exercises it suggested. It said I could actually twist my arms to boost my bust! Of course, the result wouldn't be as instantaneous as Skipper's, but hey! I had the whole summer bursting in front of me.

So I started with what the article called the "flex and squeeze." Ten to fifteen repetitions of this regimen, it instructed. Flex and Squeeze. Flex and Squeeze.

"*Pucha naman*", I silently cursed as I stopped to examine my progress. My breasts still looked the same, though my armpits were enflamed. I was doubly disappointed but not discouraged enough to stop.

Flex and squeeze. Flex and—

I was startled by a sudden, furious knock on the door.

"Ligaya? Are you done showering yet? What's keeping you? C'mon, we don't have much time!"

I mouthed, "Mother! Oh, no!" as I hurriedly put on a *duster*, a loose cotton housedress. I unlocked and flung open the bathroom door with a nervous grin, hoping that my face wouldn't show what I'd been up to.

My mother, Aurora, stood by the door arms akimbo. Her matronly body was swathed in a colorful duster. Our Saturday summer outfits.

"You spend too much time in the bathroom," she admonished. I felt warmth and color rise on my cheeks, but thankfully, her back was already turned away, *tsinelas*-ed—native slippers—feet already marching towards her aromatic kitchen.

"C'mon, it's time," she said as she flip-flopped her slippered feet on the kitchen floor.

"Time for what?" I asked myself as I followed her. "Time for what?" For a frantic second, I thought she knew what I'd been doing. And now, she was going to take it upon herself to give me advice on how to perk up my breasts, a frank mother-to-daughter bonding. No way! I stopped. My mother sensed it and spun around.

"What's the matter now, Ligaya?" my mother asked as she impatiently tapped her *tsinelas* on the hardwood floor, freshly waxed with a solution of kerosene and melted *esperma*, red candles.

I instinctively placed my arms across my chest, my imaginary puffed up breasts.

"Is this how you're going to be acting for the duration of our lessons, my ingrate child?"

Lessons?!?

"But, I'm already getting some tips from *Gorgeous*!" I blurted out before I could even think. *Oh no!*

It was my mother's turn to look confused. On her mestiza face, even a bewildered look was still pretty.

"*Gorgeous*? The magazine? *Aba*, since when did that women's magazine start publishing Filipino food recipes? Have they gone *loka?*"

Have you gone crazy?

Oh. Oh! Oh!!! *Dios ko!* Oh God!

"Is this what it's all about? Cooking lessons? You're giving me cooking lessons?" I stammered, sure that my face was boiling at its crimson best.

"What do you think?" she asked, rolling her eyes. Then she added: "And since when have you started reading *Gorgeous*? *Hoy, Ligaya, lumalandi ka na ba?*" Ligaya, are you learning to flirt?

Dios ko, she knows what I've been up to, I thought, as I covered my breasts instinctively. My mother gave me a quick once-over as she harrumphed her way towards the kitchen. I squirmed, a kid caught in the act.

"Hoy, Ligaya, I'm waiting!" Mother shouted from the kitchen.

I rolled my eyes but ambled towards the kitchen anyway.

I crinkled my nose as I inhaled the garlicky, oniony, soy-saucy, and vinegary aromas in the kitchen. I shuddered at the thought of being stuck in the kitchen all summer. Cooking lessons? Not my cup of tea. Not my bowl of rice. But what's a bust-less thirteen year-old to do?

ℯ

It was a time-honored tradition, this business of handing down recipes and cooking tips from mothers to daughters, and occasionally, for reasons only mothers knew (or sensed), to sons as well.

That summer in the Philippines, my mother Aurora, decided my time had come to learn most, if not all, about cooking Filipino dishes she had learned from *Lola*, my grandmother, who passed away before I was born. Cooking tips she'd steadfastly picked up and stored away in her brain. Oh yes, it was time to pass them on. Forget the sweltering heat of the Filipino summer. Forget that it was my last summer before high school and that I had much better things to do, like perking up my breasts in time for my fall debut.

"Someday, you'll thank me for this," she said over my protestations.

I gave her the look, the best *simangot* I could muster.

"Now let's start, shall we?" Mother said, "and wipe that pout off your mouth. It won't work, Ligaya."

So it was goodbye disco lessons at Debbie's. Goodbye John "the Point" Travolta. Goodbye flexing and squeezing. Goodbye two months of summer fun.

Hello onions.

I cried and cried as I chopped them as finely as my hawk-eyed, sharp-tongued mother instructed me to.

"Teardrops, falling down my cheeks, trying to forget now while peeling onions!" my mother off-keyed, to the tune of that annoying lounge song, "Feelings." I glared at her, *que baduy*! How corny! She waved a dismissive hand at me.

"*Oy Ligaya*, what happened to your sense of humor?"

Maybe the onions washed it out of me.

"Here," she said, picking up a piece of chopped onion, "place this on your head. It'll keep you from crying when you chop them."

"Yeah, right," I muttered to myself.

Hey! What the—?

Hey, it worked! I was no longer crying! Was this some kind of voodoo or what? I was impressed, but I didn't say so. I was still steaming at the thought of being cooped up here the rest of the summer.

"Ligaya, did you know that there are *bakla*, homosexual, crabs?"

Uh-oh. Don't push it, Mother. The onion trick was one thing, but this?

"It's true!" she declared excitedly, both hands raised for dramatic emphasis. I giggled at her extraordinary theatricality. Move over, Meryl Streep!

Mother grabbed two crabs from a huge pile in a ceramic basin. She fastidiously held each one in each hand. The poor crabs wriggled with great vehemence.

"See here?" she continued, "this is a male crab. Notice the pointed, narrow apron on his backside." The poor crab writhed, embarrassed at being displayed so vulgarly. Hey, I'm no *Bomba*, bold-star, put me down!

"And this one with a wider, heart-shaped apron is a female. Female crabs are more sought after because they contain the delicious *aligi*, roe."

"But!" Mother continued as she gestured like a stage actress delivering her most dramatic line, "But, occasionally, by a quirk of nature, you will find male crabs with this precious roe, too. These ones are mischievously called *bakla*, homosexual."

Yeah, right!

That evening, as my nuclear family, which included my father, Pantaleon, and my older sister, Maria, feasted on crabs boiled in coconut milk and *siling labuyo*—hot green pepper—over steaming rice, I found a male crab endowed with the delicious orange-hued roe. I excitedly showed it to my mother.

"Aha! Now you believe me!" she said triumphantly. "Tomorrow, I'll show you how to detect a tomboy milkfish."

I looked at her in disbelief, my eyes widening alarmingly. She broke into a guffaw, crisp, hearty, and perverse.

"Just kidding, my gullible daughter," she said as she brushed away laughing tears, "just kidding!"

Chapter One

LUMPIA

I was ambivalent about the next day, the day I would depart for America. It was the same ambivalence I had felt towards my mother's cooking lessons of long ago. Excited and fearful. Thrilled to learn to cook a new dish, afraid I'd burn it.

America. The land of milk and honey. An exciting land, a strange land. Oh say can you see?

I was in my mother's kitchen, the very same one where I had my very first cooking lesson some flexing and squeezing years ago. By the way, that hadn't work. I finally er…blossomed, towards the end of my senior year. Naturally, no breast implants were needed, thank you. As for that magazine's advice, I say stuff it. Which is what I had to do for the junior prom. *Dios ko!*—My God!—I must have tried everything as bra stuffing. Tissue paper, cotton balls, silk handkerchiefs, *pan de sal*. No kidding. That yummy Filipino salt bread is perfect. The right size and the right softness. And if you experience hunger while fooling around…

I gripped the pure carbon steel cleaver—the only one Mother ever recommended for its long lasting sharpness—with enough force to turn my knuckles white. I chopped the onions in front of me with maniacal abandon as hot tears welled up in my eyes from both the damned onions and my hysteria, which was swelling to gargantuan proportions. I continued to chop frantically, reducing the onions to fine, fine pieces, making them a suitable ingredient for *lumpia*, classic Filipino egg rolls. I felt my panic subside, fading into a sense of catharsis. *Had I just elevated chopping onions to an art form?*

"As a *lumpia* ingredient, onions should be chopped very, very finely," my mother had taught me a long time ago in her unique, riveting way. "You want to taste just the essence of the onions, not bite into a huge piece that might ruin your kissing breath."

I continued to chop, continued to cry. I had forgotten one other food preparation tip from Mother. To keep from crying when chopping onions, place a little bit of the onion on your head.

Ah damn, I could use a good cry anyway.

1

er

Six years before, my mother, Aurora, left for America as an immigrant, a year after my father died suddenly of heart failure. Mother's younger sister, Auntie Soledad, who lived in New Jersey, had started an all-out campaign to get Mother to go. Being an American citizen, she could actually petition for my mother.

"Not my bowl of rice, Soledad," Mother had said at first.

"A new life, a better one!" my Auntie propositioned in one of her countless letters aimed to uproot my Mother, to turn that "not my bowl of rice" into "life is a bowl of cherries."

"Not just for you, but for your daughters as well, because you can petition for them too, in due time.

"And *doncha* worry about feeling homesick. We are here to take care of you. New Jersey is really teeming with Filipinos. Our church even has a Filipino priest. Our malls make public announcements in *Tagalog*. There are plenty of Filipino groceries and restaurants! Why, even our mailman came from Visaya, the South! He's a widower. Short but cute." My Auntie's advertising campaign became more and more a hard sell.

"Aurora, it would be wonderful to be with you again. Please say yes. My *amigas* here need another corner filled for our weekend mahjong sessions. Remember how you used to reign as the mahjong queen back home? Humph! Always getting all the *pungs* and the *chais*. Well, I am the best player here, so they say, but I wouldn't mind you challenging that position."

Mother hadn't played that addictive game in a long time. Maria and I simply wouldn't oblige her. Her mahjong table gathered dust in the basement. Maria and I noticed that Mother salivated slightly over that mahjong sell line. You can take the *mahjongera* out of the country but…

After reading my aunt's airmail letters, my mother would reverently place them on the family altar as if imploring the triumvirate ivory statues of Jesus, Mary and Joseph to help her make a decision. In the unique Filipino Catholic tradition, Jesus would, of course, have said "Yes," Mary would have answered coyly in the negative; and as usual, Joseph would have taken the Fifth, offering no opinion at all. In a locked decision like this, Mother would first scowl at Joseph for his cowardly neutral stand, then do the next best thing. She would wait for a sign, the tie-breaker.

My Auntie finally convinced my mother to go to the States when she wrote exasperatedly: "Aurora, do you really want your daughters living there? With all the troubles in our *politica*, all those brownouts, all those *pilas* -long queues- everywhere?" The worsening situation in the country because of the Marcos' martial law was as good a sign as the proverbial comet announcing the advent of war, the onset of pestilence.

et

Ringgg! The call came early, at two in the morning. I was awakened out of some hazy dream set in some distant golden-hued rice field by the mechanical crowing of a cock.

In a few seconds, Mother, Maria, and I were in the living room, staring bleary-eyed at the phone. My mother broke into tears, sure it was tragic news. I thought it was probably about my aunt. She must have been mugged and left to die on some dark corner in Newark, New Jersey. In her letters, my aunt had warned us about Newark, New Jersey.

In the '80s, a telephone call at two in the morning was still the equivalent of a telegram in the '60s: a harbinger of horrific news. The three of us huddled around the phone, already mourning a lost yet unnamed relative. Finally, Mother nervously picked up the receiver and tentatively uttered a tearful hello.

"Hi, Aurora. It's me, Soledad!" Mother's mournful face shifted into a surprised expression and eventually darkened into an utterly irritated one.

Auntie Soledad's cheerful voice instantly told her that no one had died. It also reminded her how inconsiderate Auntie Soledad could be sometimes. Maria and I picked up the extension phone, fully awake now, anticipating Auntie Soledad's gossipy call.

"Soledad, d'you realize what time it is here?" Mother scolded as she embarrassedly brushed away hot tears.

"Oh, sorry about that. I forgot again. Well, it's two in the afternoon here and I just got my mail!"

"Well, open it so you can pay your bills on time. Goodbye, Soledad!" Mother said through gritted teeth.

"Wait! Wait! *Susmariosep naman*, Aurora. Always irritable. Your heart, *sige ka*."

My mother simmered as she waited. We were still edgy when it came to talking about heart and health.

"I called because there's something in my mail that pertains to you!"

Mother shot both of us a look that commanded, "Put down the extension phone!" So we did, but we hung out in the living room as they talked, flopping on the rattan sofa, half asleep.

The phone conversation went on and on as Maria and I stared sleepily at a moth lying singed on the family altar, beside the candle flame it once adored.

Finally, looking flushed, Mother put down the phone. We both looked at Mother expectantly.

"Soledad says my petition's been approved. I should be hearing from the U.S. Embassy very soon. Now go back to bed." And with that, Mother flip-flopped back to her bedroom. Maria and I exchanged surprised glances, eyes chattering away.

As I resumed my sleep, I dreamt not of golden rice fields but of humongous malls, malls with shops where price tags on the dresses were in dollars. American dollars.

e

Maria married her high school sweetheart a few months after our immigration petition forms were submitted. It angered my mother. She boycotted their marriage, sending only a Hallmark card and a check for three hundred dollars.

Another aunt, Auntie Rosa, who'd been staying with us since Mother left, hoping she could persuade my mother to change her mind, called her collect. To her dismay, Mother did not even accept the call. There was a lot of lip biting prior to the wedding.

The message was clear. What Maria did was, to put it politely, not my mother's bowl of rice.

During the traditional dance of the bride and groom, in which guests pin peso bills to the bridal gown to invite the gods of fortune into the couple's new life, I playfully pinned a photocopy of the check which had been cashed to partially pay for the wedding. The groom grinned, but Maria looked horrified. She angrily tore off the check and stomped into the refuge of the reception hall's ladies' room, the one with the stylized drawing of *Maganda*, the Filipino Eve, on the door.

"Maria, I'm so sorry. That was a bad joke," I stammered, flushed with embarrassment and remorse.

"*Dios ko*, Ligaya, what were you thinking?" Maria screamed.

"Please, forgive me. I'm really, really sorry." I started to cry.

Maria offered a hug at once.

"It's okay. I guess I overreacted too," she said, now feeling guiltier than I.

Maria began to unpin the peso bills from her gown. I stopped her, aware that tradition and superstition dictated they should remain pinned to her gown until after the last guest left, or the gods of fortune would feel slighted as if they've been asked to leave before the party was over and would surely curse their marriage for life.

"Come on, Maria," I goaded her, "there's a party out there with your new name on it, Mrs. Maria de Guzman-Alcala!"

We shared a giggle in the way only two sisters/girlfriends can.

"You know," Maria said as she fixed her eyes," I'm really not surprised that Mother didn't come home for my wedding."

"Look, Maria, Mother's just disappointed because now you've nullified your trip. You know how hard she'd worked on this. She'll get over-"

Maria interrupted me with a bomb: "I was never her favorite daughter."

"Now, that's not true!" I protested.

"It's true and you know it," she said, fixing her freshly made-up eyes on me. "C'mon, Ligaya. Think back. Think back to when we were still kids."

It's true. Mother had always had this lukewarm attitude towards Maria. An outsider would never have noticed it, but I did, even then.

Mother had—for want of a more accurate word—a somewhat formal demeanor whenever she'd talked to Maria, whenever she'd assigned a chore, or even praised a good deed. When I was younger, as in immature, I actually secretly embraced this with glee. It had meant more toys thrown my way, more new dresses, more enthusiastic praise for good grades, which were always inferior to Maria's. More of this, more of that, while kind, gentle, selfless Maria watched from the sideline, seemingly unperturbed.

One day, I grew up and finally had the guts to ask Mother about it.

"What are you talking about?" she had answered, sincerely surprised and offended I had asked such a question. She added, "How dare you ask me that?" As in, I don't want to talk about it. A subject that's "Not her bowl of rice."

I never brought it up again, which left me unsatisfied, questioning all these years.

And now this. The confirmation that Maria wasn't the thick-skinned, I-don't-care-if- Mother-treats-you-better-than-me person after all. Oh, Maria!

"Don't get me wrong," Maria broke in. "I know in my heart of hearts that Mother loves me too, but I've always felt that she held back some. Remember my graduation? It was one of the happiest days of my life. You were there, Father too. And Mother, oh Mother. She was this beautiful queen in a new dress and a new perm. She smiled, then she embraced me, a long embrace. It was the first time she'd done that. I clung on, not wanting it to end. It felt sooo good! Then suddenly, she struggled to break free as if I were choking her, instead of enveloping her with love. Enough, she had protested. It's getting corny, she had joked. But her flushed face had said something else. I never forgot that look. She was flustered, but her eyes were emotionless, vacant. Like a door slammed shut."

Maria's eyes swelled with tears again. I looked at her eyes, alarmed, as Max Factor brown shadow began to run, transforming bride into raccoon.

"Maria, please, there are guests waiting for you," I pleaded.

"Do you know why I decided to marry now?" she asked as we headed for the door. "It's because I don't want to go to America. I don't want to be where I'm not really wanted."

6

er

So I was going to travel alone to America. I was sad, because I was really looking forward to sharing the trip with Maria. I felt my sadness begin to turn into anger, but squashed it down, chastising myself for thinking in such a selfish manner. Maria had a new life now, though it would still be lived in the house my mother owned. I thought I should be happy for her and her good husband, Ruben Alcala.

I decided to bring *lumpia* as my *baon*, in-flight dinner. You see, I've heard countless stories about airline food, about how there are only two choices: chicken or beef. And about how both taste terrible, as in tasteless, like cardboard.

Years later, I read the real reason airline food often has no taste: thousands of feet up, our sense of taste and smell is extenuated so that even the most flavorful, spiciest dish tastes as bland as baby food.

At that time, however, I was not privy to that piece of trivia, so I was not taking any chances. I wasn't doing any *Bahala Na* attitude. I was bringing my own airline food. I went through the recipes that my mother had bequeathed me. I decided on *lumpia*. That was it! I mentally snapped my fingers, the way black divas do with such a flourish on the new channel on Philippine television, the MTV. *Lumpia*. It would beat the hell out of tasteless airline chicken or beef.

Lumpia is the Filipino version of Chinese egg rolls. It can be prepared rolled in a delicate egg wrapper or spring roll wrapper. It can be served fresh or fried.

For my trip, I prepared a version known as *Lumpia Shanghai*. To answer your question, no, I didn't think *Lumpia Shanghai* originated in Shanghai, China.

Pedring had an interesting theory. He thought *Lumpia Shanghai* was invented by some enterprising Chinese restaurateur in Manila's Chinatown as part of his pseudo-Chinese menu for non-Chinese customers, very much like fortune cookies. Like the eggroll, you will not find a fortune cookie in China. Confucious say, "Egg rolls and fortune cookies not Chinese inventions."

Anyway, whatever the real story was, there's one thing you should know when preparing *Lumpia Shanghai*. When you buy the *lumpia* wrapper, which is available in most Oriental stores, be sure to ask for the spring roll wrapper. Chinese egg roll wrappers made with wheat flour are thicker and will not produce the delicateness and crispiness of fried *Lumpia Shanghai*.

Pedring had numerous notions about food, most of them bordering on the gross. For instance, he thought that the main ingredient of a certain Filipino dish is suspect. I grew bug-eyed when he whispered the ingredient to me: canine meat! I gave him a *kurot*, a painful but playful pinch. *Ay Naku*! Gosh! Pedring was a bundle of mischievous fun! Very cute, too. He was one of the people I'd miss most of all, despite what happened to us.

Who's Pedring? Well, until a few weeks ago, he was my steady boyfriend of almost two years. A month after we started to date, I told him of my pending petition. I was very honest in telling him that America was part of my long-term plan. Pedring's reaction to my news was blase. I behaved more Danielle Steele romantic, foolishly believing that our relationship could survive distance and transcend time.

Do I hear violin music?

In spite of myself, I giggled as I recalled a totally unrelated event, triggered by the word violin.

"*Tito Joe naman*. I'm havin' a hard time learning the guitar, <u>violins</u> *pa*!" complained a famous Filipino movie star when asked by a famous celebrity interviewer what she thought of sex and <u>violence</u> in the movies. This same movie star once declared that her favorite foods were Chinese diseases.

Pedring's matter-of-fact attitude was what we call *Bahala Na*. A pre-disposition to fate. A belief that things would eventually go one's way if fate would have it.

One day, Pedring was caught red-handed with his *Bahala Na* attitude. I was finally granted my visa and summoned to the U.S. Embassy for the last time. I waited at the crack of dawn for the embassy gates to open, along with hundreds of other hopefuls seeking entry into America. It was a long, sweaty wait, but the visa stamped on my passport was worth it. I tried to stifle a cry but couldn't. The officer who interviewed me grinned and offered me his handkerchief. *The land of milk and honey, at last!* I thought as I blew my nose into this kind man's handkerchief.

There was an impromptu celebration that night. Such a happy occasion, but Pedring grew morose as the night wore on. I guess it had finally hit him. His *Bahala Na* attitude backfired and he sulked all night. He drank a whole bottle of *Ginebra*, local gin, with no chaser. I tried to console him the best I could. I joked that as soon as I was settled, I'd send for him. Pedring, in his drunken state, thought that was an insult to his Filipino machismo, to the pre-feminist idea that the man provided and dominated. That night, in front of family and friends, he actually made me choose between him and America. Door number one or door number two? I showed him to door number three, instead.

I didn't see Pedring again until a week later.

On an early Thursday evening, I found him waiting for me outside the church. I was there for my weekly novena to St. Jude, the now deposed but still very much in-demand patron saint of the impossible. I credited St. Jude with interceding in the speed by which I was granted my visa. Don't laugh, I still know of some people who are still waiting for theirs, and I never see them in St. Jude's church either.

"Pssssst!" Pedring called rudely from behind a decorative coconut tree in the churchyard a hundred yards away. My cousin Anita, a St. Jude die-hard who prayed mostly for impossible luck in lotteries, was startled. Even from this distance, I could smell *lambanog*, a brew of native wine.

"It's Pedring. He looks drunk!" Anita exclaimed. Duh. "Don't go to him, please."

"It's alright, Anita. Why don't you go on home and prepare the rice for dinner? I'll be home soon."

"But…he's really drunk. *Dios ko!*" she exclaimed again, quickly crossing and re-crossing herself in Catholicism's universal sign.

"Pssst, Ligaya, come over here!" Pedring called out hoarsely as he leaned drunkenly on the tree for support.

"Ligaya, please come home with me," my badly shaken cousin implored, her eyes wide with fear.

"I'll be okay, really. Don't be silly. I know Pedring. C'mon, please go on home. I won't be long, I promise."

"Well, okay, but…here. If he tries to do something…evil." My cousin handed me her rosary beads. The beads were made of ivory,

9

the cross sterling silver. It looked invincible, but hardly a weapon, unless Pedring had turned into a vampire. I wanted to snicker, but my cousin looked too serious. I took the rosary. Anita reluctantly walked towards home, a good ten blocks. "Be careful," her voice trailed away as I approached Pedring, now staggering to maintain his balance.

I grimaced. Pedring was punch drunk and shabby with his shirt and pants covered in food and mud stains. His Converse rubber shoes were unwashed and caked with mud. His short black hair was unpomaded, sticking out wildly. He looked awful. He reminded me of the *hurimentado*, a madman who went on a killing spree in our town three years ago with a sharp bolo. His wife and children had left him and he snapped. When the madman was finally cornered and captured by the local cops, he was wild-eyed and disheveled, much like Pedring now. I felt the small hairs on the back of my neck rise.

"Hello, Pedring. *Kumusta?*" How are you? I tried to sound calm. *I should have gone home with my cousin,* I silently scolded myself.

"Ligaya, Ligaya. How could you do this to me? I thought you loved me!" He swayed as he talked, like a young fragile bamboo tree.

"Pedring, I do love you," I began in a tentative voice. "But you have to understand, I worked so hard and so long for this trip. My mother would be very disappointed. You knew this would happen. But you must also know that my leaving doesn't have to mean the end of our relationship, you know?"

The words just flowed out, a frantic attempt to save an already doomed relationship. He stared at me, his expression like that of a wounded animal. He reeled. I tried to support him. He was too heavy. We both collapsed, he on top of me. I gagged at the smell of his breath. He tried to kiss me.

"Pedring, let go! Please!"

It was almost dark. The *sacristan* -altar boy- was probably still inside, cleaning up. Should I scream for help? Suddenly, Pedring rolled over. He squatted beside me and started to cry with his head bowed. I nervously reached out to console him. He pulled away, starting to curse.

"*Putang ina mo, Ligaya. Putang ina mo!*" he wailed repeatedly. We both sat there on the cold grass. He continued to curse silently.

The coral tints in the sky faded into the darker hues of evening. I got up, brushed off bits of grass from my skirt and walked away. I was sad and angry at the same time.

"Putang ina mo, Ligaya!" he screamed after me one more time, adding an unsavory shade to the evening blue.

"Your mother's a whore, Ligaya!" Pedring cursed repeatedly. My mother would have thrown a royal fit! My hands trembled as I tightly clutched my cousin's rosary beads. I should have strangled Pedring with this, I thought grimly.

𝒆𝒯

My hand tightened again on the cleaver at the thought. I was now dicing celery, which gives *Lumpia Shanghai* that nice crunch. Pretty soon, I'd be finished preparing all the ingredients for the lumpia filling. I thought of Pedring again. I hadn't heard from him since that ugly twilight encounter in the churchyard. Maybe Pedring was with some other *dalaga* -maiden- now.

I shook my head angrily at this thought, the cleaver barely missing my finger. I noticed that my hands were shaking.

"Shhh. Shh-h-h-h!" I whispered to steady them.

I felt depressed. I remembered how Pedring used to compliment me on my *Lumpia Shanghai*.

"Simply the best, *mahal*!" he'd say delightfully, in between tasty bites of the crispy delicacy. *Sayang* - too bad. I tried to think of happier times, like the summer when I attempted to flex and squeeze my breasts into forced womanhood. And I realized there are some things you can't hurry.

LUMPIA SHANGHAI

Ingredients:
    1/2 cup ground pork
    1/2 cup ground beef
    1/4 cup finely chopped onions
    1 egg

3 cloves garlic, minced
1/4 cup finely diced celery
1/4 cup grated carrots
1 tsp. oil
soy sauce and pepper to taste
spring roll wrapper
oil for frying

Combine all filling ingredients and mix thoroughly. Put at least a teaspoon of filling one inch from the edge of each spring roll wrapper and wrap into a thin roll. Seal with well beaten egg or water.

Place wrapped lumpia in the freezer for at least 2 hours.

Fry until golden brown. Let cool. Cut into serving pieces, about 3 inches in length per piece. Serve with sweet and sour sauce or vinegar with crushed garlic and pepper.

Chapter Two

PANCIT GUISADO

It was now almost four in the afternoon; too late for a *siesta*, an afternoon nap. It was quiet in the kitchen and in my heart.

The cleaver had been put away. My panic had taken on a dull edge, though I felt a headache coming on. I massaged Tiger Balm into my forehead to prevent a full-blown migraine. Tiger Balm was my cure-all. I used it for headaches, backaches, and every kind of joint ache. But I drew the line at heartaches. *Dios mio*, Tiger Balm can only do so much!

The *lumpias* had been rolled and were now stacked nicely in the freezing compartment of our Frigidaire. A tip: don't rush *lumpia* into the fryer. Freezing them for about two hours can make them much crisper when fried; therefore, much more enjoyable. Remember, there are some things you can't hurry if you want the best results.

By the way, our refrigerator is not really <u>the</u> Frigidaire, we just got used to calling it that. The same way we referred to our toothpaste as Colgate even when we actually used Close-Up. My cousin, the advertising man, had a fancy term for it: brand association. It's when a popular brand name becomes synonymous with its product category as in Kodak for cameras, Kleenex for facial tissues, and Kotex for sanitary napkins. You get the bloody picture. My cousin was a hotshot senior copywriter in an advertising agency. His smart head knew a whole lot more than mine, though I doubt he had any clue at all that to make *lumpias* crispier, you had to freeze them for at least two hours prior to frying. At least two hours. Time it with your Rolex, which I am sure isn't really a Rolex.

Which meant that at around seven, I could deep-fry half of the *lumpias* I made for my *Despedida* party, my very own going- away bash.

A few days ago, Maria insisted on this shebang. I reasoned that I'd rather have quiet time with her or, wistfully, with Pedring, but she wouldn't hear of it. Emigrating to America was a major event, bigger than a birthday party or a christening, she had said. So she had

13

rounded up relatives, friends, and a few ex-officemates at the bank where I'd worked as a teller.

It was a potluck affair; everybody was expected to bring a dish. It would be an eat-til-you-drop-and-if-you-can't-eat-no-more-here's-a-doggy-bag affair. Very typical of Filipino parties. Eat just one serving and you offend the host forever. What!? You don't like my cooking?

My sister had volunteered to cook *Pancit Guisado*. It is a dish of very brittle, thin, translucent rice noodles.

It was actually Mother's idea. Yesterday, she called long distance to give me last minute instructions. Don't forget your passport! Don't forget your plane ticket! Don't forget your immigration papers! The same things she had reminded me of the week before. She also reminded us to serve *Pancit Guisado* at my going-away party. That way, she added, I was assured of a long, prosperous life in America.

"When you reach 65, you get Medicare and Medicaid. That means free doctor visits, free hospitalization, and free medicine. Isn't that wonderful?" Mother, already getting the hang of stateside living, had exclaimed as she extolled the advantages of geriatric living in America. Long life. Hey, bring on the *Pancit* for longevity in the Land of Plenty!

&

I was in my bedroom, which would soon be Maria's, because it was much roomier than Maria's old room. It used to be our parents', and then Mother's when Father died. I don't exactly recall how I ended up with the bigger room. Was it Mother's idea? Did she play favoritism again?

I stood in front of the full-length mirror. I smiled as I recalled the many times we spent staring at our images here, the three women in Father's life. I snickered as I recalled that this wasn't exactly my favorite mirror.

Mine was the one in the bathroom. I smiled as I unbuttoned my blouse, right after checking if the door was locked. I stared at my breasts. I certainly didn't need any more of that flexing and squeezing shit now. And hey, I could say shit, too, but only in private. I'm a grown woman, but still a Filipina.

There was a knock on the door. I panicked as I experienced a sense of deja-vu.

"Ligaya, are you done showering yet?" For a split second, I was 13 years old again.

"Ligaya!? It's Maria. Can I come in?"

I looked around for something to wear. I spotted my favorite duster, the one with the flowered print. It was lying blooming on the floor. It either fell off its hanger or I was becoming a slob. 25 year-old slobs, America wants you! I picked it up and put it on.

I unlocked the door. Maria held up a pair of huge, imitation-leather suitcases.

"Ta-da!" She struck a pose like one of Bob Parker's girls on *The Price Is Right*, a very popular game show in the Philippines.

"Maria, you shouldn't have!" I said, touched by the gesture.

She breezed in, happy that I was delighted with the going-away gift, though in reality, I was more than willing to settle for the ancient hand-me downs gathering dust in the basement.

The luggage bags were a beautiful, mahogany imitation leather with rugged straps and nametags emblazoned across the front in the brightest patriotic red, blue and white. The tags clashed violently with the leather. "So you can spot your bags easily when you claim them at the airport," she reasoned hastily when she saw my amused look. *Oh, say, can you see my Filipino bags?* I silently sung.

Alone again later, I re-thought the bags and decided that with one look at this very American luggage, the U.S. customs officer would surely let me by with no harassing questions, as the myth had it.

Or maybe not...

Inside one of these suitcases, I planned to stuff three pieces of *Santos*, antique religious statues. They were family heirlooms my mother had specifically instructed me to bring to America. One was a *Santo Nino*, a century-old ivory statue of the child Jesus. I worried about the U.S. customs again. I tried to recall the laws about bringing antiques to America. Is the *Santo Nino* considered a national treasure?

Over the phone, I had had a heated argument with my mother about bringing these antiques to America. It smacked of smuggling, I had argued. I had visions of scenes from the movie, <u>Midnight Express</u>, where the *bida* -hero- was incarcerated for smuggling hash or opium. *Santos*, same thing. "Declare them as *pasalubongs*! (gifts)" my mother had haughtily instructed me.

I was having this vision of the customs officer giving me the who-do-you-think-you're-fooling look. I started to sweat. I shrugged off the nagging thought and took a shower. As I lathered, I thought maybe I'd hide the *Santos* inside the *Terno*, butterfly-sleeved Filipino formal dress, which my Auntie Soledad ordered. That's a perfect hiding place for the *Santos*. After all, who'd dare look under a woman's skirt? Safer, too. The soft *Pina* -pineapple fiber- material would protect them from damage as well.

Feeling a lot better, I put on a pair of Levi's (they're not really genuine Levi's). I also put on an embroidered blouse and clipped my hair into a ponytail. I looked younger than my 25 years. Eat that, Pedring.

Uh-oh, I felt sad again. I hummed a jingle that a copywriter cousin once wrote: "When the world was happy, Levi's gave the Blues." My witty cousin had won many local advertising awards. My party energy started to build up. "Blue Levi's made the world happier!"

I opened the door to smell my sister's *Pancit Guisado*. I was happy, even if my Levi's were not really Levi's.

et

At seven, the first guests arrived. A boo-boo since we Filipinos regard punctuality as an impolite trait. Such a prompt appearance makes the guests seem too eager and greedy for food. In Filipino culture, it is customary to be late. Ten to fifteen minutes after the appointed time is considered punctual. But Grace and Tessa, tellers from the bank I used to work for, seemed oblivious to this custom. They waltzed in carrying a delicious chocolate mango cake. It colorfully declared: "Von Boyage!" I got the feeling they bought the cake ready-made, frosted lettering and all. Someone's vacation cruise was probably cancelled, or someone refused the cake because of its egregious misspelling.

"Ligaya! We miss you already!" Grace said, kissing the air to the left of my cheek, Filipina-society-girl-style.

"This is from the staff. Open it!" Tessa excitedly handed me a pink envelope. It said Hallmark on the flap. (Remember, as the commercial says, it's OK to look!) It must have been an imported greeting card purchased at the American-run PX goods store. I opened the envelope and grew misty-eyed as I read the personalized messages. One, in Pentel pen, read, "Beware Of the White Men! They'll Break Your Heart." It was unsigned, though I recognized the penmanship. It was penned by Ike, the chief accountant at the bank. He was gay.

Coincidentally, he suddenly materialized at the door dressed in black pants, a blue-striped oxford shirt, and a colorful tie that saved the outfit from being total working man's haberdashery. The bank had strict conservative dress codes, even for men, but Ike managed to be stylish anyway by wearing ties with outrageous designs. This one had black musical notes floating all over a sea of neon red. Among my ex-office mates, I would miss Ike the most. I greeted him with open arms. He did the same, only more theatrically.

"*Ate-eeeeee!*" he screamed into my face. "*A-te*", the colloquial word for sister, was only a two-syllable word, but he managed to stretch it to six. "Welcome to America!" The party had officially begun.

Abligurition. When I was in high school, I came upon that word as a Spelling Bee contestant. It's a noun meaning extravagance in cooking and serving. A typical Filipino party has abligurition. Food is always in abundance and the service is always deluxe. My despedida party had so much abligurition that I was developing an encephalalgia. Did I tell you I won that Spelling Bee contest? My winning word was braggadocio, in case you're wondering.

I focused on the social business at hand. More guests arrived and my headache increased alarmingly. Three aunts arrived simultaneously, three queens from the Orient bearing gifts of more food. One of them, Tita Trinidad, secretly slipped an envelope into my non-Levi's back pocket. When I went to use the bathroom later, I opened it to reveal two crisp new fifty-dollar bills. Bless her soul! Tita Trinidad was a spinster who regarded men as unnecessary to one's life's progress. She may have been speaking the truth: she got fabulously wealthy on her own. She operated a fleet of jeepneys, a cheap mode of public transport that abounds in Manila and its suburbs. When the World War II Americans left, they left behind war babies and surplus equipment, jeeps in particular. Filipino ingenuity took care of both. War babies became beautiful movie stars and jeeps became colorful jeepneys.

Two schoolmates from a word processing class I took arrived next. Six months ago, I had enrolled in the class to improve my chances of getting a job in the States. It was an expensive class, but my mother had sent me the necessary dollars to pay for it. She had told me that many help wanted ads in the paper require computer knowledge. "These jobs pay top dollars," she had said. "You'll get promoted faster! Soon you can be supervisor!" she had added enthusiastically.

My two schoolmates had committed a social faux pas worse than arriving on time. They had not brought any food with them to share. They sheepishly apologized, explaining they came straight from their word processing class.

"Don't worry," I assured them, silently thankful they had no new additions to the obscene display of palatable extravagance on the buffet table. Then I escorted them to the buffet, determined to make them gain at least 20 pounds each.

"Wow, *Pancit Guisado*, my favorite! Who cooked this?" Josephine, already forty pounds too heavy, exclaimed while spooning a heapful of the Long Life treat onto her plate. I doubted it would give her longevity, but tonight was hardly the time for diets or other morbid thoughts. With that in mind, I also spooned a second helping of the long life infusing *Pancit* onto my plate. At the rate I was going, I would grow to be 100 in the States. My mother says you get featured in the weather-forecasting segment of a morning show if you do. Very impressive.

I was in the act of stuffing my face with another forkful of *Pancit Guisado* when Pedring showed up. I didn't notice him at first because I was turned away from him. What I first saw was Josephine's reaction to his arrival. Her mouth flew open, the still unmasticated noodles hanging like shredded buntings from her ample teeth. Her expression clearly announced the arrival of a gatecrasher. I whirled around, ready for confrontation.

"Hello Ligaya..." Pedring said timidly. His hands were hiding something behind him.

"Hi, Pedring! Come...on...in!" I stammered as I put down my fork. It missed the table and hit the floor with a loud clatter. Guests turned around, startled.

"It's okay! It's just the fork!" I assured everyone while bending down to retrieve it. Pedring ran towards me and crouched instantly. Our eyes and hands met as we simultaneously reached for the fallen utensil.

"*Uuyyyyy*! How romantic!" someone shouted from the gallery. Someone else let a snicker slip. Soon, the crowd around us was laughing uncontrollably. It was such a relief. It could have turned ugly with the sharp fork and all.

Pedring picked up the box he had dropped when he came to my rescue. It was beautifully gift-wrapped and tied with a fanciful red ribbon. He handed it to me without a word, just a misty smile. He looked a lot better today than when I had last seen him in the churchyard. He was even wearing a tie! I felt a pang of sadness.

Breaking a Filipino custom of not opening gifts in front of the giver, I gamely unwrapped the box. Almost everybody was crowded around us including my sister Maria, looking worried, and Anita, my religious cousin, looking even more worried. Anita made the sign of the cross, so sure was she the box held a small ticking bomb ready to explode and annihilate us all. Instead, the box revealed a relatively harmless cookbook. The title on the handsome Filipino art deco cover read: Recipes of the Golden Archipelago. I was genuinely thrilled at this going-away gift. I kissed Pedring, who instantly reddened. He didn't say a single word, but his eyes said volumes.

"Would you like some *Pancit Guisado*? It's really delicious," I said, straight from my heart.

He nodded. I could tell he was trying to keep from crying. He looked so sad I had to turn away. I started spooning *Pancit* onto a plate and then handed it to him with a table napkin, a fork, and a concerned look.

"Ligaya..." he finally said.

"Eat," I replied nervously.

He tentatively rolled a forkful of the noodles and brought it to his mouth.

"Well? How is it?" I asked as he chewed.

"Delicious," he said, managing a toothy smile. Some morsels stuck to his white teeth. I giggled as I pointed at them. Catching on, Pedring started laughing. All around us, there were sighs of relief, giggles of glee and chomping sounds of *Pancit Guisado* being consumed with relish.

PANCIT GUISADO

Ingredients:
>1/2 cup boiled chicken (flaked)
>1/2 cup boiled shrimps (sliced in long narrow strips)
>1/2 cup boiled pork (sliced in long narrow strips)
>1 cup shredded cabbage
>3 lemons, sliced in halves
>2 tbsp soy sauce
>1 lb rice noodles
>2 cloves of garlic, minced
>1 onion, sliced
>Salt and pepper to taste
>Vegetable oil for frying

Fry the garlic, onion, shrimps, pork, and chicken separately. Set aside a portion of each for garnishing the dish. To the rest, add soy sauce, shrimp juice, salt and pepper. Simmer for about five minutes, then add the cabbage, mixing well. Simmer until almost dry.

Blanch rice noodles in boiling water for about two minutes. Quickly fry in vegetable oil, then add to the mixture. Arrange on a platter and garnish with set aside ingredients and slices of lemon.

Chapter Three

BIBINGKA

It was the crack of dawn. A luminous line of gold stars tinted the horizon. A rooster gaily crowed the start of a new day. It was joyous magic yet I felt only sadness.

I slept fitfully. Before dawn, I was already wide awake, roused by a dream that I could barely remember. All I knew is that it must have been a sad one, for I awoke with a heaviness in my heart and tears in my eyes. I slowly got up and ambled to the window. The sight of the sunrise and the sound of the rooster crowing only made me cry more. I sat and sobbed shamelessly, the tears of a homesick girl, shed in advance.

The party had ended a little before midnight. The last guest happily left with Tupperware containers full of leftover food. "Go to bed, we'll clean up later," my sister had said while barely concealing a yawn.

Now she was entering my room, possibly awakened by my loud sobs. "Ligaya, are you crying? What is it?" she asked worriedly. She smelled of Lifebuoy soap. I had not awakened her after all.

"Ah...yes. I had a bad dream, that's all," I lied as I hurriedly wipe away tears, overcome by a sense of *amor propio*, false pride.

"*Ay naku*, it's just excitement," my sister said dismissively. "Imagine, same time tomorrow you'll be in the States *na*. Stop that crying. Think of the exciting things waiting for you in the States...*bagong buhay*!" A new life!

I sobbed even more.

"Ligaya, did I say something wrong? Oh, you very sentimental girl!" Maria said, finger wagging in mock rebuke. Then she hugged me. It felt comforting, safe, and very brief. She promptly pulled back, looking alarmed.

"*Dios Mio*! My *Bibingka*! They might burn! Excuse me!" She rushed to the kitchen as if late for a momentous meeting with the Kitchen God. My sadness turned to annoyance.

Bibingka is a delicious native cake made of ground rice called *Galapong*, butter, and eggs. It is not your everyday breakfast fare, so you can be assured that my sister must have risen at least an hour earlier to make the preparations. The tantalizing aroma wafted into my room, my *sarat* -pug nose- following its source hungrily.

Maybe she hadn't even slept at all. The house was already spotless! Except for the lingering garlicky smell of food, there was no tell-tale sign of the previous night's all-you-can-eat feast.

This house will be in good hands, I thought, as I let out a soft slow whistle of admiration. Until last night, my sister lived with her family in a rental in another suburban city called Marikina. Since my sister got married, I had been living in this house, which mother owned, with only a cousin, an all-around maid, and a laundry woman for company. My mother had suggested that we rent out the house when I left. I counter-suggested that Maria and her family should move in instead.

Initially, she had bristled in that annoying 'not my bowl of rice' attitude of hers, but I argued, appealing to her *sintido comon*, a utilitarian sense of self-preservation.

"The house will be better taken care of, Maria will see to it. Besides, when you come visit, where will you stay?"

She relented. I doubt if she would have had I argued that allowing them to housesit this adobe dwelling would help them economically. It drove me crazy that Mother treated Maria that way. I made a mental note to confront my mother about this in America.

The cookbook from Pedring lay on the coffee table. Its glossy cover was gleaming in the semi-darkness of our *sala*, living room. I squinted at it, picked it up and saw something I had missed seeing at the party amid the din. On the inside cover page was an inscription. "I'll miss you," it stated simply but in elegant calligraphy. Pedring had taken up calligraphy in a Manila art school. He had told me it would come in handy when we begin to address our wedding invitations. It was truly sweet of him, considering the lessons were not free and the commute through potholed Manila streets hellish.

I involuntarily clasped my hands to my bosom at this thought. Sweet Pedring. Sweet, temperamental, egotistical Pedring. If only things were different. If only his *macho delicadeza* weren't as deep seated. Last night, just as we were beginning to have a pleasant, amicable talk, someone made an innocent, albeit tacky, remark about my good chances of meeting successful men in America. Pedring had reddened and quickly motioned to leave, mumbling something about having to work early. I reluctantly saw him off at the door. He had simply said, "Take good care, Ligaya. Keep in touch, OK?" Then he was gone before I could even respond, walking rapidly away with his head bowed, hands shoved into his pants pockets. "Pedring," I had uttered, relishing the name for perhaps the last time.

I sadly padded toward the kitchen. The sweet, buttery aroma of *Bibingka* immediately buoyed me. It smelled perfect, not burnt.

"Ligaya, sit," Maria motioned toward a rattan dining chair.

"Here, the first *salang*," she said, offering me the very first baked *Bibingka*, an honor accorded to prized guests. I should have bristled with self-importance. Instead I felt like a death-row convict eating her last meal.

"Maria, sit down *muna*. Join me. Let's talk while the kids are still asleep," I suggested, welcoming the fact that the kids and her husband were probably still snoring away. Caught in the frenzy of pre-departure preparations, Maria and I never really had the opportunity to talk in earnest.

"Can't, these *Bibingkas* are so delicate. They burn easily. I have to constantly watch them. Go ahead and eat. Don't let it get cold," she said as she continued to fuss over the *Bibingka* oven.

A *Bibingka* oven is a stovetop-style baking pan made of clay, lined with banana leaf softened by an open flame, and covered with a galvanized iron sheet containing live embers.

"Maria, what's your plan *na ba*? Are you still interested in going to America?" It obviously caught her attention since she whirled towards me, momentarily forgetting the delicate chore at hand. She was frowning.

"How can I, with two kids growing fast and a husband? No, better we stay here! Rent-free house, what more can I ask for?" she added with a touch of bitterness and sarcasm.

"You wanted to see America, too. Don't deny it," I offered, remembering the excitement we had when we finally got our petition documents. "America here we come!" we had shouted in unison.

"Well, I did…once. But I'm married now. Things are different now," she said with a sad smile.

"Mama can still petition for you and your family. It's been done before! It might take longer, but it can be done."

"The question is, is Mama willing to petition for my family?" she questioned bitterly. *"Ewan ko ba.* I get the feeling that sometimes Mother thinks she only has one daughter-" Maria suddenly stopped, realizing her slip.

"Oh Ligaya, I'm so sorry. I didn't mean it that way," she said, wide-eyed and red-faced, frantic to rectify what she considered a breach of tact. "I'm sorry..." her voice trailed off as she began to sob.

"No, Maria, that's not true. Mama loves you too," I whispered. My mouth felt dry.

"Really? She sure has a strange way of showing it." She gazed at me, her face crumpled with many years of bitterness from being treated like a second-hand daughter. She quickly turned around to mask it as Ruben, her husband, entered, yawning and bleary eyed.

"Strange way of showing what?" he innocently asked through a yawn.

His eyes grew wide with glee as the enchanting aroma of *Bibingka* fogged his concentration. "Mmm, *Bibingka*! I want some."

I silently blessed my brother-in-law's light soul. Maria and I exchanged furtive glances. The discussion would have to wait, now that the whole household was awakening.

"Bibingka! Sarap. Yipeee!" Maria's two kids shrieked as they entered, still in their pajamas, though their energy levels were at a play clothes high. Maria glanced at me with warmth and composure returning to her pretty face. A sense of pride too. She had produced good kids, just like Mother.

The *Bibingka* tasted heavenly! I washed it down with freshly brewed *Batangas* coffee, a blend of industrial-strength local beans. *Batangas* is strong enough to wake even the *Patay*, dead. The kids had *tablea tsokolate*, a thick chocolate drink, with theirs. The whole family was going to be seeing me off. Cousin Anita and Tita Trinidad were to be at the airport too. It was all possibly a ruse to make sure that I was really leaving. Hmm, maybe that was a nasty, juvenile thought. Natch. I took another bite of the *Bibingka*, hoping I didn't choke on my sarcasm.

The jeepney that would take me to the airport was idling in the driveway. A mutated American jeep with art deco pretenses, the jeepney has become the most common mode of public transportation in the Philippines. In the back, squat small benches that face each other serve as passenger seats. A low top painted in every bright color imaginable covers the whole structure. An American writer once described jeepneys as Carmen Miranda on wheels.

My brother-in-law made a decent living driving the jeepney. On a good day, starting at dawn, he could make about five hundred pesos, enough to feed his family of three decently. Today, he would lose his entire day's earnings because of me. I had offered to take a cab to the airport, but he refused. His *utang na loob*, sense of gratitude, would not allow him to do such an unthinkable thing. Freeing his family's apartment rent budget would allow them extra luxuries. That alone was worth losing a day's earnings, or so he said. Still, I felt guilty. It was not even my house that they were getting rent-free.

The ride to the airport was long, hot, and dusty. We left a little before ten in the morning, to give us plenty of time to catch my two o'clock flight, allowing for traffic and the expected occasional breakdown of the rickety jeepney. I sat in the back with my niece and nephew. Maria sat in front with her husband. The luggage was squeezed into the narrow aisle. My hand-carry bag, with the *lumpia* in Tupperware, rested on my lap.

As we traversed the jammed streets, I observed the unhealthfulness of my surroundings. Dust and exhaust fumes permeated the air while smoke billowed from burning sidewalk trash. Small children on the curb covered their noses and coughed like 2-pack-a-day smokers. It was a nauseating sight. Maria frowned at me. I sat silent, sullen and sweaty. The slow movement of traffic, usually blamed on the proliferation of potholes sarcastically referred to as moon craters, aggravated us all.

"*Pasensiya ka na.*" My sister broke the silence, apologizing for something she had absolutely no control over.

"Don't be silly. I'm used to this. You're treating me as if I were a *Balikbayan*. I haven't left yet, remember?" I said, laughing. Everybody joined in except my sister. She remained unamused.

"At least you won't be experiencing all this any more. There, only smooth roads, huge freeways. No potholes!" she said, spitting out the last two words.

The anger in her voice alarmed me. "I'm sure there are potholes too. America's not a perfect world, you know," I said defensively, amicably.

"Maybe not, but I'm sure of this. No potholes!" As if on cue, we bumped over one. My head hit the low ceiling as the jeepney rattled dangerously.

"*Kita mo na?*" You see? My sister declared smugly as if the accident was a confirmation that America roads are pothole-free.

The jeepney approached Roxas Boulevard a few miles from the airport. We passed by the piece of artificial land that was reclaimed from the sea to make way for many of ex-First Lady Imelda Marcos' capricious edifices: the Cultural Center, the Folk Arts Theater, the Coconut Palace and the Manila Film Center. Every time I would pass the Film Center, I would shiver at the memory of one of the most horrible tragedies in Philippine construction history. Several floors of the Center collapsed while being hastily built for the Manila International Film Festival. Many workers were killed. The exact count was never known because details of the accident were quickly shrouded by official Marcos regime secrecy and silence. There were reports that many of those killed were trapped in quick-drying cement and that no effort was made to recover the bodies simply because the building needed to be completed in time for the holding of the festival. It is said ghosts now haunt the Film Center. A cineaste friend of mine, while seeing a movie there, once felt a cold, clammy hand grab at her ankle.

We finally reached the Benigno Aquino International Airport an hour later! The airport was formerly known as the Manila International Airport, but when Cory Aquino became president, it was renamed after her husband, who was murdered on the airport tarmac. It was in this airport that our country's journey toward regaining our long-curtailed freedom had begun. Approaching it, I felt the usual sense of pride, but this time the feeling was mixed with guilt.

We went directly to the check-in counter of Philippine Airlines. It would be a direct flight to Honolulu, my port of entry, then a connecting flight to my final point of destination, Newark Airport in New Jersey. I checked my two colorfully tagged, imitation alligator leather suitcases.

"I am halfway there," I thought as my luggage was slowly ferried away by the conveyor belt into the inner recesses of the plane, on its way to New Jersey, U.S.A.

"See you later, alligator," I whispered in the direction of my imitation leather bags, snickering at my own bad pun.

et

"Take care of yourself," my sister said finally, pressing her hand into mine.

We exhausted a 36-exposure roll of film. I posed with my cousin, my aunt, my nephew and niece, my brother-in-law, my sister. Then we had a group shot, taken by an accommodating airport attendant. It all seemed very silly until I realized morbidly that it could be my last day on earth; this could be the final preserved memory of me. So I posed for one more shot.

Then I was worried that the sweet-smelling *Sampaguita* garlands around my neck might be staining my new silk blouse. The thoughts of a traveler ran the gamut from profound to preposterous.

It quickly became time to board the plane through a small iron gate marked 24. My brother-in-law gave me a hug, a courageous act from a very reserved man. Others followed suit. Cousin Anita slipped me her rosary beads, the same ones she had lent me to ward off Pedring's drunken advances. My nephew offered a kiss, wet and smelling of strawberry-flavored rock candy. My niece simply stood at my side, bawling.

"Don't leave us, *Tita Ligaya*!" she pleaded. My heart was instantly broken.

"Don't worry, your *Tita* will be back," my sister said gently, trying to appease her. My niece continued to cry.

"Hey, if you don't stop crying, she won't send you stateside toys and clothes *sige ka*!" my aunt said with mock warning.

"Won't...send...me...toys...and clothes?" my niece said in between hiccoughs. Soon, she stopped crying, buoyed by the bribery. I stared at my aunt, who was looking triumphant.

Then finally, my sister's turn. "Be careful. Write as often as possible," she said, gripping my hand. "Take care of Mother..." She

27

was desperately trying to retain her composure. Tears began to stream down her cheeks, filling me with love and sorrow. We hugged for a long time. There was no rush this time, for there were no *Bibingkas* to burn.

BIBINGKA

Ingredients:
    1 cup thick *galapong* (see recipe below)
    1/2 cup white sugar
    2 tsp baking powder
    2 tbsp melted butter
    4 tbsp powdered sugar for topping
    3 eggs well beaten
    1 cup coconut milk
    3 tbsp grated cheddar cheese

To make *galapong*:
    Soak white rice in equal amount of water overnight. Grind and let stand until the following day.

Add sugar to the *galapong*. Add baking powder, melted butter, eggs and coconut milk. Mix well. Pour a thin layer of this batter into a traditional *Bibingka* oven. If a traditional *Bibingka* oven is not available, bake in a regular oven pre-heated to 350 degrees.

Check sporadically. When almost cooked, sprinkle grated cheese and sugar on top. Continue baking until golden brown. Brush top with melted butter and serve hot with grated sweet coconut.

Chapter Four

ADOBO

I had been wrong about airline food. At least about the food they serve on Philippine Airlines. The food was delicious and plentiful. There were more choices than just chicken or beef. There was even *Adobo*!

Adobo is a wonderful dish of chicken or pork, redolent with garlic and black pepper. It is *the* Filipino people's contribution to international cuisine. Having become a favorite among world travelers, it had now been adopted on many international flights, even on flights not originating or landing in the Philippines.

The *Adobo* came with Oriental fried rice. Eating it, I was on cloud nine, literally and figuratively.

The airline had Filipina stewardesses, all outfitted in uniforms designed by a leading Filipino couturier. I smiled with pride. The Philippines can hold its own when it comes to fashion. Some of our designers have even won awards in international fashion competitions.

I chuckled as I remembered a cousin of mine, Esteban, who once dabbled in fashion design when he was in the Philippines. He now lived in San Francisco, California. I made a mental note to call him the moment I got a chance and perhaps visit him once I was settled in New Jersey.

It was a good nine-hour trip from the Philippines to Hawaii, which was long enough for me to recite all the mysteries of the Holy Rosary and long enough to repeat them twice over using my cousin's ivory and silver rosary.

I had never been on a long flight like that, much less traveled across the ocean into another world. I had been on one-hour flights back home, Manila to Bicol mostly, to visit a rich uncle, but nothing had prepared me for this.

After dinner, there was an American movie shown, but I was too nervous by then to enjoy it. We were having a rough flight. We kept bumping into air pockets. I kept losing my place on the rosary beads. The lighted sign that read "Fasten Your Seat Belt" was blinking constantly. I didn't need to fasten mine, because I had never unfastened it from the moment we took off.

I worried that the *Adobo* I ate would make a repeat performance. I thought of the uneaten *lumpias* I brought and how they must have wasted into a cold, soggy pile by now. Maybe the elderly man in the tacky Hawaiian shirt beside me would like them. Nah! He was already into his third cocktail, oblivious of the possibility that we could crash at any moment.

A Filipino movie star was also on the same flight. The stewardess had asked her earlier if she'd care for a cocktail. She had looked at the stewardess quizzically, then brightened and said enthusiastically, "Yes! Fruit cocktail please!" I could still hear the snickers of the stewardesses behind the curtain. I couldn't wait for the Filipino movie tabloids to print that.

The plane continued to rattle dangerously, at least in my mind.

Then it suddenly stopped. We were cruising evenly, solidly. A few minutes later, the lighted "Fasten Your Seat Belt" sign was turned off. I didn't unfasten mine, but most people did. I could hear the unison clinking sound of metal against metal. Some stood and headed for the bathroom.

A long line of heeders of nature's call soon formed, some squirming as they tried to control their bladders. I giggled. The man in the Hawaiian shirt turned and sized me up through drunken eyes. I continued to giggle. He turned around and shook his head, perhaps too drunk to deal with me. I grasped my rosary beads and began to pray again. Perhaps this was what saved us all, my long drawn-out rosary prayers.

We reached Hawaii without any other incidents. I was nervous again. I had heard stories about how brutal the custom officers in Hawaii could be. I suddenly remembered the uneaten *lumpia* and panicked. *What should I do?* The plane was taxiing down the runway. I took the Tupperware container from my hand-carry bag and swiftly inserted it into the hanging magazine rack behind the seat. I covered the exposed top with the unused vomit bag. I hoped the Hawaiian guy was still too drunk to notice. He must have downed a dozen cocktails! I looked at him. He was still dozing. "Aloha to you too," I whispered.

er

I slowly inched toward the customs desk. I clutched my hand-carry bag, mentally trying to remember if it contained any contraband. I had already taken out my passport and the huge envelope which contained among other immigration documents, my clear lung x-ray, proof that I was tuberculosis-free.

An individual with active tuberculosis was prohibited from immigrating to the United States. Applicants for immigration visas had to show a clear chest X-ray before legal entry was granted. Because of this, there was a thriving black market for clear chest X-rays from healthy people that applicants could purchase to pass off as their own. However, X-rays do not always show inactive cases of tuberculosis. Because of this, immigration authorities in America had recently started to install chest X-ray machines at entry points, which rendered the fake chest X-rays useless. I glanced around and saw that this entry point had no X-ray machines yet, so my X-ray would suffice.

"Hello, welcome to the United States of America," the gray-haired, chubby customs officer beamed at the old Filipina in front of me. She must have been in her sixties and no taller than five feet. She was probably petitioned by a spinster daughter. She was visibly nervous as she offered her bag to the officer. He opened the bag with a wide smile, a man used to his job. Suddenly his smile dissolved into a frown.

"What do we have here?" He was gingerly holding a brown package. It reeked. The officer opened it and looked horrified at the sight and stench of 3 dried milkfish called *Daing* (pronounced dah-ing). "What are these?"

"Those are *Daing*, sir!" the Filipina nervously answered.

"Dying? These are dead!"

People within earshot broke into laughter. The elderly woman was as red as a herring.

After the customs, I was herded into a little cubicle where my photograph was taken for my green card. I dreaded how I would look in the photograph. I would find out in a month when I received the green card in the mail.

After posing, I hurried down to the luggage claim area. I had another plane to catch in an hour.

There were passengers looming like vultures over the revolving luggage container. Their bodies involuntarily smooshed closer as the first of the suitcases appeared. From what I could see, it wasn't mine. I waited nervously as suitcase after suitcase popped onto the conveyor belt. None resembled mine. I began to feel very nervous. Then the chute stopped spitting out luggage. I still didn't see mine.

On the verge of hysteria, I frantically scanned the room for an officious- looking person. I spotted a lady in an airport security uniform leaning against one of the ceiling struts. I approached her and related my predicament. She escorted me to the luggage area where we both looked for my suitcases. The crowd around had thinned as passengers left the area heading for their destination gates, suitcases in hand. I had a plane to catch soon too, but I'd be damned if I left without my suitcases! I started crying.

"Well, they're apparently not here. Let's go to the lost and found office and see if they have them there, okay?" the lady officer said, giving me a sympathetic look. I nodded and followed her while mumbling a supplication to St. Anthony of Padua, the patron saint of lost or missing objects.

They weren't in the lost and found either. I was bawling like a baby now, oblivious to onlookers.

"What could have happened to them?" Then I remember the *Santos. Oh No!* I thought, then aloud: "Oh No! Oh No!"

"Lady, calm down. We'll locate your luggage one way or another. Let me get the lost luggage forms for you." She said this with the naïve optimism of a public servant who was oblivious to the success rate of following her procedures and forms.

"Oh, no! This can't be happening! St. Anthony, please help me," I kept repeating to myself as I tried to fill out the forms. I never knew there were so many varieties of luggage until I saw those forms. Each luggage type was carefully illustrated. Did my suitcases look like any of them? I checked what looked like a medium-sized rectangular-shaped suitcase. *St. Anthony, please help me!*

The kindly airport officer escorted me to my next plane. I was the last passenger to board.

"Hello! Welcome to United Airlines!" the cheery stewardess greeted me.

I looked at her through eyes enshrouded in runny mascara. Her smile faded into a crooked grin that screamed, *We have a possible hijacker in our midst.* She took me to my seat and headed back to the front of the plane. I'm sure she took serious note of the seat number, just in case.

They didn't serve the vinegary, garlicky *Adobo* on this plane and, it turned out, they had more meal choices than just chicken and beef. Neither mattered to me, though. I was feeling too upset to eat.

CHICKEN ADOBO

Ingredients:
    3 lbs chicken
    3 tsp salt
    1 tsp black pepper
    2 bay leaves
    8-12 cloves garlic, crushed
    3/4 cup white vinegar
    1/3 cup soy sauce
    3 tbsp oil

Clean chicken, rinse and wipe dry. Cut into large pieces and rub with salt and pepper. Put pieces into a deep saucepan and add bay leaves and crushed garlic. Pour on vinegar and soy sauce and marinate for an hour.

Cook over moderate heat until chicken is tender, adding a little water or stock as the liquid evaporates to keep meat moist. When chicken is cooked, turn up heat for a few minutes to dry out any remaining liquid.

Pour oil into pan and fry on high heat until chicken pieces are dark brown and crisp on the surface. Remove from pan and drain well before serving.

Chapter Five

ARROZ ALA VALENCIANA

Most Filipinos are devout Catholic Christians, but that doesn't mean we don't know how to party. There is always an excuse for a celebration. To honor patron saints, we have elaborate town fiestas. To give thanks for good harvests, we hold harvest festivals that last for days. To welcome a new child into the world, we have extravagant christening parties. Christmas, weddings, and birthdays are all events we invoke for the sheer purpose of partying and these merrymaking festivals are very colorful, oftentimes excessive and always fun! With typical Filipino exuberance, we throw open our homes, inviting in friends and sometimes even total strangers to partake of our feasts. Filipinos believe in sharing and what better way to express that than a party?

It was my twenty-fifth birthday, my first in America, and a grand birthday celebration was in order.

Mother had invited every aunt, uncle, cousin and friend she could possibly locate in the New York-New Jersey area. Our neighbors, my mother's personal care physician, her regular dentist, even her postman, had also been invited to her 2-bedroom apartment for my birthday party.

The living room was typical of a Filipina in America who might resort to design elements that reflect her ethnicity. There was a collection of *Muslim Kris*, ceremonial swords of the Muslim, hanging on one wall, a pair of bas relief sculptures of Philippine pastoral scenes on another wall, a hanging macrame planter by the window, and a three-tiered *capiz*—Philippine seashell—chandelier dangling from the ceiling.

The dining room had a woodcut painting of the Last Supper. It hovered over a table laden with dining accessories like *capiz* coasters, rattan placemats, and napkin holders made of seashells. The wall across from the Last Supper wall was adorned with an over-sized wooden fork and spoon that Mother had bought in Baguio, the Philippines' summer resort, before she left for America.

Mother and Auntie Soledad are the bona-fide interior decorators of this *Pinoy-centric* home. It was really their home away from home, in every way imaginable.

The guests milled about in the dining and living room areas. I spotted Mother talking to two tall Caucasian women. It was a funny sight, Mother's diminutive figure flanked by these two giantesses.

Mother introduced me to her Caucasian friends. "My favorite co-workers," she gushed, from the store where she worked, K-Mart. They were both salespersons, like her. One was older than the other, probably early fifties, with horrible blue hair. The other, perhaps mid-thirties, was a peroxide blonde. I said hello to them, craning my neck. They towered over the mostly Filipino guests.

"So this is Lee-gay-yeah. What a pretty girl!" Katherine, the older one, intoned. I winced at the way she pronounced my name.

"It's LiGAya," I said with a smile, correcting her. "Ligaya, broad A, accent on the second syllable."

"Lee-GAH-yah!" she bravely mimicked.

"Well, that's good enough!" I cheerfully approved.

"You know her name means happy," my mother chimed in.

"Happy? Then it should really be pronounced Lee-GAY-yeah!" Katherine he-hawed, spilling some of her third margarita on the carpet.

"That's right! You're a Gay girl," agreed Lucy, the younger one, as she laughed along.

I was sorely tempted to say something nasty, but checked myself. They were, after all, my mother's guests.

I had been in the States almost three months. I had just gotten a job a few weeks before as a word processing clerk at the <u>Jersey Daily</u>, a local newspaper. It didn't pay "top dollar" as my mother had predicted, but it would do. My mother hadn't demanded yet that I pay part of the rent, nor had she asked me to chip in on the food. I wondered how long my mother would let me stay in the honeymoon stage. Maybe until tonight, then the party's over.

Food abounded at my first American birthday party. It was potluck, although I don't remember seeing Mother's two American salespeople friends bring anything. I mentally reviewed the rules and etiquette of a potluck party. Hmm, they were surely in breach.

I looked for them. They were by the macrame planter, stuffing their faces with a dish called *Arroz Valenciana*. I didn't blame them. The dish was truly delicious, especially the way my mother made it: moist tumeric rice mixed in with tender chicken, fresh seafood, wonderfully cured sausages, and a host of heavenly spices. It was a dish that was Spanish in origin, like a lot of Filipino dishes. After all, we had four hundred years of Spanish rule, the influence naturally showed: in our skin, our language, our music, our clothes, our food. Philippine history can be summed up in the phrase "400 years in a convent, 50 years in Hollywood," which referred to the two very different eras of colonial domination, first by Spain and then by the U.S. Both eras began with naval actions.

I looked around, checking out a different kind of action going on in the room. What a nice party! Too bad my sister Maria wasn't there to enjoy it. Earlier, I had called her long distance after confirming she was at home to receive my call. Because of the time difference, it was imperative that we knew the party we were trying to reach was there to receive the call. How did we do this? It's an old trick that a lot of people with far-away relatives do to avoid additional charges. Our folks back home placed a long distance call to us, collect. They told the operator that they wanted to speak to so-and-so, a pre-arranged fictitious name. The operator called us, asking if we wanted to receive a collect call from so-and-so. We would say, "I think you have the wrong number" or "Sorry, so-and-so is not here right now so we can't accept." Naturally, we weren't charged for the call, but through this gimmick, we learned that the person we had wanted to call was at home and could receive our call. Then we made the call. Not illegal nor ethical, but a very imaginative survival trick for immigrants in America. Check it out in the American Immigrant Survival Tips 101 handbook.

Maria was overjoyed to hear from me. She had a thousand and one questions about America, but we kept the conversation short due to time and cost constraints. At over one dollar per minute, even her inquiry about the missing luggage went unanswered.

We still hadn't heard from the airlines about my missing luggage. Numerous calls to the airline only resulted in their sending me another claim form. They were willing to pay up to $1200 per missing suitcase. Those *Santo* statues were priceless. My mother didn't seem too disturbed though. Maybe she preferred the cash. After all, she had bought me a new work wardrobe from K-Mart, at a 20% employee discount, but still expensive enough to have broken her budget. In addition, she had bought me the party dress I was wearing. I had already worn this party dress a little too often for it to be a "party debut," but it was either this or the 100% wool K-Mart outfit that makes me itch and is too hot to wear inside my mother's over-heated apartment. She cranked the thermostat to *Impiyerno*, Hell.

"Well, how is it to be twenty-five and in America?" It was Katherine again. She was balancing a plate full of *Arroz Valenciana* with other goodies in one hand and gingerly dangling a glass of freshly mixed margarita from the other. She was dithering, slurring through her sentences. "Well?" she impatiently asked.

"It's okay, I guess," I answered, acutely aware of her swaying.

"Oh c'mon, there must be more! Okay, how about a birthday wish? Any special birthday wish, Lee-GAY-yeah?"

I wish you'd leave me alone. I smiled instead and said, "Birthday wish? Mmm, well, just a healthy life for me and my mother."

"Why that's absolutely boring, my dear. How about something like a good looking boyfriend or winning the lottery?"

"Oh wait! Actually, I do have another birthday wish," I said, touching her shoulder to steady her.

"Out with it, dear. Maybe the old fairy godmother will grant you your wish."

"Well, I wish to keep my hair forever dark, lustrous, and free of gray so I don't have to resort to using cheap hair dyes." I gave her a full smile, staring at her blue-tinged hair.

This must have taken her off guard or she must have been really drunk, because she staggered and almost fell, except I caught her in time.

"Oh goodness me, thank you, Lee-GAY-yeah," she said breathlessly. She focused on her plate of *Arroz Valenciana*. "This dish is really delicious! Love it! And these delightful slices of sausages, what are they called, dear?"

"Oh, that, it's Spanish sausage called Chorizo de Bilbao."

"Chorizo. I get that, sausage, yes? But what is Bil—bilbao, dear?"

"Oh Bilbao, well, you know I'm not really sure, but I think it is a breed of," I whispered the last word in her ear, "dog."

"What! Are you kid- goodness - no-"

She was pale as she backed away, disappearing into the crowd. She was a haze of blue in a sea of black.

"Enjoy your *Arroz Valenciana*!" I called out to her.

er

Later that night, I apologized profusely to her for my trick. She accepted with a game smile but refused the take-home doggie bag of *Arroz Valenciana* that my mother offered.

ARROZ VALENCIANA

Ingredients:
    1 whole chicken, cut into pieces
    1/2 lb beef, cut into pieces
    Salt, pepper, and paprika to taste
    2 segments garlic, macerated
    1 onion, sliced
    1 cup tomato, sliced
    6 potatoes, quartered
    2 pieces Chorizos de Bilbao, sliced
    Slices of sweet red pepper
    1/2 cup sweet peas
    1/4 cup green olives
    3 cups tumeric rice, boiled in 3 cups water and 2 cups coconut milk
    2 dozen shrimps, boiled and shelled
    2 crabs, boiled and cracked into pieces
    1/2 cup shortening
    Slices of hardboiled eggs

Season chicken and beef with salt, pepper and paprika and fry until slightly brown. In a deep pan with cover, fry in sequence garlic, onions and tomatoes. Add the potatoes, then the chicken, beef, and chorizos. Mix well, cover the pan, and cook until the meat and potatoes are tender. Add water if necessary. Add the sweet pepper, sweet peas and olives. When the meat and vegetables are done, remove some of the stock from the pan and set aside. Add to the meat mixture the cooked rice and mix thoroughly until well blended. Add cooked shrimp and crabs. Add remaining stock and seasoning to taste. Cook on low heat until mixture becomes quite dry.

Place on a wide serving platter, garnished with slices of hardboiled eggs. Optionally, also garnish with stuffed green olives and red pepper slices.

Chapter Six

HALO-HALO

The Philippines is made up of either 7,107 or 7,108 islands, depending on whether it is low tide or high tide. A Miss Philippines beauty pageant contestant once wittily said this when asked about the number of islands in the country and won the title. Nothing like the winning combination of beauty and brains, huh?

Weather-wise, the Philippines is typically tropical. It is hot and humid year-round with an average temperature of 32 degrees C (90 degrees F). Although the weather pattern is fairly complex, it can be roughly divided into the dry season (January to June) and the wet season (July to December). I think the same beauty contestant mentioned above became a weather girl for a local television news program and it was from watching her that I came to know these facts.

But that was so long ago and far away. I was now in New Jersey, roughly 7,000 miles from my 7,107 or 7,108 islands, experiencing my first summer in America and it was insanely hot. Peter, a fifty-ish bachelor with salt-and-pepper hair who lived across from Mother's apartment, packed up and left for some cooler place. "I am getting the hell out of hell!" he quipped as he jumped into his pick-up truck and drove away. Why Peter was still a bachelor after all these years, besides the obvious fact that he told real eye-rollers for jokes, remained a mystery and a favorite topic of conversation among the meddlesome neighbors, Mother and Auntie Soledad included. I didn't think Peter should ever return to that horrible Jersey neighborhood, but don't tell Mother and Auntie Soledad I said that.

It was a Saturday afternoon. I sat on a white plastic chair on the backyard porch wearing a pair of shorts and a white T-shirt already soaked with perspiration. The chair was part of a patio set that Mother had bought from K-Mart. "It was on Blue Light special— 50% off! Plus, with my employee discount, almost free!" she had gushed. In the Philippines, this set would be a prized possession owned by only a privileged few. Here, everybody had one. The humble patio set, America's great equalizer! I forgave the umbrella's garish design because it did provide a bit of cooling relief from the sweltering heat, though the chair stuck to my exposed legs.

Mother came out of the back door dressed in a bright yellow duster, balancing two tall clear glasses of *Halo-Halo*. *Halo-Halo* literally means a "mix-mix" of ingredients: corn kernels, crisp cereals, assorted tropical fruits, and sugar, topped with shaved ice and a scoop or two of your favorite ice cream. It's a delightful summer dessert that has saved many a Filipino from a heat stroke during the excruciatingly hot summers of the Philippines.

"Remember this, Ligaya? Halo-Halo!" my mother loudly reminded me, as if I'd been away from the Philippines for decades. "Here, taste!" she said as she handed me one of the ice-cold glasses. "I made this specially for you. I got all the authentic ingredients at the Oriental store. *Nangka*, jackfruit and *macapuno*." Coconut meat. "Ay Ligaya, just like in the Philippines!"

I took the glass. It was cool to the touch. "Thank you, Mother. This is such a treat!" I exclaimed, genuinely. With a long handled spoon, I mixed the ingredients while holding the tall perspiring *halo-halo*-filled glass.

Filipino culture is sometimes likened to *Halo-Halo*. The ice cream, which is a Western ingredient, floats on top of the tropical fruits, the Eastern ingredients. As the ice cream melts, it blends with the fruit underneath forming a concoction better than either ice cream or fruit alone. Think Reese's Peanut Butter Cups. It is East meets West in a tall clear glass. Try making a Broadway musical out of that! *Halo-Halo, Dolly!*

"So, *anak*, daughter, are you enjoying your job at the <u>Jersey Daily</u>?" Mother asked, referring to my new position as a classified advertisement taker in a Jersey City newspaper. "*Swerte mo naman*! A nice job just within a few months of your arrival here!" She said this with a mouth full of *halo-halo*.

Swerte means good luck; *malas* means bad luck. In Philippine culture, especially among the urban poor, there is the fatalistic idea that any life situation is unchangeably either *swerte* or *malas*. *Bahala na.* Come what may.

"And of course, you're a smart girl!" Mother hastily added when she saw that my face had fallen. "And, *ay naku*, goodness sake, a very sensitive one!"

"Oh, this heat! Not my bowl of rice, really!" she said, changing the topic.

Was it really out of *swerte* that I chanced upon the job opening at the <u>Jersey Daily</u>? Or was it out of *malas*? I was waiting on the Jersey City PATH terminal platform to board the train that would take me across the Hudson Bay to Manhattan when I felt the need to use the bathroom, badly. *Damn!* I cursed myself silently for not going before I left the house.

I left the train platform and headed for the ladies' bathroom. I was now intimately familiar with the train station's layout, having been subjected to multiple dry run tours from my mother and Auntie Soledad. They had been worried I would get lost in the morass that is the PATH train system: platform 1 goes to downtown New York near the World Train Center; platform 3 goes to midtown where Macy's Department store is located; and platform 2 sometimes goes to downtown, other times to midtown. You have to listen carefully for the announcements on the public address system, which are often garbled and usually played at the same time that another train is screeching into the station. And then there's the process of paying for the train ticket. You must use exact change or you will not get through the metallic turnstile. So God bless my Mother and my aunt for their doting.

A sign on the ladies' bathroom door said, "Closed for Clean-up." *Malas!* Bad luck. I glanced around and spotted the men's bathroom just across the corridor. Its sign-less door beckoned me. *Swerte.* Good luck. I rushed towards it to find the door locked. *Malas!* I jiggled the doorknob violently to no avail.

"Hey, excuse me! What'cha doin', Ma'am?" a PATH train staff person called out to me.

I turned around to spot a black, pot-bellied man wearing a now familiar blue and white PATH train staff uniform. He sported a set of dazzling white teeth when he smiled. "Can I help you?"

"Sir, I just need to use the bathroom and the ladies' is not available." He stepped to the door and knocked.

"Wait a frigging minute! I'm still using it!" The voice sounded strained.

The PATH Train person shook his head. We looked at each other. We both sensed a long constipated session. He let out a sigh.

"Why don't you leave the station and use the bathroom in the
<u>Jersey Daily</u> building across? I'll let you in again when you're
finished, okay?"

I looked across the street. Somehow I never really had noticed
that building before. A large sign outside the 4-story brick building
announced in old English script: "The Jersey Daily since 1956".

"Do you think they'll let me use their bathroom?" I asked the man
while fidgeting.

He grinned. "Just tell them Jim sent you, okay?"

I nodded thankfully and rushed across the street.

I entered the building. I was amazed at the expanse of the inside
of the building. At the reception desk sat an obviously Filipina
receptionist, despite the flaming red hair.

"Hi, can I help you? What can I do POR you?" she inquired,
pronouncing the "f" as "p." It was a forgivable mistake, being from a
nation of people whose alphabet does not include the letter "F."

"Oh, yes, hello. May I use your bathroom, please? Uh, ah, Jim
from the PATH station told me I could—"

Rolling her eyes, she pointed to a door nearby. "Ay, *dios ko*, my
God, I swear that PATH train toilet must be cursed!" I heard her say
as I rushed into the bathroom.

ә

Whew! Thank God! I muttered, relieved, as I exited the bathroom.

I approached the receptionist to thank her.

"*Pilipino ka ba?*" she asked before I could even open my mouth.
For future Filipino immigrants, be ready to be bombarded with this
question everywhere you go. Are you Filipino? I must have heard it
asked of me a thousand times already. I had grown tired of asking
myself why. Is it a need to seek a friendly face? A longing for news
back home? I didn't look Filipino enough? Or was this some kind of
a code like a question with a hidden meaning?

I nodded. "*Ikaw rin?*" I asked back. Are you also? Up close, I
saw her hair was actually deep orange. Ike, a gay friend back home,
told me if I ever decided to dye my hair for some crazy reason, to

avoid red—it would only turn orange on a black (or deep brown) haired person. I controlled the urge to giggle.

"*Ako si Stella.*" I'm Stella. She offered a manicured hand.

"Ligaya." I smiled.

"Bagong dating ka ano?" New in the states, huh? *Oh dear!* I wondered if I had that "fresh off the boat" look, as my Auntie Soledad had teasingly chided not so long ago. How could she tell?

I nodded, suddenly feeling insecure about my appearance. "I'm on my way to New York to look for a job. In midtown, through some placement agencies."

"Hey, that's PANtastic! But—" she gestured for me to come nearer. I did and almost gagged at the heavy perfume emanating from her. She lowered her voice to barely above a whisper. "You know, we happen to have an opening here right now. D'you know word processing?"

Memories of all those months of Mother nagging me to take that word processing class washed over me like a cool swim in the river.

"Oh, yes. Yes! *Puede ba ako mag-apply dito?*" I answered gratefully. Can I apply?

"Of course! *Pero teka, hindi ka TNT ha?*" she eyed me suspiciously. You're not TNT, are you?

TNT. *Tago-nang-Tago.* It was not dynamite, but it was equally dynamic in meaning. *Tago-nang-Tago* means "well-hidden." It was a term used to refer to aliens who stayed illegally in America beyond their visa expiration dates. I didn't sympathize one hundred percent, but I totally understood why so many would rather go underground than leave this land of milk and honey.

"NO, of course not. I have a green card!" I answered defensively.

"Okay then." She pulled out an application form from her desk drawer and handed it to me. "I guess you won't be going to Manhattan today, apter all," she grinned.

And just like that, with both *malas* and *swerte* on my side, I found myself a job in America. *Malas? Swerte?* Is life really completely random or can we control our lives in every way?

et

I had been with the <u>Jersey Daily</u> for a month and a half, working as a word processing clerk and training for a classified ad taker position. The ad taker position entailed being on the phone all day taking all kinds of classified ads, from help wanted to used bikes for sale. It was not that interesting, but it paid better and it wasn't like the word processing clerk position was overly stimulating.

The ad taker position had opened up a few weeks after I started working at the <u>Jersey Daily</u>. Stella, who knew practically everyone in the company, had urged me to see the supervisor of the classified department.

His name was Picard Lancelloti. I sat across from him in his office, which had a see-through glass window that overlooked the department. I looked out and saw multiple sets of eyes looking back. I hoped they weren't as nosey as they appeared.

"What I can offer you now is an entry-level position, but I'm sure that in due time, you'll easily be one of the top classified sales people." I must have seemed reluctant for he continued on. "Ligaya, the goal of the entry-level position is not simply to get a paycheck. It is to start you off towards learning how the world of American work operates on a day-to-day basis, how to deal with co-workers of varying mentality, how to take direction from your superiors—uh, that would be me, in your case—and finally how to take responsibility in the American system." He exuded confidence and something else I couldn't place at the time.

"Thank you. I promise to do my best, Mr. Lancelloti."

"Picard," he corrected me. "Call me Picard. Everyone else does."

I thought that was cool. I had never been on a first name basis with any of my bosses in the Philippines. That would have shown much disrespect.

"What do you think?" Mr. Lancelloti, I mean Picard, offered a hand to clinch the offer.

"Yes, I accept. I think this is a great opportunity for me. Thank you again, Picard." I flinched a bit as I accepted his hand. It was sweaty and hairy and the handshake seemed a bit tight. It was a small price to pay. I was now a classified ad taker.

From the beginning, almost everyone at the classified department made me feel utterly welcome. There was Anita, a loud but totally friendly Puerto Rican; Loretta and Delilah, both borrowed-from-the-bottle blonds, always flirting with walk-in classified ad customers; Armida and Ruthie, the mother figures, both close to retirement and sporting blue hair; mousy, bespectacled Joanna, the richest in the department, always exceeding her sales quota, always getting all the bonuses; Christopher, the department's Prince Charming, a guy who actually wanted to be a fireman someday; and Tuwanda, the personification of the "black and beautiful" attitude.

I tried to stay out of Tuwanda's hair as much as possible, which was an almost impossible feat because I was assigned a desk next to hers.

What I really liked about working in the department was taking incoming calls from all of the advertisers of different ethnicities in this "melting pot" city—Latinos, Japanese, Koreans, Indians, and of course, the Filipinos who speak about 87 different dialects. Accents arise from foreign speakers mismapping the sounds of a language to their native language's sounds, so you can imagine the dizzying number of accents that we had to deal with on a daily basis. But I quickly learned to attune my ear to different accents so it became equally easy to understand Mr. Yamato, who was Japanese and a regular advertiser of flea market items, when he greeted me with "Haro Rigaya" and Mr. Patel, an apartment manager who hailed from Bombay, when he referred to his overdue tenants as "ideeeooots."

et

The *Halo-Halo* was halfway gone when we heard the front doorbell ring.

Mother said, "*Siguro si Soledad.*" Maybe it's your Aunt Soledad. She frowned. "I told her I'd call her later." She rose and headed for the front door, still carrying her glass of *halo-halo*. I followed.

Mother squinted into the door's peephole. She did a double-take.

"*Aba, mamang Kano!*" Hey, it's an American guy! "Wonder what he wants?"

"Yes? What do you want?" she called out, refusing to open the door to a stranger.

"I'm from the airlines, ma'am. We have a delivery for a Miss De—De Guzman!"

Mother and I looked at each other, amazed. I opened the door before Mother could stop me.

Malas. Swerte. This was how my imitation leather suitcase found its way back to me. I almost didn't recognize it. The handle was broken, the sides had scratches, and the bag was now held together by unsightly ropes that had taken the place of the original carry straps. But my nametag sat undisturbed in its patriotic red, white and blue. I burst into tears. The sweaty *Kano* grinned. He had seen these theatrics one too many times.

Wiping his damp brow, he asked us to open the suitcase to check if everything's in there. I remembered the antique *Santos*. Mother nodded in encouragement. I reached for the bag with shaking hands.

My clothes were all there. I shyly covered some underwear that lay on top. I pressed down on Aunt Soledad's *terno*, formal dress, and felt the satisfying hardness of Mother's antique *Santos* statues pressing back.

"I think there's nothing missing." I said and smiled at the *Kano*. I silently thanked St. Anthony of Padua, the patron saint of missing objects for a favor granted, no matter that it came a few months later. *Dios ko!* I was a such a nervous wreck that day in the Honolulu airport, sobbing and shaking while uttering a supplication to St. Anthony to help me find my missing luggage. "Yes, nothing missing." I repeated, more to assure myself than the smiling *Kano*.

"Alrighty, then. Just sign here, please."

"Oh, sir, would you like some *Halo-Halo*?" my mother blurted out before I could stop her.

The *Kano* frowned a bit. "Halo-Ha—what is that?" My mother showed him the tall glass in her hand.

The *Kano* took one look and shook his head. "Oh, no. Thank you, but I gotta get going. It looks delicious though," he added, eyeing the clear glass halfway filled with melted ice cream and bits of fruits and beans.

"It is delicious!" Mother declared. "You gotta try it sometime."

"Mother!" I said, mocking a shocked reaction.

"Well, anyway, ladies, have a good afternoon and enjoy your, uh, hal—ha…whatever that is." He gave us a final grin and walked towards his van.

"Halo-Halo!" my mother called out to him. The guy turned back and waved while exclaiming: "Hello to you too!" He entered his van, shaking his head.

HALO-HALO
(Tropical Fruit Melange)

Ingredients:
  2 tbsp nangka (jackfruit)
  2 tbsp macapuno (a variety of coconut meat sold in bottles in Oriental food stores)
  2 tbsp sweetened kidney beans
  2 tbsp sweetened garbanzos
  2 tbsp sweetened banana
  2 tbsp yam
  2 tbsp mango slices
  2 tbsp pineapple slices
  2 tbsp sweetened corn kernels
  Enough crushed or shaved ice to fill glass
  2/3 cup milk (preferably the canned evaporated variety)
  1-2 scoops of ice cream

Combine all the ingredients from the first section in a tall clear glass. Add crushed or shaved ice. Add milk and top it with a scoop or two of your favorite ice-cream flavor.

With all the ingredients in place, the halo-halo is complete, inviting, ready to be feasted on.

Chapter Seven

JAMON EN DULCE

Mahjong, the traditional Chinese game played with tiles, is one of the Filipino peoples' favorite pastimes. It is played everywhere during every occasion: birthday parties, weddings, graduations, anniversaries, fiestas. Even christening events are incomplete without a group of adults breaking out the board for some quick, addictive competition.

During long funeral wakes, it plays a vital role in keeping the mourners wide awake. Strong caffeine-laden *Batangas* coffee is no match for the eye-popping clatter that the 144 ivory or bone tiles make when mixed or "washed" faced down on the mahjong table.

Like many games of chance, it has found its way into the gambling arena. Serious stakes have been bet on the outcome of the tiles. One famous Filipino mahjong player lost his house, his car and his wife, in that order, during one marathon mahjong session. Then he committed suicide, dead from a single bullet to his head. Another player, who used to be a high Philippine official, was rumored to have made many important government decisions with wide-ranging political implications while playing mahjong with his cronies, who were not exactly impartial to the outcomes of his decisions. This led to his downfall in his political and personal lives. Now he is in jail, but during prison breaks, he still pulls out the board hoping for that elusive winning mahjong tile that will return him to the top of his game.

In America, mahjong continues to be a favorite pastime of the Filipinos. Although one can buy a cheap set of mahjong plastic tiles in select Oriental stores, many Filipinos choose to bring their most prized mahjong sets with them to America. My mother's set has tiles made of bone, which are stronger and more desirable than the more commonly used ivory. The tiles rest in an elegant wooden box with a mother of pearl inlay.

That night, this precious set was on full display, perched atop the mahjong table in the living room and brightly illuminated by Mother's humongous *capiz* sea shell chandelier. That night, a

Saturday, was my mother's monthly mahjong session with her *amigas*, lady friends. My Auntie Soledad was coming and so was another aunt who lived two cities away in Bayonne, New Jersey, Auntie Trining. *Aling* Salvacion, a retired Filipina who lived in the neighborhood, would fill the fourth corner of the mahjong table. All three were at my birthday party and a few other gatherings after that so they were no strangers to our house or to me. I was actually looking forward to seeing them again so I had offered to cook the pre-mahjong dinner for the night.

"Are you sure?" Mother asked, her voice unsure if she heard me right.

"Yeah, it will be fun. You always cooked, so now's my turn."

"What are you thinking of making? My *amigas* don't care for American food on a night like this, you know."

I often brought sandwiches for my lunch to work, rarely Filipino food. A while back, I had learned to bring American lunches only. Stella, the Filipina receptionist, had once brought *Balut* to work. *Balut* is a boiled, fertilized duck's egg. It is eaten by cracking open the wide end, sprinkling a little salt inside, sipping the broth and then cracking the whole egg open to savor the red yolk and tiny chick inside. *Balut* is popularly believed to be an aphrodisiac but that's not the reason Stella brought it that day. She just wanted a genuine Filipino lunch. She had come to my desk and offered me one.

Tuwanda crinkled her nose at the sight. "What the hell's that?"

"It's *Balut*, boiled egg. Would you like one? It's very tasty," Stella said, not quite honestly.

"No, no, thanks!" Tuwanda said, shaking her head. I also declined. I had two Spam sandwiches in my lunch bag.

Stella then went to the office kitchenette to warm up her *Balut* in the microwave. There was a small gathering of employees in the room, waiting to warm up their lunches as well. Stella put her egg in the microwave, overestimated the time factor and left it in too long. There was an explosion! Everyone stared at the smoking microwave oven. Splattered on its glass door was the disgusting duck fetus, much like those Garfield-suction cup toys clinging to car windows. Many appetites were ruined that day.

er

I was tempted to serve *Balut* to Mother's mahjong guests.

"Don't worry, Mother. It will be an all-Filipino *fiesta* tonight, promise!" I said with a flash of a nervous smile. Mother still had that effect on me. I was the student who desperately sought the approval of her teacher. Memories of those long sessions of cooking lessons several summers ago in the Philippines came wafting back, like the burnt smell of food I mangled during those sessions.

"*Fiesta,* huh? Can you really make something that will do justice to that word you just used, *Fiesta*? You know a feast is like a king's dinner?" Mother teased but I believe she, the one who taught me all about cooking one summer many moons ago, had just dared me to outdo myself in the kitchen that night. Boiled eggs a feast will not make, fertilized or not.

"Alright Mother, I'm going to make *Jamon en Dulce* tonight!" I declared before I could even think. *Oh no!*

My mother gasped, "*Anak*, daughter, that's perfect but difficult to make! Are you sure?"

I nodded. Laughing, Mother hugged me tight. I believed I just got an A-plus from Mother, the cooking guru. Or, as we say in Tagalog, *Guro*, teacher.

Jamon en Dulce can elicit that kind of reaction. It is a sweet Filipino baked ham that is traditionally prepared only on special occasions like Christmas or Fiesta. I had thrown caution to the wind in thinking that the festivity of a mahjong session would do. My stomach ascended on an elevator to my throat as I made a mental list of the ingredients needed for the festive ham. Too many complicated ingredients! A quick trip to the nearby Pathmark supermarket and its adjoining Oriental food store was definitely in order.

er

Storms blew away and seas became calm. I was calmer once I'd done most of the preliminaries for the *Jamon En Dulce*. I was glazing the ham with a mix of orange juice, lemon juice, coca-cola and brown sugar when the doorbell rang announcing the first of the arrivals of *Mahjongeras*, mahjong participants.

It was Auntie Soledad. She breezed into the kitchen, already munching garlic peanuts and holding a glass of *calamanzi,* Filipino lime, mixed with something alcoholic, no doubt.

"*Hoy Ligaya.* I heard you're serving us *Jamon en Dulce* tonight." She greeted me with a rum/lime-laden air kiss, mindful of her full make-up and my sweaty face. "*Wow, Iha, tumama ka ba sa lottery?*" Did you win the lottery?

I was surprised to see our aging bachelor neighbor, Peter, following behind her. "Hi, Ligaya, how's it going?"

He had a bottle of champagne in one hand and a glass filled with the effervescent drink in another. Auntie Soledad once told me that the bubbly was Peter's drink of choice. *Makes me feel like I'm celebrating something every time I drink it*, was how Peter explained his choice. I thought but did not say aloud, *That's a creative way to defend one's effervescence for alcohol.* I left Peter alone that way. He was a nice enough man. Kind of like an uncle.

"He may be in his 50s but, really, he's still a growing boy," my auntie, who had grown very fond of Peter, would sometimes say in defense of him.

"Yeah, growing around the middle," Mother would retort.

"Mmm, smells good in here," the growing boy inhaled deeply and noisily.

Mother walked in. "Hey, are you guys checking out my daughter's special treat for all of us? *Jamon en Dulce,* can you believe it? I taught her how to cook that when she was just a small girl, you know?"

She tapped Peter on the shoulder. "*Jamon En Dulce.* Do you know what that means in English, Peter?"

"No, ma'am, but I bet it's something tasty." Peter licked his lips for emphasis.

Auntie Soledad frowned. "Mmm, you *Kano*, no imagination. Tasty, delicious, good, great! Boring words to describe such a culinary creation! This dish is heavenly, scrumptious, mouth-watering, delec-!"

"Alright, alright! Geez, what do they give you immigrants at your port of entry, a thesaurus?" he said, slapping his thigh as he broke into guffaws.

Auntie Soledad and my mother glared at him while I giggled in the corner.

"So champagne makes me funny and witty. Sue me. C'mon, loosen up. You both look like you just swallowed a whole herd of canaries! Oh wait, I meant, a flock of canaries! Or a group of canaries? Or is it a pack of, or a host of, or a team of, or a colony of—"

I lost it right there as I joined Peter in a full-bodied, jaw-cracking explosion of mirth. Mother and Auntie Soledad were shaking their heads but they were also letting a giggle or two slip.

"Oh that was good!" said an out-of-breath Peter, wiping laughing tears from his eyes. I did the same.

"Alright, okay, let's leave Ligaya to finish her masterpiece," Mother finally said, pushing them out of the kitchen. Peter placed his arms around both women as they exited. As he left, he gave me a drunken wink.

I dismissed them with a wave of my hand clutching a glazing brush.

Peter, now there's a happy and contented man, like a carabao in a mud pool, I thought to myself as I continued glazing the ham. It was looking egregious, flagitious, and saporous! Hey, I used to be a Spelling Bee champ, remember? I just hoped this rich dish didn't give them cardialgia.

ღ

Thank goodness no one suffered mild indigestion from eating the *Jamon en Dulce*. What? You thought cardialgia was a serious disorder of the heart?

Everyone had high praise for the meal. Auntie Soledad, tipsy from too much *calamanzi* and what I guessed was rum, slurred great eulogies abut my cooking.

"...and I'm the one who taught her and now, it seems the student is a better cook than the teacher!" Mother chimed in. She did not drink, so she wasn't just saying this because she was tipsy. I took it as a compliment and smiled at her.

Peter left to go back to his empty home or the cocktail bars in Newark. Who knew?

Auntie Trining was snoring away in Mother's bedroom. She had played 4 sets of mahjong and excused herself. She had had the most to drink tonight, not to mention 3 helpings of *Jamon En Dulce*. She was a possible candidate for cardialgia-itis.

So there I was, having been designated the fourth player, the South Wind, to replace Auntie Trining, who no doubt would be waking up tomorrow with a throbbing headache and a nasty stomachache. In preparation for this, Mother had placed a bottle of aspirin and a roll of Tums by her bedside.

Both Auntie Trining and Auntie Soledad brought with them small overnight bags in anticipation of the marathon mahjong session and in case one of them became too drunk to drive back to her respective apartment.

I was nervous as we started to mix the tiles, face down so we couldn't see the suits. After what seemed to be an endless mixing and rattling of the tiles, we arranged them into equal stacks, 2 tiles one on top of another, in front of us. Joining all stacks, we made a perfect square.

The designated dealer, otherwise known as the East Wind, in this case Aling Salvacion, rolled the dice to start a new game. I felt very inadequate as I examined the concentrated faces of Mother, Auntie Soledad and Aling Salvacion. Lips shut tight, eyes narrowed to a squint, all three mahjong experts gathered up their tiles and with magician's hands adeptly arranged them in order of suits. I did the same, only much slower, like a magician's newly hired clumsy apprentice.

"C'mon Ligaya, the night is not getting any younger," Auntie Soledad teased while impatiently drumming her manicured fingers on the mahjong tabletop.

"I'm almost finished, almost—" *Okay, okay. Balls go with balls. Bamboos go with bamboos. Characters, oh I only have one. Flowers, I declare and replace with...oh, another character so now I have two.* I felt their impatient eyes as I finally got my tiles in order. "There, I'm ready!" I flashed them a nervous grin.

Mother immediately discarded a tile.

"*Pung!*" Auntie Soledad yelled, retrieving the discarded tile and adding it to her two other identical tiles in hand. She then discarded a tile to replace the one she just acquired to make a winning *Pung*.

"*Chow!*" Mother called out, grabbing the discarded tile to form a 3-4-5 sequence. I was flabbergasted. I was no match for these professionals. In my competitive little heart, I secretly wished this were a Spelling Bee competition instead of a marathon mahjong session. That I would've aced.

"*Pung* also!" Aling Salvacion shouted out, grabbing the winning tile.

"Hoy, Ligaya, your turn!" Aunt Soledad exclaimed, trying to interrupt my daydream of standing at the podium spelling my award-winning word: braggadocio.

"What's the meaning?" I asked the pronouncer.

"A noun meaning a braggart. Arrogant pretension. Cockiness," he answered.

"Could you please pronounce it again?"

"Braa ga doe see yoe."

"Any other way to pronounce it?"

"Braaga doe shee yoe."

"Language of origin?"

"Italian."

"Hoy, Ligaya!" Mother was screaming in my ear. I snapped out of my daydream. These ladies' mastery of *mahjong* had robbed me of any amount of braggadocio.

"So slow. Hoy, when your mother was cocktail waitressing in a Bayonne nightclub, she was quick as *kidlat*, lightning. C'mon- oh my!!" Auntie Soledad's hand flew to her mouth.

Mother and Aling Salvacion were both as pale as *puting bigas*, white rice.

"Cocktail-waitressing? Mother, you told me you were the manager of a restaurant in Bayonne. I didn't know you—" I glared at my mother, awaiting her response.

"Hey, I'm just kidding. Sorry, Aurora." Auntie Soledad tried fruitlessly to salvage the situation. Mother scowled at Auntie Soledad. Aling Salvacion was suddenly pre-occupied rearranging her mahjong tiles.

I looked at my mother, uncertain. She slowly shook her head and dropped her shoulders in a sad, resigned gesture.

"Okay, so the truth comes out. So I served cocktail drinks at a club in Bayonne in my early days here. I couldn't help it. I couldn't find a better paying job. Your auntie here was kind enough to recommend me to the club owner who was her friend." My mother's voice was hoarse, defensive.

"Why hide it from me? Why sugar-coat your past life here in America for me?" I said the words before I could process them in my brain.

"You need not know, Iha. *Nakakahiya!*" It's shameful! "The sacrifices we have to do to reach this level of comfortable living. The menial jobs I was forced to take." My mother's eyes started to frighten me. There was hurt, shame, and sadness there.

"Akala mo basta na lang makakuha ng magandang trabaho dito?" You think good jobs are handed out just like that here? "You're lucky you have college education, but what about me? *Matanda na, hanggang high school lang?*" I'm old and just a high school graduate.

"Hoy, tama na 'yan ha? Tama na!" Okay, enough of that, Auntie Soledad said sharply. "Enough! Look, Ligaya, your mother did what she had to do to make ends meet. I helped her every way I could but you know how she is, proud as a peacock. But this I can tell you *iha*, no matter how menial the jobs that she took, she never compromised her honesty, integrity and morals. You should be very proud of her." Tears began to flow in Auntie Soledad's eyes as she pleaded with my mother. "Aurora, *patawarin mo ako.*" Forgive me. "Me and my big mouth." She sobbed.

The pain swelled in my throat until I no longer cared. I burst into tears. The east, the north, the west, and the south corners of the mahjong table were soon in tear-soaked turmoil. We Filipinos are a very sensitive bunch.

Auntie Soledad was anxious to end this line of talk, this emotional *tsunami*. She quickly wiped her wet face. "Let's continue playing, okay? C'mon!" She discarded a tile.

Still crying, I drew one. It was a tile that I needed. I inserted it into my row of tiles and discarded another.

"*Pung!*" Mother's voice was hoarse as she picked up the discarded tile and threw another. "I also worked as a cleaning woman in a home for the aged, you know?" Mother was unstoppable. "Oh yes, all sorts of odd jobs before I landed this sales clerk job at K-Mart."

"*Kang!*" Aling Salvacion's eyes were still wet, though there was now a shine in them, perhaps brought on by the fact that she had just won a four of a kind. She displayed her winning tiles proudly as she said, "Your mother even had to sell Tupperware. Now that job was fun!"

"- and Avon. 50 percent commission!" Auntie Soledad chimed in.

Mother was smiling now, though her eyes were still moist.

"*Mahjong! Mahjong!*" I declared, grinning. I laid down my tiles to display the winning suits. Everyone was shocked.

"What the—?" Auntie Soledad was speechless. Mother and I faced each other, laughing and wiping the tears from each other's eyes.

"Okay, enough of that drama. *Para naman tayong mga artista sa radyo.*" We were just like radio soap opera stars. "Hey, let's have some more of that delicious sugar-coated ham of yours, okay?" Auntie Soledad rose from her seat, tapping each of us on our proud shoulders.

I excused myself. I had had enough of the *jamon*. "Time for me to go to bed now. I'm afraid I'm feeling a bit of languescence," I said, yawning. Auntie Soledad, Aling Salvacion, and my mother were already busy carving what was left of the ham, too engrossed to listen to an ex-spelling bee champion's sleepy lament.

JAMON EN DULCE

Ingredients:
  1 pc. boneless ham (5-7 pounds)
  2 cups orange juice
  1 cup brown sugar
  1 cup coca-cola
  1 tsp salt
  1/4 tsp cinnamon

2 pcs. orange slices
2 pcs. cherries, halved
1/2 cup lemon-flavored iced tea crystals

Combine orange juice, brown sugar, coca-cola, salt, and cinnamon in a pot. Add ham and simmer for 20 minutes. Remove ham and simmer sauce for 5 more minutes. In the meantime, roll ham over iced tea crystals. Place ham in 375 degrees F oven and use sauce to glaze. Cook ham for 5 more minutes while glazing continuously.

Top with pineapple slices and add cherries to the center of each slice. Cook ham for another 5 minutes.

Cool and serve.

Chapter Eight

EGG FO-YUNG

One of Auntie Soledad's numerous Filipino friends had a story about the first time he interviewed for a job in America. It was February, the height of winter, when he was interviewed for an accountant's job in Manhattan.

Dressed in many layers of winter clothing, he took the subway to a midtown Manhattan office. He had been in America for only a few days, had not seen much of it, and had certainly not experienced an actual snowy day.

In the company's office, he was seated across from the interviewer, which afforded him a good view of the streets outside. The interview started with the usual preliminaries: educational background, work experiences, hobbies. It was going well until it started to snow outside. What a glorious sight! Something that we never saw back in our tropical homeland: the miracle of water vapor turning into ice. The guy was soon mesmerized, fascinated by the snowflakes falling from the American sky. He stared at the blankets of white, completely oblivious to the questions that the interviewer was asking him. The interviewer soon brought him back to Earth with some gentle nudging, but the damage was done. He did not get the job. The reason? Apparently, the person being replaced was flighty and the hiring manager had requested that the person hired must demonstrate an ability to totally focus on the job at hand. What is the moral of the story? Get acclimated before doing job interviews!

Adapting to America's work environment involves some must-haves:

You must have a valid social security number. This is an essential form of identification. You cannot work (legally) in America without it. The employer needs it to report your income to the Internal Revenue Service.

My Auntie Soledad accompanied me to the Social Security office on my first day of work. There was a long line. It took us half the day to reach the front of the line, but I left the office later with a card in my hand and a smile on my face. "By golly, your own social security number!" my Auntie Soledad said excitedly as if I'd just won the lottery. In a way, I had. One's social security number is an invaluable tool for navigating American life. Besides needing it to work, one also needs it to open a bank account, apply for a credit card, and apply to college.

You must have an Alien Registration Receipt Card, or "green card." When you arrive in America with an immigrant's visa, you will be given a temporary green card status stamped on your passport. You will receive your real green card in the mail a few months later. Make sure the Immigration and Naturalization Service (INS) has an accurate mailing address for you. If more than six months goes by without the green card in the mail, visit or write the INS to straighten matters out. By the way, this card is not actually green, though it once was.

Obtaining the green card is the goal of all immigrants in America. It gives all the rights and responsibilities of a citizen (except voting and consular protection abroad) and a first step toward citizenship. Employers are penalized for hiring illegal aliens so they check documentation more carefully than in the past.

You must have Proof of Residence. Often telephone and utility bills with your name and address on them will suffice. Mother still pays our utility bill but she had it changed to my name for this purpose.

No amount of mastery in word processing or word-of-mouth recommendation from my first friend, Stella the receptionist, would have gotten me the job at the Jersey Daily if I weren't in possession of one or all of these must-haves. It sounds corny, but I really do go to work every day feeling lucky I have all the necessary tools to be legally employed in America.

But one day, I entered the office not feeling lucky at all but feeling a weird sense of nervousness and impending doom.

The day before, my boss, Picard Lancelloti, had asked me to take over the obituaries task since Marla, the regular obituary ad taker, was taking a few days off.

Taking death notices was not a popular job. Of course, there was the morbidity factor, but there was also the work schedule. It started at the ungodly hour of six in the morning.

I was rightfully hesitant but Picard insisted it would be good training for me. "It will make you a really well-rounded ad taker, familiar with all types of advertisements," he had said while leaning on my desk, breathing distance from my face. Tuwanda hadn't said a thing, but I saw her cringe.

"You know he likes Asian women," Tuwanda gossiped to me a few days after I was hired in Picard's department. "His former girlfriend was Japanese," she added.

"Former? So what happened to her?" I asked. Tuwanda answered with a shrug. Picard could see all his subordinates through the glass window. We never discussed the matter again. I was tempted to ask know-it-all Stella but was afraid it might find its way to Picard's desk, knowing Stella's reputation as the company's unofficial walking newsletter.

I went into the office; it was deserted. I walked to my desk and deposited my handbag and my breakfast, an egg sandwich. In a rush to arrive on time, I had forgotten to bring lunch.

Mother had prepared the egg sandwich in a hurry when I declined the tempting *Tapsilog*, a typical Filipino breakfast of cured beef, fried eggs and fried rice she had prepared for us this morning.

"I have to take over the obituaries ad for the next few days, because the girl in charge is on vacation and the calls from the funeral homes for these death notices start coming in at six! At six dollars per line, we can't afford to lose these customers," I explained while sipping a cup of instant Nescafe.

"Obituaries? Death notices? I didn't know those are paid notices," Mother said, surprised and scandalized.

"Everything is charged except when someone's placing an ad to give away pets for adoption. It's the only classified ad we take free of charge." I grabbed my bag.

"That doesn't seem right." Mother shook her head as she handed me the wrapped egg sandwich.

"Mother, it's business." I rolled my eyes, which only provoked her further.

"Yeah, the business of taking advantage of the dead!" she shouted at me as I walked out the door.

Filipinos pay much respect to their dead. Our funeral ceremonies and rituals are often lengthy and colorful. We have wakes or vigils for the dead that last as long as seven days. Notices are mostly spread through word of mouth, never through paid, printed obituaries unless the deceased lived in a big city where word-of-mouth communication is not feasible. Friends are expected to grieve with the members of the deceased's family, give *Limos*- monetary contributions - and keep vigil until the interment.

The vigil usually takes place at the home of the deceased where the embalmed body is on display in an open casket. A steady stream of friends and relatives pay their respects, especially when the deceased was a well-loved one in the community.

A pig or a cow is bought and butchered to feed all who come to mourn. Refreshments such as soft drinks, *calamansi* juice, *salabat* - ginger tea-, coffee and cocoa are served to those who join the wake. Alcoholic drinks are also consumed discreetly.

On the final day of the viewing, the relatives view the body and the children, if there are any, are asked to kiss the hand of the deceased. Then the lid of the coffin is nailed shut to much loud wailing by the relatives.

Filipinos believe in life after death and the possibility of the return of a loved one from beyond. As the bearers lift the coffin, all the household members of the deceased pass under it to prevent the spirit from coming back to haunt them. Then everyone heads to the cemetery where the coffin is opened for a final viewing.

Novena, prayers, are said for nine consecutive nights. On the final night, a sumptuous meal is prepared in celebration of the end of the *novena.*

The period of mourning extends up to a year. During this period, very close female relatives, like widows, mothers and daughters, wear all-black attire. (If it weren't for the dead, it would make for a very chic New York look.) Men wear a simple black pin on their shirts. Milestones and events such as birthdays and fiestas are downplayed during this period out of respect for the deceased. A year later, the mourning period ends with a jubilant mass followed by an elaborate banquet.

er

I almost dropped the cup I was carrying when I saw Picardi in the kitchenette. He was pouring a cup of freshly brewed coffee. The robust smell made me heady and uneasy. *What is he doing here so early?*

"Good morning, Ligaya. Care for some coffee?" he asked casually as if he usually arrived for work before sunup.

"Mr Lance-Picardi! Hello, go—good morning! You're early?" I stammered.

"Well I thought I'd help you out seeing that this is your first time to ever take death notices from the funeral homes. It can be, er-deadly, you know?" he said, laughing at his own bad joke. I managed a weak chuckle.

"Oh, no need, Picardi. Ruthie was kind enough to rehearse me on this yesterday. Sorry you had to trouble yourself to be here this early and—"

"Oh nonsense. I don't mind. Not at all. I'll just be around in case a problem comes up. Besides, I wouldn't want my most promising ad taker to be working so alone and unprotected this early."

There was something in the tone of his voice that made the hairs on the back of my neck stand on end.

"Hey, are you okay?" he asked, rubbing my back with his hand! I pulled away, stunned.

"Hey, hey no need to do that." He smiled but his voice had a threatening tone.

"What?" That's what I said: What? Not "Excuse me?" or "Beg your pardon?" It's funny how easily we forget our manners when under duress.

"You know, you're a very pretty woman, Ligaya. And a smart one. I can see you becoming a top money earner for my department soon." I may have imagined it but I swear I saw the front of his trousers rise a bit. "Like I said, no need to do that," he repeated.

My head was spinning! I was seeing multiple Picardis!

The phone rang. I scampered away to answer it.

It was the funeral home, calling in a death notice. I tried to concentrate but could not. Picardi hovered nearby. I asked the caller to repeat himself. I explained that I was new at this, just filling in for the regular gal, Marla. Though he sounded impatient, he obliged. I was grateful for the molasses-like transaction on the phone. "Can you please repeat that again?" I was trying to buy time the way I did during my spelling bee days, *Can you pronounce that again, please?*

I glanced up. Picardi was walking towards the main door. He looked back before he disappeared outside. He shot me a look I will never forget. I finished the transaction and put down the phone. My heart was thumping violently and my hands were shaking.

er

The rest of the morning was a disastrous blur. I kept making mistakes taking the classified orders. Tuwanda noticed and asked, "Are you alright?" Not out of concern, but because I was distracting her with my fidgeting and nervousness. Picardi did not attempt to talk to me after that kitchenette incident, though every time I looked up, I saw him eyeing me through his glass window.

I was thankful when lunchtime came. I grabbed my purse and barely said two words to Stella, who must have been surprised to see me go out to eat since the girls usually huddled in the kitchenette and made *chismis*, gossip, to while away lunchtime.

Lunchtime. I was in a Chinese restaurant two blocks from the Jersey Daily. I had just ordered a lunch of Egg Foo Yung. My mother referred to it as a Chinese omelet. It was simple to prepare, but could be quite complex in taste with its delicate ingredients of eggs, green onions, bean sprouts, onions, peppers and sometimes, mushroom, chicken or crabmeat.

The Chinese waitress arrived with the Egg Foo Yung. She lay the steaming plate and a small dish of Egg Foo Yung sauce on my table, smiling. "Enjoy!" she said and went mechanically to a table where a yuppie couple waited to order.

The fragrance of the Egg Foo Yung suffused me with sudden hunger. The egg sandwich I had brought for breakfast lay untouched inside its brown paper bag on my desk in the office that seemed a thousand miles away at that moment. I realized I was ravenous. I poured some sauce over the Egg Foo Yung and, as Americans would say it, dug in.

er

I entered the <u>Jersey Daily</u> building and saw Stella by the reception desk. She beckoned me.

"Hey, good lunch?" she asked in a tone meant to convey: "I'm hurt you didn't ask me to have lunch with you, my Friend." In my mind, Stella always pronounced the letter F as F.

I decided to ignore it. "Yeah, it was okay. I went to the Chinese place. *Ano yun, Stella?*" What is it, Stella?

Stella let out a sigh: her way of saying she forgave me and said, "Mr. Lance- Picardi was just here, looking POR you. He said POR you to see him at his oPPice soon as you come in."

I started to feel queasy and swallowed hard.

"Hey, you okay?"

I did not answer. I bit my lips.

"Hey, could be good news, maybe a promotion, *di ba*?" Right?

Wrong! I stared at her. A sickening feeling of nausea overcame me. I rushed inside.

"Hey, Ligaya! *Sandali lang!*" Ligaya, wait! Stella called out but I was already inside the classified department.

I walked towards Picardi's office. As I did this, I avoided eye contact with all of my classified officemates but I felt their eyes.

I saw Picardi watch me come in. He stood and paced. I entered his office. I was shaking.

"Ligaya," he greeted me, still standing up. "Look, I think there's some misunderstanding about this morning's—"

I stared at him. The feeling of nausea was so strong. I started to retch.

"Ligaya, are you OK?"

I spattered Egg Foo Yung all over him, his shirt, his pants, his wing-tipped shoes.

I looked up at his eyes and bravely, but hoarsely, declared, "I quit."

65

et

According to a recent national survey of over 400 Asian American women, over one-third of Asian American women have experienced sexual harassment on the job and almost two-thirds of them knew other Asian American women who had been harassed. This type of harassment has been assigned the term, "intersectional discrimination," which is when sexual harassment is combined with the harasser's utilization of particular stereotypes of women of color. This type of harassment is finally gaining attention at the Equal Employment Opportunity Commission (EEOC) because in America a large number of workers are now women of color.

When this happened to me, I was unaware of my rights in the workplace concerning harassment. I did not know that employers are liable for ensuring their supervisors do not sexually harass their employees. We certainly did not have sexual harassment resources in the Philippines. I did not report the incident. I didn't even tell my mother. Instead, I made up some lies about how I'd rather do catering work or find a job in Manhattan where the pay was better and the work experience was more enriching. She accepted this rambling excuse with a frown and muttered, "Giving up such good opportunity, that's *stupida*." Stupid.

I know better now so the next time it happens to me, I will be fully armed. I will also make sure my stomach is full of Egg Foo Yung again.

EGG FOO YUNG

Ingredients:
  6 eggs
  1 cup bean sprouts, raw or blanched
  1/2 green onion stalk, minced
  1/2 tsp soy sauce
  1 clove garlic, minced
  4 tsp peanut oil

NOT MY BOWL OF RICE

salt and pepper to taste

Optional: meat or seafood—chicken pork, shrimp, crabmeat, etc.

Beat eggs well. Add bean sprouts. Stir in other ingredients except peanut oil.

In a skillet (preferably non-stick), heat the peanut oil over medium heat. Pour in 1/4 of the egg mixture. Cook until the bottom is browned and the top is almost set. Flip the omelet over and quickly brown the other side. Repeat this process until all omelets are cooked.

SAUCE

1 tsp sesame oil
1/2 cup chicken broth
3 tsp soy sauce
1 tbsp sugar
1 tbsp cornstarch
1/2 cup water
1 green onion, chopped

In the same skillet, make the sauce by heating the sesame oil, chicken broth, soy sauce, and sugar. Blend the cornstarch with water, then stir the mixture into the pan. Return to a boil and cook for a minute or until the sauce is thickened. Stir in the green onions.

To serve, pour a small amount of the sauce over each omelet.

67

Chapter Nine

RELLENONG MANOK

Courtship in the Philippines often involves the boy courting the girl <u>and</u> the mother as well. There is a period of courting in which the boy works alongside the parents of the girl, allowing the parents to observe the fitfulness of his character. To win the heart of the girl's mother, a boy does all sorts of chores in the girl's household: gathering and chopping wood, fetching water, fixing a broken staircase, tilling the girl's father's farm. If the boy's behavior does not find favor with the parents, the parents usually end the courtship. The parents' decision is irrevocable and indisputable, like the word of God. According to folklore, if the couple elopes against the wishes of the girl's parents, barrenness, or other equally painful tragedies, will surely ensue. It is a parental curse arising directly from the couple having ignored the parents' mandate.

I was determined to buck this age-old Philippine tradition here in America. Dating in the western culture was done with little or no parental supervision at all and with little regard for the parents' wishes. I, being a mature, responsible twenty-five year-old woman, was determined to embrace American ways, including dating who and when I wanted. Brave words from someone who was raised under the umbrella of an ultra-conservative Filipino society. But we would see. We would see.

I was in the Liberty State Park in Jersey City. With the Manhattan skyline, the Statue of Liberty and Ellis Island looming in the distance, Liberty State Park has one of New Jersey's most spectacular backdrops. I was in one of its many buildings' function rooms catering a fundraising dinner party for the Filipino Veterans of New Jersey.

I was one of the three Filipinos hired to cater the event. Since my resignation at the <u>Jersey Daily</u>, I had had no luck getting a new job. Or maybe I was still paranoid about applying for a new one. Regardless, catering had been both a diversion and even a money-making venture for me. I had been daydreaming about the possibility of making a full time career out of it. "Ligaya's Catering Service," my card would have said.

My usual escorts/chaperones, Mother and Auntie Soledad, decided to skip this event and instead joined a group of Filipinos on a chartered bus tour to Atlantic City. The allure of "777" and "bar-bar-bar" across a slot machine payline was stronger.

Filipinos love to gamble. Like food, song, and language, the love of gambling is a trait that unites Filipinos in the Philippines with Filipinos in America. And it is not limited to any generation, class, or immigration status. While the poor pitch pennies, the rich wager diamond necklaces.

The earliest wave of Filipino immigrants found work in Hawaii on the sugar cane plantations. It was a hard life filled with long days of back-breaking, low-paying work toiling the fields and shucking cane. These Filipinos saw gambling as a glimmer of hope. Many plunked down their hard-earned cash on *sabong*, cockfights, hoping for the elusive windfall that would allow them to board a ship to the United States mainland, to the "true land of milk and honey."

Times have changed but Filipinos have not. Many on the mainland still equate the American Dream with a gambling windfall, but today, we have many more choices: Lotto, Keno, bingo, slot machines, and of course, mahjong.

Sabong, though illegal, is still a highly enjoyed underground gambling activity here in America, though more so in the Philippines where it is legal. A cockfighting aficionado once said that there were more cockfight arenas in the Philippines than churches. The fact that a bloodsport in which two roosters, each with a razor-sharp blade tied to its legs, are placed in a pit to fight to death is more popular than religion in a highly conservative Catholic country, says pages about our affinity for gambling.

So while Mother and Auntie Soledad plunked their hard-earned quarters and dollars into the slot machines hoping for a jackpot, here I was, alone and unchaperoned. I was excited at the prospect of meeting new faces, especially away from my mother and Auntie Soledad's scrutinizing eyes, but I saw only a few people my age. The crowd was mostly made-up of old Filipino veterans and heavily made-up matrons dressed in butterfly-sleeved *Ternos*, Filipino formal evening gowns made popular by the Philippines ex-First Lady, Imelda

Marcos. *It's going to be a long night.* I sighed. I immediately scolded myself for such a thought and went about placing the food I brought for the affair on the buffet table.

"Hello Miss Ligaya!" I was startled by the voice. I looked up. It was Ditas, one of the event planners for this fundraiser.

"Hi Ditas, *kumusta?*" How are you? I greeted her cheerfully and gratefully, happy to see a familiar face. She was the one who recommended me for the catering position.

"Eto, tumataba!" Fine but gaining weight, she said, gesturing to her tummy. "It's all your fault! It's your delicious cooking that's responsible for this. Like this fantastic *Rellenong Talong!*"

It was really meant as a compliment so I thanked her. "*Salamat,* for making me one of the caterers for this affair. I hope you're not disappointed?"

"Who, me? Oh no! No! *Puede ba?* In fact everybody here loves your *Relleno.* In fact, there's someone who wants to compliment you *nga eh! Nasaan siya?*" Where is he? She looked around.

"Hoy Ramoncito, halika. Eto ang cook!" Hey Ramoncito, come over here so you can meet the cook. She called out to someone whose back was turned. He turned around. I gasped! He walked toward us. I started to shake. I held on to the edge of the buffet table for support. This man was walking, no, gliding towards us.

I was completely smitten by this handsome man in front of me, Ramoncito Macalalad. He is what is called a *Mestizo,* a hybrid of Malay and Spanish blood, giving him that gorgeous bronze complexion, aquiline nose and impressive height that we usually refer to as "tall for a Filipino." He wore a *Barong Tagalog,* a richly embroidered Filipino men's formal wear made from *Piña,* a fine fabric extracted from pineapple leaves. It is one of the most delicate fibers in the world. He looked very regal in it, like a *principe,* a prince.

I was enthralled. I did not realize he had just asked me a question: Did you make this *Rellenong Manok?*

Ramoncito's hazel eyes were still smiling when he repeated his question: "Did you make the *Rellenong Manok?*" And a little concerned: "Hey, are you okay?"

I'm sure my face was pink. I touched it. It felt warm. "*Dios ko!* I'm sorry," I replied, taking a deep breath and exerting a supreme effort to focus. I nodded vigorously. "Yes! Yes to all your questions!" His brows knit but his smile stayed.

"Yes, I made the *Rellenong Manok*. Yes, I'm okay. *Dios ko*, I'm sorry," I answered, still very flustered.

"Well, I just wanted to say that this is the most delicious *Rellenong Manok* I have ever tasted. You're an excellent cook." Still noticing my flustered look, he added: "Look, I'm sorry, I didn't mean to be a bother to you but I just had to meet the creator of this, this masterpiece, so I asked Ditas here to make the introductions."

"Thank you." I stammered the response but my heartbeat was slowing down. I saw that Ditas was still standing between us, a wicked smile playing on her face. She grinned revealing crowned front teeth. "Well, now that I have done my (clears her throat) duty, I leave you guys in peace...or love...or whatever!" She took a slice of the *Rellenong Manok* and made her exit. I followed her with my eyes and sure enough, she looked back and smiled again, full of wicked meanings. I glared at her, blushing again.

In the Philippines, Ditas' actions could be considered as *tuksuhan*, teasing. It is part of the courtship process. Love is hinted at, not by the admirer or the object of admiration herself, but by their friends. It is done through playful proddings, gentle teasing, easy laughter and stolen glances. The girl welcomes this if she secretly favors the boy and the boy must be quick to notice the hints.

Ramoncito had moved a bit closer to me. I could smell his cologne, which was subtly spicy.

"So," Ramoncito said as he teased with his eyes, "how does one go about creating this delicious dish?"

I examined his face. I was not sure he really wanted to know the intricate details that went into making *Rellenong Manok*. In Philippine culture, we are amazed when men cook and women can't. Our culture has assigned to women the task of planning, preparing and serving meals as a gender role, as part of being women. To men, our culture has assigned the task of, in American parlance, "bringing home the bacon," earning the livelihood, providing for the family. A woman who can't cook will tend to be apologetic or defensive while a man will just shrug his shoulders and say, "I can't even boil eggs!" If a man manages to prepare an intricate dish, it is the talk of his family and friends for days. No such praise for the woman who makes an average of ninety meals a month.

"C'mon, you don't really want to know," I teased back, "it'll just bore you to death."

"No, it won't. Please, I am really interested. I cook too, you know. Alright, I admit, maybe not as good as you, but I try." His face was earnest. I took a deep breath.

𝒆𝒓

When the Spaniards came to the Philippines, the food influences they brought had new flavors and ingredients: olive oil, paprika, olives, saffron, ham and cured sausages. They brought new names as well: *paellas* meaning rice-based dishes; *ensaymadas* meaning brioche-like buttered and cheese-sprinkled cakes; *jamon en dulce*, sweet ham; and *relleno*, the process of stuffing festive turkeys, which is now also applied to chicken and fish.

Making *Rellenong Manok* is a very intricate, time-consuming process. De-boning the chicken takes time and much skill. First, you have to cut along the backbone from neck to tail. Then you have to carefully free the meat from the bones, using a very sharp paring knife, starting at the neck and moving slowly towards the tail, making sure not to pierce the skin. Then you must marinate the cavity with *calamansi juice,* local lime juice, salt, sugar, soy sauce and pepper. This takes a good hour or two.

While waiting for the skin to fully absorb all of the delightful flavors of the marinade, you combine the rest of the ingredients and stuff the de-boned chicken with it. Then you sew up the opening, stuff the chicken into the oven, and do a thousand and one more things to it.

𝒆𝒓

It was a grueling process for me to make *Rellenong Manok*, but I was rewarded with the handsome man who stared into my eyes as we sat on one of the benches in the Liberty State Park picnic area. We decided we both needed a more private setting for my cooking lecture, so we left the party room and walked across the sprawling lawn to the picnic area where we were treated to a glorious view of the Statue of Liberty and the Manhattan Skyline with its Twin Towers. It was stunning, romantic and wonderfully innocent.

"Wow!" he muttered.

"Is that a comment on my very scholarly explanation of making *Rellenong Manok?*" I teased. I was a bit winded. I just finished a 20-minute dissertation on the intricate art of making *Relleno.*

"It is wow to everything! This view, this night, this moment. Your wonderful *Rellenong Manok.*" He gestured around, then touched my face. "Your wonderful eyes, your wonderful you."

Oh god! I am afraid to breathe. I am afraid to breathe.

He took my hand. I almost pulled it back but I could not move. We kissed, breaking a cardinal rule in Philippine dating: no kissing on the first date.

We kissed. And kissed.

Afterwards, we shared leftovers of the *Rellenong Manok.* We were both non-smokers. The savory food was a good substitute.

Just kidding! We kissed. We just kissed!

RELLENONG MANOK
(Stuffed, De-boned Chicken)

Ingredients:
  4-5 lb roasting chicken
  2 tsp calamansi or lemon juice
  3 tsp soy sauce
  1 tsp sugar
  1 tsp salt
  1 tsp pepper
  1 cup pork, finely ground
  1 cup chicken meat, chopped
  1 cup Spanish sausage, sliced
  1/3 cup celery, chopped
  2 tsp parsley, chopped
  1 medium onion, finely chopped
  1 small box of raisins

3 raw eggs
1/2 tsp white pepper
4 shelled, hardboiled eggs, quartered
4 tsp melted butter

Rinse chicken in cold water. Dry thoroughly. De-bone, following Ligaya's instructions in her story.

Combine lemon juice, soy sauce, salt, pepper, and sugar. Marinate the cavity in this mixture for at least an hour.

Combine all the remaining ingredients, except the hardboiled eggs and the melted butter and mix thoroughly.

Drain the marinade from the chicken. Stuff the chicken with the mixture. Press the hardboiled eggs into the stuffing, putting at least 2 slices on each side of the chicken.

Sew up the opening (ordinary needle and thread will do). Truss, to keep the stuffed chicken in place.

Place breast side up in a roasting pan with a rack, and brush all over with melted butter. Loosely cover pan with foil. Bake in pre-heated 350 degrees F oven for 1-1/2 to 2 hours.

Remove foil during the last 30 minutes to brown the chicken.

Cool before slicing. Serve with gravy.

GRAVY for *Rellenong Manok*:
    4 tsp pan drippings from roasted chicken
    4 tsp flour
    2 cups chicken broth
    Salt and pepper to taste

Combine pan drippings with flour in a saucepan and place over moderate heat. Slowly add broth, stirring continuously with a whisk. Add salt and pepper to taste. Scrape all browned bits clinging to the pan. Simmer, stirring constantly, for 5-10 minutes or until thick and smooth.

Chapter Ten

EMPANADAS

I was about to be bestowed the dreaded "Parental Curse." Ramoncito Macalalad was not entirely unacceptable to my mother but our plan to live together without the benefit of marriage was.

Ramoncito and I had been dating for four months now. Although our dating process was not exactly very Filipino in ways and norms, it wasn't very American either.

Ramoncito did not woo me with a *Harana,* serenade. The *Harana* involves the man standing before the girl's bedroom window on a moonlit night and, while playing guitar, unburdening his feelings in a song. The girl, wakened by his serenade, responds with her own song. The singing goes back and forth until they reach an understanding.

Nor did he court my mother by doing her laundry or food shopping, or changing the light bulb in her kitchen.

And Mother and Auntie Soledad did not leave us alone either. It had not been a parentally-supervised courtship, but more like a constant scrutiny of Ramoncito's and my current standing in the whole scheme of dating. Nag. Nag. Nag.

So one day I told Mother that Ramoncito and I were planning to live together.

"You mean get married?" Mother asked hopefully.

"No, no marriage yet. I don't think we're both ready for that," I answered, my heart rising to my throat.

"Are you telling me what I think you're telling me?" Mother's voice had taken on a hard edge. I was telling her exactly what she thought I was telling her. And I was regretting it as her brows rose up to there.

In the Philippines, free love and pre-marital sexual relationships are not recognized nor accepted. Our conservative society condemns them for two of the reasons America once did: the shame of the female becoming pregnant out of wedlock and the risk of sexually transmitted diseases. But, unlike American culture, Filipino culture is tightly intertwined with Catholicism. This adds a third reason:

disobeying the sixth commandment given to the people of God. It is this third reason that solidifies the taboo status of premarital dalliances. In the eyes of society and God, pre-marital sex cheapens the relationship.

Living together without the benefit of marriage was the ultimate blow. It was the greatest sin in a pre-marital sexual relationship. Mother was livid.

I bowed my head. It was the most sublime answer I could give to her question.

"You and Maria are so alike!" my mother screamed.

What! I looked up and stared at my mother. *What do you mean by that?*

"Mother, that's not true and that's not fair! Let's leave Maria out of this."

"Why? She also disappointed me, just like you're doing now. Hah! Marrying so quickly so she can avoid coming to join us in America. And now you! Wanting to - to live in sin with this man so you can avoid living with me. You two are alike. *Walang galang. Walang utang na loob!*" No respect. No sense of gratitude. *Aray!* Ouch!

"Mother, Maria and I are both adults. We both have the right to decide what's good for us. Please, Mother. It is not my intention to abandon you. Certainly not Maria's."

"Oh c'mon, you think I didn't sense it? Maria didn't have the slightest intention to join me here in the States. *Di ba? Di ba?*" Am I right? Am I right?

This is it, I thought to myself. I stiffened and took a deep breath.

"You are damn right, Mother!" Mother gasped. She had heard me say the d-word before but never in such a damning way as this.

"Maria did get married to avoid joining you here in America. Is that what you wanted to hear?"

"*Ano?*" What?

"Oh, I'm sure she loved her husband very much and her kids. Your *apo*." Grandkids. "But yes, she did admit it. On her wedding day—the wedding you boycotted—she said that she didn't want to be where she wasn't really wanted."

Mother's hand flew to her mouth.

"Yes, Mother. That's exactly what she said. And can you blame her? Ever since we were kids you never really showed her the kind of affection that you so willingly and lovingly showered on me. Oh, Mother, you treated me like a princess. And Maria, like shit."

Her open palm hit me full force across the face. I was stunned. My face was red and twisted. Hers was white and stony. I bit my lip to stifle a cry, but my eyes were moist. After what seemed like an eternity, Mother broke the silence when she spoke in *Tagalog*.

"You want to know why, as you put it so eloquently, I treat you and Maria so differently? Sit down. I will tell you. I will force myself to dig into the long ago past. Sit down, Ligaya."

I did not do it. I stood, still defiant, face still stinging from the force of her slap. She let out a sigh and continued.

"Let me tell you a story of long, long ago..." she began in her perfect *Tagalog*. She had a pained expression that almost tempted me to stop her before she even began.

"I did not always look like this, you know? There was a time when I didn't have these wrinkles on my face, these age-spots, these skin tags. I was once young and beautiful. It's not show-off, it's genes. I inherited my father's features, your *Lolo*, grandfather, who was pure Spanish. He was fair-complexioned with deep-set eyes and an aquiline high bridge nose. Not *sarat*, pug nose, like yours, which you got from your father, so not your fault." I felt hot in the face but I didn't dare say a word.

"I was born several towns away from where you and Maria know to be your hometown. It was a much larger town, the home of many well-to-do families, like your *Lolo's*. We lived in the prestigious district of town, in this huge Spanish-type house with a courtyard and a garden that my mother, your *Lola*, filled with rose plants, rows and rows of different varieties of roses. And we had two cars, a luxury in those days. They were called *Berlinas,* which your Lolo acquired from the only car dealer in the province.

"Life was luxurious. I was a very popular girl. Do you know what that means? I was always invited to parties, picnics, fiestas and dances. And so many suitors! But only one caught my fancy. Norberto Marasigan. The only son of the only doctor in our town. And no, Ligaya, he isn't your father," Mother added as she read my questioning look. I swallowed real hard.

77

"Norberto Marasigan soon proposed and I accepted. A party was given by your grandparents to announce our engagement. They spared nothing for this party. It was huge. The entire town was invited. Pigs, chicken, goats and cattle were slaughtered for the occasion. The house was decorated and lit like one of your Auntie Soledad's tacky Christmas trees. An orchestra from another town was hired, for it was to be a dance party. Did you know I can dance the *rhumba, cha-cha,* waltz, tango? Yes, I was a decent dancer. In those days, my dance cards were always filled. There was always this long string of eager men who wanted to have a dance with me. But I'd chosen Norberto and that night, we were to make our relationship formal.

"For that event, your *Lola* ordered this long, flowing pale blue gown from Manila. It was made of silk as sheer and perishable as gossamer. It was delivered a few days before the party in this big box that bore the logo of a famous Manila couturier. And your *Lola* lent me her collection of diamond jewelry so I was decked out in diamonds from head to toe! Earrings, a necklace, a bracelet, a diamond-encrusted brooch. My hair was fashioned in an upswept hairstyle with a diamond pin.

"That night, all eyes were on Norberto and me. The girls were wide-eyed with jealousy over my diamond jewelry and over landing the most eligible bachelor in town. And the boys- oh those boys, they just couldn't take their eyes off me which made the other girls all the more jealous."

I was mesmerized by Mother's expression. She seemed transformed into a young girl. Her face was luminous. A light shone in her eyes. A knowing smile played on her lips.

"Mother?" I inquired, a bit alarmed.

"Do you have any idea what that kind of attention can do to a girl, *ha,* Ligaya?" Mother continued, her expression suddenly turning hard and stony. "It can make your head spin, your mind imprudent, you body reckless. I was drunk with happiness that night.

"In between dances, I had sips of wine but avoided food because I was afraid that my dress might lose its nice fit. The dance hall started spinning! I excused myself and ambled over to the bathroom. It was locked. I hurried outside to the rose garden. There, I retched and vomited, right into your *Lola's* precious rose bushes. I believe it was on one of her prized hybrids, the Bette Davis she called it. It was deep, deep red, very thorny.

"And so I was standing there, catching my breath, cringing at my handiwork on your Lola's roses when this hand, this awful hand wrapped around my mouth. I was wide-eyed with shock. I curled my fist to strike the intruder but someone else hit me hard in the face. *Dios ko!* There were two of them! I started to fall, blacking out. As I closed my eyes, I saw two shadows looming over me, coming closer and closer. I couldn't even scream. *Dios ko,* I couldn't even scream.

"I awakened to someone's voice crying in my ears. It was my best friend, your Auntie Soledad. I opened my eyes. I was surrounded by faces. The girls who were jealous of me. The boys who were admirers of me. My family. The whole town. And then there was Norberto staring down at me, but keeping a distance. I cried out to him. He didn't budge. In fact, he retreated a bit. The expression on his face was something that I'll never forget. It was a look of disgust. I looked down at my silk dress. It was ripped and stained. I screamed. I screamed. I screamed. Your Auntie Soledad held me, whispering, 'Shhhhh, shhhhhh.' I must have passed out again for the next thing I knew, I was on my bed, wishing it all was just a *bangungot*, a nightmare.

"There were two versions of that horrible event. Mine, the one I'd told my parents and the town police to the best of my recollection, which wasn't much. It wasn't even enough for the police to make arrests. And then there's the whole town's version. A filthy, malicious story that went from ear to ear, from house to house. That I was drunk and flirty that night. That whatever happened to me, I brought on myself.

"Soon, my parents started looking at me differently, poisoned by the entire town's toxic tale. The front windows were ordered closed by my father, the better to stop anyone from seeing me: a disgraced woman. Norberto called off the engagement. He never visited me again. His parents sent him away, I heard. No one visited me except your Auntie Soledad. It was as if in that one night, I lost all my friends, all my admirers. And then, to my horror, I discovered I was pregnant! My father was horrified. My mother wailed for a long time. More windows were shut closed in our household.

"A few weeks passed. Then one night, there was a knock on my door. It was my father with Pantaleon, our gardener. Yes, it was your father, Ligaya." She answered a question I dared not ask.

"I frowned at them, puzzled. I covered my bulging stomach. Pantaleon's head was bowed when my father ushered him into the room. My father held both my shoulders and said, "*Iha*, this is the only way." His voice sad, resigned, defeated, ashamed. They had paid Pantaleon and his family handsomely: hectares of rice field, a house, six *carabaos*, who knows what else? In exchange, he was to marry me. He was to give my baby a proper name.

"What else could I do? No one in town would ever look at me again with respect. I was like a broken porcelain vase put back together by glue. Who would ever want that? I married your father, moved to another town and bore Maria. And no, abortion was never considered an option. Better a disgraced woman than a murderess, you see? A disgraced woman can still go to heaven. A murderer, straight to hell."

"In the Philippines, the first conception is considered a happy event, a kind of good luck. Of course mine was exactly the opposite. Oh, the nausea, the vomiting, the dizziness! I had this desire to sleep all the time. Always feeling cold, always irritable. And my cravings and aversions! I hounded your father for unripe mangoes, young coconuts, young guavas. And anything that smelled of garlic and onions made me throw up. Even the smell of your father's pomade!

"The day I felt labor pains, your father ran like a mad dog to fetch the *komadrona*. She helped me deliver Maria after hours of excruciating pain because Maria was such a big baby. A sharpened piece of bamboo was used to cut her umbilical cord. Afterwards, the *komadrona* gave me a glass of warm milk with a piece of the placenta burned and added to prevent a *bughat,* or relapse, in me.

"My family heard of Maria's birth, of course, but my father never visited us. He never set foot in that town. My mother managed a few secret visits and then I heard she became very ill. I wanted to go see her but, shortly thereafter, she died. And my father, your *Lolo*, followed her soon afterwards. I blamed myself for their deaths. I destroyed their names. I broke their hearts.

"I lost my mind after that. I would wake up at night screaming, unable to bear even the sound and the feel of the wind. And when it rained, I imagined our house being washed away. Even those little insects, *aninipot*, fireflies, frightened me. Your father finally summoned a doctor. He diagnosed it as a nervous breakdown.

"It took months before I had the courage to visit your grandparents' graves. To do that, your father and I had to sneak during the night like thieves! Your father drove me to my old town, to the cemetery one evening, when no one was around. Somehow the visit brought me closure. I never went back to that town after that. Your father took care of selling what was left of my parents' property.

"Oh, your father, he was such a good man. But I didn't love him for a long time after we were married. We slept in different beds. When we ate, there were no words exchanged. But, *dios ko*, he was such a patient man. When I raged, and I did a lot of that, he just let me. When I would throw a plate against the wall, he would pick up the broken pieces and discard them. When I would punch a hole in the wall, he would silently spackle it the next day. If I refused to get out of bed, he let me sleep all day.

"Eventually, my anger ran out. I started noticing things again like the sunrise, birds chirping in the trees, the blooming fruits of our *Kalamansi* tree. I started to see your father in a different light, in his true light. A kind, patient, not-so-bad looking man. In the end, I learned to love him. And then we had you, our labor of love. We named you *Ligaya* because when you were born, I felt really happy for the first time in a long, long time.

"Do you now understand why I have not been able to give Maria the kind of love that I know in my heart of hearts she deserves? I have tried, oh how I have tried! Countless prayers, countless *novenas*, countless times walking on my knees in the church, begging for enlightenment. But every time I look at her, I only see those two shadows in that dark rose garden. I only see evil. It is unfair, I know. Maria has nothing to do with what happened to me that night. But what can I do? No matter what my brain says, my heart still horribly beats that way."

So now you know. What do we do now?

"What do we do now?" Mother repeated the question. I was startled to realize I was standing again, tightly holding the back of the chair. Mother was looking up at me from her chair, her eyes red-hot from crying.

81

"I—Mother, I don't know," I answered, feeling instantly foolish. For some stupid reason, all I could think of at that very moment was that now I knew why Mother refused to touch alcohol.

Mother shook her head and started toward the kitchen.

"Mother...?" I opened my mouth, determined to put in my most profound thoughts on this most revealing story.

She turned around, offering me the saddest smile. "I have to prepare the *Empanadas*. I promised your Auntie Soledad I'd have them ready for her mahjong session this Saturday."

Then she left the room. I held on to the chair, willing myself not to cry. I began to tremble, terribly. In the kitchen, I heard the opening and closing sounds of cabinets as Mother gathered the ingredients for her *Empanadas*.

Empanadas are baked or fried pastries of dough, similar to a meat turnover, filled with virtually any type of meat and savory vegetables. They take a little more effort, a little more patience, a little more time than most other dishes because of the lengthy process of making the pastry shells. They are truly a labor of love.

EMPANADA

Filling Ingredients
    1/4 cup cooking oil
    1/2 cup sliced onions
    2 cloves minced garlic
    1 cup diced carrots
    1 cup peas (canned or frozen)
    1 tsp salt
    1 tsp pepper
    1 cup seedless raisins
    1 cup diced potatoes
    1 lb ground meat—beef, pork, chicken, or turkey or a combination

Pastry Ingredients
    4 cups all-purpose flour
    1/4 cup granulated sugar
    1/2 cup cold butter, cut into 1/2 inch cubes (or 1/3 cup oil)

1/2 cup water

1/2 tsp salt

3 egg yolks (save the whites for sealing the *empanadas* and brushing on pastries)

Cook the filling:

In a large wok or casserole, heat the oil. Sautee the onions 1 to 2 minutes. Add meat, garlic, potatoes, carrots, and peas. Sprinkle with salt and pepper. Mix in the raisins. Set aside.

Prepare the pastry:

In a mixing bowl, combine egg yolks, flour and sugar. Cut the butter into the mixture and blend, using a pastry blender or your hands, until the butter is well distributed and the mixture resembles semi-dry sand. Pour in the water and mix well to form a solid dough. Dust the worktable and the rolling pin with flour. Roll out the dough, putting a little pressure on the rolling pin so that the dough will spread out evenly. You want to spread out the dough to a thickness of about 1/8 of an inch. To be able to achieve this, turn the dough as often as possible. Constantly dust the table and the rolling pin.

Start the Filling Process:

Using a 4 to 5- inch diameter circular cutter (using the circular edge of a cup or a drinking glass will serve the purpose as well), begin cutting thin circles from the dough. Place about 2 teaspoons of the filling in the lower half of each circle of crust. Brush the edges of the crush with the egg whites. Fold the two ends of the crust together with your fingers or with the tines of a fork. Repeat process with the remaining crust and filling.

To bake empanadas:

Arrange on a thoroughly greased cookie sheet. Prick surface of each empanada with a fork to allow steam to escape. Bake at 400 degrees F for ten minutes. Remove from the oven and brush again with the egg whites. Bake for another 10 to 15 minutes or until golden brown.

To fry empanadas:

Deep fry on medium high heat using corn, canola, or peanut oil until golden brown and drain on paper towel.

Chapter Eleven

BITTERSWEET CHOCOLATE POUND CAKE

Filipinos are overly sensitive to criticism, insults and other personal affronts, whether real or imagined. Folks can become ruthless enemies for reasons that Westerners would deem trivial, not worth losing sleep over.

Amor Propio is a Spanish word that means self-love. It is a typical Filipino trait, a sense of self-esteem that prevents a person from swallowing his own pride. *Amor Propio* is ego defensiveness, dignity or personal pride.

Pricking a Filipino's *Amor Propio* can have devastating consequences. An abandoned wife will often refuse to seek financial support from her husband, no matter how financially destitute she is. A daughter will not ask to be taken back by a mother who previously disinherited her. And a mother will sever all communications with a daughter who, in the past, has disobeyed her authority.

My mother and I have pricked each other's *Amor Propio*.

er

Despite my mother's strong disapproval and her heartbreaking story of rape, I moved in with Ramoncito Macalalad. It was simple really. I was in love with Ramoncito. A piece of paper wouldn't change how I felt about him.

Ramoncito had a two-bedroom condominium by the Hudson River in Jersey City. From its windows, I could see downtown Manhattan and the Statue of Liberty. Ramoncito joked a lot about how those landmarks were so close he swore he could touch them if only he had longer arms. It did not matter. His arms were long enough, especially when they were wrapped around me, comforting me through my loneliness for my mother.

Ramoncito worked as an accountant for a major television network in their offices in Manhattan. He was almost a cliché, as accountants and nurses are two of the Philippines' major exports to

America. This brain drain has dwindled the number of nurses and accountants in the Philippines, but ironically has boosted the Filipino economy, because these professionals send back money to their families on a regular basis. That is a very Filipino thing to do: send money back home. It does not matter if your relative in the Philippines is a brain surgeon and you are flipping burgers, you will still send back money because you are *in America* and therefore, must be better off.

Ramoncito would take the PATH Train from New Jersey to Manhattan, then transfer to a crowded subway train to get to his office on Fifth Avenue on the Upper East Side.

I only took the subway once, with Auntie Soledad, just to experience riding it. It was an uneventful ride, so unlike the many horrible but enthralling stories I had heard about the New York Subway from friends, relatives and office mates here in America.

There was one story about a gang of young kids wearing colored baseball caps who harassed an old lady with razor blades they carried in their mouths. They forced her off at the next stop to kill her in full view of everyone on the train.

There was another story about a Chinese couple carrying dozens of eggs, who disposed of the bad eggs on the subway car seats when they discovered that many of the eggs were broken. Many passengers were unaware they sat on the eggs until they felt the wet, sticky substance permeate their underclothes. It wasn't a joyous Easter egg hunt.

And another about two elderly lady friends packed in with the other passengers during the evening rush hour when a scruffy man, smelling of garbage and body odor standing next to them, started to moan and shake. The two women were frightened and got off at the next stop. On the platform, one of the women looked down at her shoes and noticed a load of semen smeared on her pants and shoes.

And, of course, the story about an old man bent over with his pants around his ankles defecating in full view of passengers on a Bronx-bound train platform. And the teenage couple who were hugging, kissing and petting very heavily and left a "pretty mess" on the seats when they left the train.

My personal favorite was about the old bag lady who was scratching her leg under her long, faded denim skirt. She would shove two fingers underneath her skirt, place them up to her nose and inhale deeply as if to savor the aroma. She did this several times before lifting up her skirt to reveal a leg sporting an open pus-filled sore. As she exited the train, she left her mark on New York by dragging her sticky fingers across all the seats and train poles.

Ramoncito's favorite story was less gruesome. It was about a Wall Street stockbroker who proposed to his girlfriend on bended knees as the train chugged along on its way to a PATH train transfer station. Ramoncito claimed to have witnessed this romantic interlude himself. I often daydreamed that I was the girl being proposed to and that Ramoncito was the dashing man on bended knees.

er

In the Philippines, marriage is viewed as a permanent contract, an inviolable social institution. There is no divorce in the Philippines except among the Muslims and some indigenous religious groups.

Legal separation involves separation from bed and board but does not allow for a second marriage while the first spouse is still alive. It is not too common a practice, primarily because of the legal complications involved in a formal court separation process and the social stigma attached to the process. There are religious and cultural forces that keep couples together, so most couples will stay together regardless of their feelings for each other.

Unlike in western cultures, marriage is seen not so much as the joining in matrimony of two love-struck partners but rather as an inter-family alliance deliberately created for sound economic reasons. In many Philippine rural areas, it is not unusual for a wedding to be sanctioned through a group decision by the parents and relatives of the bride and the groom. Therefore, relatives of both parties take a keen interest in making sure the couple, once married, stays married. An easy way to ensure this is for the couple to live near the relatives. This is known as *Bantay sa MagAsawa*, marriage surveillance.

The eyes, ears, and tongues of the relatives are effective tools for stopping a man and woman from doing things bad for the marriage. In America, this can be categorically termed as "harassment from the in-laws".

What divorce is to the Westerners, the *querida system* is to a few Filipino husbands. And note that this system exists all in the spirit of making sure marriages are kept intact. The *querida* system is a way of life wherein a married man takes on a mistress or a *querida*. The married man provides for this second woman to the extent of giving her a monthly allowance, even a home. This situation is usually temporary. The husband soon tires of the *querida* and abandons her. The way for a *querida* to avoid abandonment and guarantee that the provisions continue is for her to bear a child. A man may not support an abandoned mistress anymore, but he can be coerced into supporting a mistress' child, who is his own flesh and blood.

How does the wife get her fair share of retribution? Filipino wives feel sex is primarily the husband's pleasure so it can be denied if he behaves badly. Outside the *kulambo* (mosquito net) is a punishment meted out to a husband who has been caught by his wife having an affair with a *querida*. This denial of man's primal craving can last for days or even months, as long as the Philippines' dry season.

ℰ

Ramoncito tried to bridge the gap between Mother and me. He sent gifts as peace offerings to my mother through our mutual friends, even through Auntie Soledad, who was amazingly neutral through all this. Auntie Soledad likened herself to Switzerland's stance during World War II, although I was sure my mother harrumphed at her stance, reminding her that after the war, the Swiss got burned for not taking a side. Mother returned all the gifts to us. I knew she would. The vicious cycle of *Amor Propio* at work.

I told myself it didn't matter. I was having the time of my life cohabitating with Ramoncito. Back in my Spelling Bee days, cohabitation was just another word that I had to learn to spell correctly. Now that I was living it, it had taken on a greater meaning.

Cohabitation is a living arrangement between two people who are committed to each other but are not ready to go as far as marrying each other. It is convenient for a number of reasons: it's less expensive to share costs of living; it's easy access to—Mother will hate this and agree totally—sex anytime you want it; and, as most Americans will tell you, it's a good way to determine if you and your partner are really compatible before taking the plunge.

Part of Mother's vehemence towards our arrangement was this: she thought that this was too easy a way to establish a relationship. Easy how? Did she really believe that only married people worked at relationships?

We had a long argument over that. Easy to establish? Yes, I agreed with her. Especially when you consider that in America, an average wedding costs around $25,000 and takes almost a year to plan. Yes, because there is no need to get a state license for the relationship. But NO, finding a life-partner is rarely an easy thing, though I felt blessed to have found Ramoncito.

What Mother didn't realize is this: our day-to-day relationship was no easier than that of a married couple. We had household bills, finances, chores, dealing with differences of opinion, balancing work schedules (my catering jobs were mostly at night while his accounting work was a nine to fiver), dealing with in-laws (good thing Ramoncito's parents lived on the West Coast!), deciding on purchases both major and minor. And, of course, the occasional mending of wounded feelings from a careless remark or an unintended insult ("Sweetheart, that dress makes you look thinner!"). But most importantly, loving each other through every hardship. Cohabitation may not be a hard-to-spell word but it was a hard-to-live lifestyle. And *salamat sa dios*, thank God, my Ramoncito made it all worth it.

Ramoncito was a sweet, funny, responsible and considerate man. He was a damn good cook too.

One night I came home worn out from another catering event. I entered the living room to a fragrant, familiar aroma. I rushed to the kitchen, calling out "Ramoncito?" and there he was, slaving over the dish that brought us together for the first time: *Rellenong Manok*.

"Happy six month anniversary!" he shouted, grinning through the sweat on his face. I broke into tears. Never mind that the *Rellenong Manok* was burnt a little and lacked a few ingredients. It was the most delicious meal I had had in months.

For our dessert, I offered to bake a Bittersweet Chocolate Pound Cake. The classic pound cake gets a bittersweet boost in this rich chocolate dessert. It is a case of food imitating life.

BITTERSWEET CHOCOLATE POUND CAKE

Ingredients:
   2 cups all purpose flour
   1 tsp baking soda
   1 tsp baking powder
   1-1/2 cups water
   2 tsp instant coffee powder
   3 bars bittersweet (unsweetened) chocolate baking bars, broken into pieces
   2 cups granulated sugar
   2 sticks butter, softened
   1 tsp vanilla extract
   3 eggs

Rich Chocolate Glaze
   1 bar bittersweet (unsweetened) chocolate baking bar
   3 tsp butter or margarine, softened
   1-1/2 cup powdered sugar, sifted
   3 tsp water
   1 tsp vanilla extract

Optional: coarsely ground nuts, powdered sugar, very tiny slices of dried fruit for topping.

Preheat oven to 350 degrees F. Grease a medium size pound cake pan. Combine flour, baking soda, and baking powder in a small bowl. Bring water and instant coffee powder to a boil in a small saucepan. Remove from heat. Add the bittersweet (unsweetened) chocolate bars. Stir until smooth.

Beat sugar, butter and vanilla extract in a large mixer bowl until creamy. Add eggs. Beat thoroughly for five minutes. Beat in flour mixture alternately with chocolate mixture. Pour into the pound cake pan.

Bake for 60 minutes or until wooden toothpick inserted in cake comes out clean. Cool in pan for about 30 minutes. Invert onto a cake plate to cool completely.

Drizzle with chocolate glaze. Sprinkle with optional powdered sugar, coarsely ground nuts, or dried fruits.

Chocolate Glaze:

Melt baking bar and butter in a small saucepan over low heat, stirring until smooth. Remove from heat. Stir in powdered sugar alternately with water until desired consistency is achieved. Stir in vanilla extract.

Chapter Twelve

LECHON MANOK

Marriage comes in many forms in the Philippines. There are the usual church weddings with the bride dressed in white and the whole pomp of the father marching down the aisle hand-in-hand with his little girl. Outside the church, there are civil ceremonies or "registry marriages" performed by a judge, mayor or minister. And there is a new phenomenon: the fast-becoming popular mass weddings. Very fitting in today's modern concept of the mass marketing of practically anything.

Traditionally, males above twenty but under twenty-five years of age or females above eighteen but under twenty-three years of age are required to get their parents' or guardians' consent to marry. A sworn statement by the contracting parties to the effect that such consent is given accompanies the application for the marriage license. There is a ten-day waiting period prior to the marriage that allows time for the parties to think over the seriousness of their intent.

Although a civil marriage performed by a justice of the peace is just as good and legitimate, undoubtedly most brides in the Philippines prefer a church wedding. The preparations for this kind of wedding are long and exhaustive.

First, a wedding announcement is formally made by the bride's parents or guardians. This usually takes place during a sumptuous party given by the parents of the bride.

A *despedida de soltera* is given in honor of the bride to be. This literally means goodbye to spinstershood. It is the equivalent of the American "bridal shower," a party given in honor of the bride-to-be by her friends. At the *despedida de soltera*, the bride is given appropriate and practical gifts, things that she would need to start housekeeping. There are no flimsy Victoria's Secret-type lingerie or naughty sex toys. Male strippers are a big no-no.

Sometimes a *despedida de soltera* takes the form of a party where the groom, his family, and close friends and relatives from both sides are invited to meet and get to know one another before the wedding.

When this happens, the occasion serves as the formal introduction of the two families to each other.

The date and time of the wedding is set. More often than not, the parents have a direct influence on the setting of the date. Certain superstitious beliefs are wisely seriously considered here. For example, calendars are consulted to ensure the marriage will take place on a day before the full moon; a day when the moon is waning is considered bad luck. Any day that marks the death anniversary of a loved one is definitely out of the question as bad luck will follow the couple through their first years of marriage and, according to superstition, leave the young couple barren.

Not all superstitions are followed, though. A rain shower on the day of matrimony is believed to bring bountiful blessings to a couple, but many are willing to forego such fortune out of preference for a bright and sunny wedding day. Some couples will actually troop to the monastery of St. Clare to offer eggs to this beloved patron saint of married couples and request the nuns in residence to pray for their wedding day to be rain-free. Sometimes, reason wins over superstition. No bride in white is crazy enough to waddle through layers of squelchy mud.

Traditionally, the groom's family pays for the wedding expenses, unlike in some western cultures, although that is changing too. Today, you'd be more likely to see the bride's and groom's families sharing expenses, and with good reason: the bigger contributor is considered to have the majority stake on the wedding guest list.

Why did I ramble on about Filipino wedding traditions and such? Because at this time, the idea of a wedding of my very own had been on my mind. It wasn't entirely my own doing. Ramoncito had been giving hints that made my heart a tingle. One day he brought home a wedding magazine, which he claimed he found discarded on a subway train. A week earlier, while helping me prepare our dinner, he playfully threw grains of rice at me. Two nights ago, while in bed, he asked me if I knew of any Philippine wedding folklore and superstitions. I had told him of a few: a bride shouldn't try on her wedding dress before the wedding day or the wedding will not push through; knives and other sharp-pointed objects are bad choices for wedding gifts for they will lead to a broken marriage; the groom who sits ahead of his bride during the wedding ceremony will be a henpecked husband (he took special note of this one); the groom must arrive before the bride at the church to avoid bad luck; altar-bound couples are accident prone and therefore must avoid long drives or traveling before the wedding day for safety.

And over breakfast, he asked me if it was proper for a mother's sister to be asked as a *ninang*, wedding godmother, considering her already close kinship with the bride. I screamed, "Of course, it's okay! There are no rules to being a *ninang* really. Auntie Soledad would be perfect!" I waited for his reaction, my heart bungee-jumping out of my chest. *Is he going to go down on his knees to propose?* Instead, he pursed his lips, raised his brow and muttered, "Mmmm, interesting."

"Ramoncito!?" I exclaimed with the impatience of a sixteen-year-old girl.

"Gotta go to work, I'm late," he said, kissing me on the lips. "And oh, *Mahal*, my loved one, keep your fingers crossed. I might get that promotion today. A raise would be good, yes?" he added, grinning from ear to ear, before heading for the door in his casual Friday attire: blue denim jacket and Raybans.

I was left with an excitement that made me restless. *Should I call my mother? Auntie Soledad? Oh god! Should I start leafing through that bridal magazine?* I decided to cook him an extra special celebratory dinner. That night I would cook him *Lechon Manok*.

In those days of cooking lessons with my mother, the underlying theme had been the old adage about the stomach being the way to a man's heart. "Good cooking is the key," she had said in that knowing tone of the wise. "That's how you bait a husband!"

It was preposterous, even to a thirteen- year-old kid in the '70s, but a neat ploy just the same: it kept me in the kitchen all summer. I couldn't help it. The saying contained a whiff of truth I so desperately and naively wanted to breathe all the way into my adolescent heart where a foolish dream once lived: that someday I would travel across the ocean, thousands of miles away to the land where disco began, meet John Travolta, and lure him into marriage with my perfect Filipino cooking. When I told my mother about this dream, she felt my forehead as if I had a fever. "Crazy kid," she murmured, "I've been keeping you in the kitchen too long."

I didn't get to meet John Travolta, though there was that one night when I went to a coffee shop in Hoboken and was excitedly told by the waitress that I just missed Mr. John Travolta and his party who had had coffee there minutes before. No, no chance meeting with the disco king but I met a disco prince, Ramoncito, who could do a passable version of the disco point, almost as well as the real thing. He demonstrated this one evening when we went out dancing in a New York discotheque patronized by many Filipino-Americans. I remembered that night, not only for the "point" but for an incident in the elevator that involved two Filipinos and an American, with Ramoncito and I as pointed witnesses. I swear to you, this really happened.

A Filipino and a Caucasian were among the passengers. On the way down, the elevator stopped and another Filipino got in. He pointed at the first Filipino with his lips and asked, *Bababa ba?* Is this going down? The other Filipino answered, *Bababa.* Yes, this is going down. We took no special notice of the exchange until we noticed the Caucasian guy's bewildered expression on his face. "My God!" he exclaimed, mouth descending on an elevator to his feet. "You people can actually carry on a conversation with just that one word, Ba? How amazing is that!" The Tagalog word *baba*, a verb, means to go down. It can be used in various situations and forms. It is used to refer to getting off a bus, getting out of a cab, going down the stairs or descending from any high place. And a single *ba* is a particle used in questions. It was a night of disco-dancing and Tagalog-word bopping.

Sometimes Americans find conversation with a Filipino-American strange because the Filipino is translating a Tagalog idiom into English word for word. Asked what the time is, a Filipino may apologetically reply "his watch is dead," a literal translation of the Tagalog phrase *"patay ang aking reloj"*, that is, his watch has stopped. Or a Filipino wanting to compliment a nattily-dressed American friend may tell the American *"Nakapamburol Kayo"* immediately followed by the English translation, "You are dressed for the funeral." What the Filipino is really trying to say is, "You are dressed to kill."

I was *Nakapamburol*, as I anxiously waited for Ramoncito to come home from work. I was wearing a dress he had bought at

Macy's Department Store with his newly acquired charge card. It had a delicate flowered print and the light lavender color truly complemented my skin tone, as Ramoncito himself had pointed out.

The table was festively set, not with our everyday Corningware plates but with Ramoncito's good china. *Noritake* it said at the bottom of each delicate porcelain piece. "No, don't break me," Ramoncito joked about this expensive dinnerware brand the first time he brought them out. I bought flowers, too, and scented candles to complete the festive look. A perfect setting for a wedding proposal, don't you think?

The *Lechon Manok* was roasting in the oven. I used a recipe I learned from a friend who hailed from Tacloban, Philippines, the ex-First Lady Imelda Marcos' hometown. A good thing came out of that town after all.

Lechon Manok became a food craze in the Philippines some time ago. Because of the low cost to start up a *Lechon Manok* business, you were bound to find a stand selling this delicacy anywhere you went in the Philippines. The first wave of entrepreneurs made a lot of money but when an enormous second wave played catch-up, many me-too entrepreneurs ended up losing money. The novelty has since worn out, but I kept the recipe.

I checked the chicken in the oven. Its skin was beginning to take on a nice golden hue. I checked the wall clock. In an hour, Ramoncito would be home. I checked my make-up. It was perfect. I pirouetted through the kitchen. At that very moment, I was a happy soul. *I wished Mother were there.*

er

I was frowning at the clock. It told me Ramoncito was already an hour and a half late. I called his office half an hour ago and his phone just rang and rang. *Think he made a stop at Tiffany's?* I giggled nervously at the thought. *I so deserved that blue Tiffany's box.*

I fell asleep waiting. The shrill ringing of the phone made me bolt upright.

"Is this the Macalalad residence?" an officious sounding voice asked on the phone.

"Yes," I answered reluctantly. My hand gripped the phone so hard it turned my knuckles white. I had a strange sense of *deja vu*. Only before it was a cleaver, not a phone, I was gripping.

There was a pause on the other line as the voice cleared its throat.

"Yes? What is it?" I inquired with fear forming in my heart.

"I'm afraid we have some bad news about Ramoncito Macalalad."

"What?" I couldn't continue. I felt something catch in my throat, a shiver flew up my spine. After exhaling slowly, the officious sounding voice continued. There was anguish in his voice.

On his way home, Ramoncito was mugged in the subway. He tried to fight his muggers, but one of them had a switchblade. The mugger fatally stabbed Ramoncito with it, in full view of the other horrified commuters.

Blackness colored this news of death as I fainted. The suckling *Lechon Manok* burned to cinders in the oven.

LECHON MANOK

Ingredients:
    I fresh, whole chicken

Marinade:
    1/2 cup honey
    1/2 cup patis (fish sauce)
    3 tbsp all-purpose liquid seasoning
    4 tbsp lime juice
    1 tbsp salt
    1 tbsp pepper

Sauce:
    1 cup pork or chicken liver (cooked and finely minced)
    1 large onion
    2 tbsp finely minced garlic
    1 cup brown sugar
    2 tbsp salt
    1 tbsp ground pepper
    1/2 cup white vinegar

2 cups chicken stock or water
1 cup bread crumbs

Prepare marinade by combining all marinade ingredients. Marinate chicken overnight. Pre-heat oven to 350 degrees F. Rub chicken with salt and pepper and roast for 45 minutes or until golden.

For the Sauce:
Mix all ingredients in a saucepan. Whisk with a wire whisk. Bring to a boil whisking to smoothen texture.
Serve chicken with sauce.

Chapter Thirteen

KUTSINTA

Patawad, forgive. I held my mother's hand and uttered this word very softly but I knew she heard me. The mist in her eyes told me so. She mouthed back, *Patawad*. We held each other tight and sobbed for a long time.

ℰ

News of Ramoncito's death made it to the <u>New York Times</u>. It was a small article on page 3, an article that Auntie Soledad clipped and put away after clucking her tongue in protest, "They misspelled his name!" The *Jersey Daily* published an obituary *gratis*, free of charge. Stella, the receptionist, called to tell me about it. She also added that Picard was no longer working at the *Jersey Daily*. I only managed a "Really?" as a reaction to that news. It seemed so trivial, no longer important.

News of his death also reached the many Filipino communities in New York and New Jersey. Flowers and cards expressing condolences were delivered daily to our home and the funeral home where Ramoncito's body was lying in an open casket for the viewing.

I had no idea there were so many Filipino organizations in America until I started leafing through the sympathy cards. Beyond the cards from our relatives and friends and from the office of the Philippine Consulate in New York, there were flowers and sympathy cards from such organizations as the Filipino-American Accountants, where Ramoncito was a member; the Association of Filipino Teachers in America; Fil-Am Veterans League; Filipino Nurses of New Jersey; National Association of Filipino Dentists of America; the Filipino Social Club of New York; and the Society of Philippine Surgeons of America.

I was touched and quite amazed. There were a lot of organizations, associations and groups out there which could potentially help Filipinos in America keep in touch with their friends, relatives and the large Fil-Am community. I made a mental note to write a thank-you note to every one of these wonderful organizations. In the Philippines, during good times, one is expected to share his blessings (through donations, sponsorship, gifts, etc.), which is commonly demonstrated during town fiestas and holidays. In bad times, one is expected to help other people who are in need through donations (in monetary terms or in kind), especially in times of disasters and calamities. The *Tagalog* term that aptly describes this form of empathy is *pakikiramay*. The extension of this Filipino trait here in America, as reflected by the outpouring of empathy from the various Filipino-American organizations, was such a comforting thought. We are Filipinos, no matter where we go. Even if we dye our hair red sometimes...

Auntie Soledad brought an accordion-type folder to store all the sympathy cards alphabetically. She also meticulously recorded every name and address in a notebook. Peter accompanied her on the night she brought us the folder. Peter gave me a bear hug as he mumbled tearfully, "I'm so sorry." Peter was such a sweet man. No wonder Auntie Soledad and my mother were so fond of him. I noticed how he held Auntie Soledad's hand during the wake. I also noticed the way my mother reacted to it. I cleared these observances from my head for there were more important issues that required my attention. Death was at hand.

In the Filipino culture, death is considered a spiritual event. Most Filipinos share in the belief that accidental death, whether from illness or a horrible accident, is due to supernatural causes such as punishment from God or an attack from an angry spirit. While this may contribute to stoicism in the face of pain or distress, it is the Filipinos' way of accepting what has been bestowed upon them. It is both a distressing and a soothing thought. It is not unusual for the dead, laid in a casket, to be surrounded by religious medallions, rosary beads, or a scapular to appease an other-worldly offender.

The rituals surrounding death can be described as "showy." Women are expected to grieve very openly, though men are allowed to be more reserved. There is a lot of sobbing, a lot of hugging the casket of the dead person, a lot of swooning, and even fainting. This kind of public grieving indicates how much the griever cared for the deceased. As the saying goes, "the more emotion shown, the more respect for the deceased."

Likewise, the family feels obligated to spend a lot of money on the death of a loved one: on the visitation casket, the flowers, the service, the burial place, and the food and drinks served during the wake which can last as long as seven days. It is not unusual for the families of the deceased to incur heavy debts as a result. This practice borders on a Filipino trait called *Pakitang Tao*. It means showing to others for the benefit of social approval. The Filipino often feels that he is being watched and evaluated whether in his office, church, school or community. This leads to subtle posing in life. And showy wakes and funerals.

As a rule, caskets, preferably top-of-the-line mahogany caskets layered in silk, are open. It is not unusual for those who come to pay their respects to touch the body of the dead person. Filipinos do not believe in cremation. They feel a body should remain whole in preparation for the second coming. You cannot resurrect a jar full of ashes, as my Auntie Soledad put it so philosophically.

Rosary sessions and *novenas* are held during the wake to help the deceased in his journey to heaven.

The funeral itself is a long procession on foot since towns are generally small enough and the cemetery close by, usually near the town's enormous Catholic church. In this procession, the mourners sing prayers while the procession leader takes them on a zig-zag course through town to the cemetery to give as many people as possible the last opportunity to pay their respects to the dead.

After the interment, families visit the grave, often for months, bringing flowers and candles. A special mass is held on the first anniversary of the death, which also marks the lifting of the mourning period.

The biggest holiday for Filipinos is All Soul's Day, celebrated every first of November. It is a day set aside for honoring and remembering the dead and keeping vigil at the cemeteries. Lighted candles and beautiful flowers adorn the clean and polished graves as relatives pay homage to their departed. It is customary to see a lot of food displayed, sometimes even on top of gravestones, during this day of the dead feast. No, the food is not an offering to the dead. It is sustenance for the living.

Considering all the pomp around death in the Filipino culture, it is not surprising that we have many superstitions surrounding death. If a black butterfly lingers around a person, it means one of his relatives just died. If a sick person on his way to the hospital meets a black cat, he will die. Pregnant women should not have their pictures taken; if they do, their babies will die. If a person's shadow appears to be without a head, he will soon die. If someone smells the odor of a candle when there is no candle burning, one of his relatives will die.

I broke into sobs. "Ligaya, are you okay?" My mother's hands were instantly placed on my shaking shoulders. I remembered the night when Ramoncito asked me all about Philippine wedding folklore and superstitions. I racked my brain. Had I told him any superstitions about death? Did I fail to warn him about his own?

Mother held me for a long time. I looked up. The funeral home was almost empty. It was late. The wall clock said midnight. The next day we would bury Ramoncito.

"Ligaya," my mother spoke to me, still holding my hand. "After the *novenas* for Ramoncito, I plan to go home to the Philippines." My mother continued in whispers, despite the fact that Auntie Soledad was the only other person present in the room. She was in one corner, pouring coffee and putting some snacks on a plate.

"Mother?" I said, a way of confirming what she had just told me.

"Yes, I will go home to be with Maria. We have to start being mother and daughter to each other before it's too late," Mother finished, breaking into tears. I hugged her. Despite the air of sadness, there was a vast sense of relief in my heart.

Auntie Soledad let us have our moment. Then she came over with a tray of coffee and a plate of *Kutsinta*, native rice cakes topped with grated coconut.

I picked one and took a bite. It tasted wonderful. I smiled gratefully at Auntie Soledad. I realized I hadn't had a bite since lunch. I took another bite as Mother reached for a piece. If hope were food, this was how it would taste.

KUTSINTA

Ingredients:
   3 cups water
   2 cups brown sugar
   1 cup rice flour
   1 tsp lye water (potassium carbonate solution sold in most Asian food stores)
   Freshly grated coconut

Bring water and brown sugar to a boil. Let cool. Add to rice flour and stir until smooth. Add lye water and mix well. Fill greased mini-muffin or mini-tart pans 3/4 full with mixture. Steam in a large pan with a cover. The water should be 2 inches deep. Cook for 30 minutes or until a toothpick inserted comes out clean. Add more water if needed until cooking is done.

Remove from mold and serve with freshly grated coconut.

Chapter Fourteen

LECHON DE LECHE

I moved back to my mother's apartment. I couldn't bear to continue living in Ramoncito's condo. His parents had put the condominium up for sale. They told me I would be getting part of the proceeds. I thanked them but said no. It didn't seem right. We were not married after all. I had no legal right.

It was Christmas Eve. I was still in mourning but Mother and Auntie Soledad insisted we have Christmas decorations and the traditional Filipino *Noche Buena*, a festive meal held at midnight.

The Philippines celebrates the longest Christmas season in the world. While Europeans and many Anglo-Saxon Americans celebrate Christmas over a period of 12 days from December 25th to January 6th, as popularized by the carol "Twelve Days of Christmas," the Philippines celebrate 21 days of festivities. The Spanish missionaries in 16th century Philippines added a nine-day *novena* and morning mass from December 16th to December 24th. Of course, one can argue that Americans actually prepare for Christmas the day after Thanksgiving. But that's more of a commercial undertaking.

The nine-day *novena* and morning mass is called *Simbang Gabi*. It means mass at night. This is a misnomer because the mass actually starts at four in the morning. After the mass, those attending eat breakfast in the churchyard where vendors in their *tiendas*, food stalls, offer such breakfast delicacies as *Bibingka*, rice cake, and *Puto BumBong*, a purplish delicacy baked inside bamboo canes along with steaming cups of *Salabat*, ginger tea, or hot chocolate. After gorging on such delicious delicacies, many churchgoers promptly return to bed to sleep off their heavy stomachs.

Colorful Christmas rituals abound in the Philippines. In the Tagalog regions, there is one called *Panuluyan*. It is a dramatic re-enactment of the weary journey of Mary and Joseph searching for shelter on that first Christmas Eve more than 2,000 years ago. A young man and a young girl, usually the town's fairest, play the parts of Joseph and Mary. Followed by a band and a string of townspeople, they go door-to-door singing an appeal for shelter. The owner of each

103

house approached apologizes in song that there is no "room in the inn" for them. This continues until Christmas Eve when, finally, one house owner sings "there is available space in a manger." In a designated area, decorated like the Bethlehem manger, the birth of Jesus is reenacted, signaling the advent of Christmas.

Another festivity is the Lantern Festival. Very large, gaily decorated and lighted Christmas lanterns representing the Star of Bethlehem, called *Parols*, are showcased. Much pride and effort goes into each lantern. Many take months of labor and cost thousands of Philippine pesos to create. Most are so huge they have to be carried by trucks. And some have so many multi-colored bulbs on them, they have to be powered by multiple generators. The lanterns are lit and displayed until Christmas Eve, when a contest for the most breathtaking and most dramatic lantern is held.

In old Manila, over 60 images of the Blessed Virgin Mary from all over the country join an annual procession. The images are clothed in rich robes and fine jewelry, and borne on lavishly decorated antique *carrozas*, carriages.

A typical Filipino home is festooned with the western Christmas tree alongside a *Belen*, the nativity scene of Mary, Joseph and Jesus lying in a manger and many dangling *parols.*

On Christmas Day, children go to the houses of their *ninangs* and *ninongs*, godparents, to receive their blessings and gifts. Though the idea of a Santa Claus is now generally accepted, many still do not include the jolly fat man in their Christmas celebrations. Auntie Soledad and my mother both agree that Santa Claus would not survive the hot tropical weather, even in December.

et

But I peered out the window and noticed it was snowing! Surely, Santa Claus was at home in this kind of weather. Without thinking, I looked up at the sky. There was no Santa or his reindeers hovering overhead, but who knew, the snow was thickening. It was hard to see beyond the white dust falling from the sky.

I called out to my Auntie Soledad and my mother, who were in the kitchen preparing our *Noche Buena*.

"What is it?" they asked as they rushed out of the kitchen.

"Look, it's snowing!" I said, excited like a child.

They looked out the window and stared at the snow. "We are going to have a white Christmas!" Auntie Soledad exclaimed. "Oh, what a great backdrop for our *Noche Buena!*"

The *Noche Buena*, literally Night of Goodness, is often referred to as *Media Noche,* Midnight, because no one is allowed to eat until after the midnight Christmas mass. One usually fasts beforehand, especially from meat, to prepare for the midnight feast. Traditionally, the feast is only shared among the nuclear family, the very closest and the very dearest, because for most Filipino families, it is the most meaningful meal of the year. But for ours, we took exception. We invited Aling Salvacion and Peter and some other relatives and friends for our feast.

My mother and Auntie Soledad worked hard to recreate a traditional Filipino midnight meal. They went to every Oriental food store in the greater New York-New Jersey area in search of ingredients for the feast. I was grateful. I knew they're merely trying to divert my mind from sad thoughts of Ramoncito.

The feast began with *bibingka, kutsinta, puto bumbong* and *suman,* a delicacy of sticky rice and coconut milk wrapped in banana or palm leaves and steamed. These are served with ginger tea and hot chocolate, made from scratch out of unsweetened chocolate balls, scalded milk and sugar. We enjoy these while singing Filipino Christmas carols.

My mind wandered to a joyous time when Maria and I joined other children Christmas caroling. She, the other kids, and I would gather bags of soda bottle caps and, with a rock, we would hammer the caps flat. We would then punch a hole in the middle of each cap and string a wire through the flattened disks to create a quaint jingling tambourine to accompany our singing.

As soon as night would fall, we would hit the streets, ignoring Mother's loud reminder to be home in time for dinner. We'd go from house to house in the neighborhood, rendering our off-key yet very heartfelt renditions of "Silent Night," "Jingle Bells" and some *Tagalog* carols. Some houses would wait until we finished our repertoire before opening their doors and handing us coins. Others would hand us coins after the first note to shoo us away. Between the two types, Maria and I might take home a hefty fifty centavos a piece for one night's work!

Of course there were others who would quickly turn off their lights to pretend no one was home. We sometimes pelted those houses with eggs.

My wandering mind snapped to attention when Mother and Auntie Soledad entered from the kitchen carrying a large tray containing our main dish. Instead of the traditional *Jamon en Dulce*, we had *Lechon De Leche* as our Christmas centerpiece. "Ligaya ruined it for Christmas when she served *Jamon* during one of our mahjong sessions, so we're serving this equally festive main dish!" my Auntie Soledad barked when someone inquired why we weren't serving *Jamon* for this Christmas dinner.

Lechon de Leche, roasted suckling piglet, is traditional fiesta fare in the Philippines. The best versions can be found in the southern part, especially in the city of *Cebu*. A *Cebuano* lechon is stuffed with *tanglad*, lemongrass, before it is sewn up and roasted on a spit, giving it a crispy delicious skin and a tender fragrant meat. Ours was roasted in the oven. The small pig fit quite nicely in Mother's Westinghouse.

A funny story about *Lechon*: a cousin of ours took his children back to the Philippines for the first time. They went to a restaurant and ordered *Lechon de Leche*. The roasted piglet was brought spread-eagled to their table and, without warning, the waiter began hacking the *Lechon* to bite-size pieces. The children screamed in horror, "What are they doing to *Babe*?" referring to a movie about a loveable pig. As the adults enjoyed the crisp skin of the *Lechon*, the children bawled.

et

There were also some tears shed over our Christmas dinner. A prayer was said in Ramoncito's honor and halfway through, everyone was choked to tears. I looked around, grateful that Ramoncito was truly well-loved in this circle. I imagined him seated beside me, enjoying this Christmas meal. I excused myself from the table. The pain was overwhelming.

I went to the living room. On one of the side tables, Mother had placed a framed photo of Ramoncito and me, taken during happier days. A tiny dragonfly was perched on the edge of the frame. *Where did it come from?* I looked around. All the windows were shut for the winter season. I squinted my eyes at the dragonfly and smiled. There is a Filipino superstition that the spirit of the dead visits his loved ones in the form of an insect, like a butterfly or a moth. The visit was like a final goodbye before the spirit advanced to the eternal realm. The dragonfly was blue with wide black eyes. I imagined Ramoncito in his denim jacket and Ray Bans, one of his favorite get-ups. I touched the dragonfly. It moved and settled on my fingertip. A strange warm feeling washed over me. Then the dragonfly took off, flying into the folds of Mother's window curtains. I rose and followed it. It was gone. I flapped the curtains. Nothing flew out of it. I felt goose pimples all over my arms.

I returned to the table more composed, ready to pounce on the crispy skin of the perfectly roasted *Lechon*.

LECHON DE LECHE

Clean a small pig well and stuff with lemongrass. Truss it with skewers or with string. Put stuffed pig on a roasting rack with dripping pan. Brush entire surface with melted lard or butter and pour 2 cups of boiling water over the pig. Cover the skin with greased paper and roast at 350-400 degrees F for 4-5 hours, basting every 15 minutes with liquid from the pan. Serve with liver sauce.

LIVER SAUCE
   1 small can liver pate
   1/3 cup vinegar
   1-1/4 cups water
   1/2 cup ground crackers
   1/4 cup sugar
   3/4 tsp black pepper
   salt to taste
   2 tbsp lard or butter
   1 medium onion, finely chopped

8 cloves garlic, pounded

Mix liver pate, vinegar, water, crackers, sugar, salt and pepper. Sautee garlic in lard or butter. When brown, set aside, leaving only 1 tsp garlic in lard or butter. Add chopped onions and fry until tender. Add liver mixture. Cook over low heat, stirring constantly. Serve topped with the rest of the browned garlic.

Chapter Fifteen

MORCON

Mother moved her departure to the Philippines from December 28 to December 29. She did so for a very good reason. Known for its odd wit and humor, somehow the Filipinos were able to turn December 28th, which is Holy Innocents Day per the biblical account of King Herod ordering the slaughter of all first- born male babies, into a Christmas equivalent of America's April Fool's Day. Known as *Ninos Inocentes* Day, Innocent Children's Day, in the Philippines, December 28th has become a day for pranksters. It is the perfect day to settle a score with a godparent who has given you a lousy Christmas gift. Mother simply refused to travel on such a day so she left the following day instead, just in time for a New Year's Eve celebration with Maria and her family in the Philippines.

The New Year's celebration is one of the most anticipated festivities by the Filipinos. It is a time of merriment for the whole family as the family gathers at home to ring in the midnight hour together. There is a traditional belief that if the family spends at least the approach of midnight together, then they will stay together for the rest of the year. So if you're out, take a cab, hitch a ride, paddle a canoe. Just make sure you return home before the New Year comes.

According to Filipino superstition, whatever a person does on New Year's Eve is what he will be doing for the rest of the year. If he gets drunk, then he will be drunk for the rest of the year. If he puts money in his pocket, then he can look forward to a bulging wallet for the next twelve months. If his family is together, then he can feel comfort in knowing his family will be near throughout the coming year.

There are a number of other interesting superstitions associated with New Year's Eve. Wearing polka dots on New Year's Eve brings wealth because the polka dots symbolize coins. A person wearing polka dots is literally drawing money to himself. Opening windows, cabinets, and doors on New Year's Eve lets good luck flow into the house. Putting out food, round-shaped food, on the table brings wealth to the household. Setting off firecrackers and other noisemakers wards off evil spirits and bad luck. Ironically, this last practice has actually led to much destruction, many injuries, and even death as careless celebrants have sent powerful flaming fireworks and stray bullets into unsuspecting places.

A stray bullet pierced through the roof of our house one New Year's Eve. Luckily, no one was hurt, only Mother's ego. The bullet landed on her signature New Year's round food, *Morcon*, stuffed rolled steak.

er

I uttered a fervent prayer for a safe New Year for Mother and Maria's family. I smiled, imagining the lit-up faces of Maria's kids when they saw the gifts we sent ahead in two *Balikbayan* boxes.

Balikbayan. The word refers to someone returning to his homeland. The *Balikbayan* box is literally a huge box measuring about 24 inches tall by 24 inches wide that Filipinos overseas send home by air or sea to their relatives in the Philippines. Our two *Balikbayan* boxes for Maria and her family contained all the love and loot we could marshal within budget: Spam, corned beef and other canned goods, candies, toys, clothes, books, vanity products, and even small appliances. We squeezed all these into the boxes and sent them ahead of Mother to eliminate the hassle of Mother lugging them around the Philippine airport, which is considered one of the most congested in the world.

Auntie Soledad, Peter, and I drove Mother to the Newark International Airport, a better, less crowded airport than Kennedy International. (Pssst, it's our secret!)

Peter and Auntie Soledad became inseparable. "They're now an item!" my mother snorted one day. How it started no one knows, though we suspected it intensified at Ramoncito's wake. Aside from the "item" remark, Mother remained tight-lipped about the relationship, though I could tell she was just dying to articulate her feelings about it. On the subject, she was like the world-famous perfectly coned-shaped dormant *Mayon* volcano waiting to erupt. Me, I was just happy that Peter and Auntie Soledad seemed to get along so well. I must admit I felt slightly awkward, especially when they started acting like silly infatuated kids - they're both in their fifties, for god's sake - in my presence. Which was what they were doing now as I tore open a letter from a cousin in San Francisco, California. It had been sent to Ramoncito's condo and forwarded to my mother's apartment.

"Okay, stop. That's more than I need to see," I said with pretend annoyance when Peter started licking Auntie Soledad's ear. Peter acceded, pouting like a sad clown. Auntie Soledad was a bit red in the face.

"*Iha*, who is it from?" Auntie Soledad asked, after clearing her throat.

"*Aba* it's from Esteban!" I exclaimed, skimming through the contents of the letter.

It was Auntie Soledad's turn to roll her eyes.

"What was that about?" I asked, catching her reaction from the corner of my eye.

"*Ang iyong mujeradong pinsan, anong sabi niya?*" Your gay cousin, what does his letter say?

"Auntie!" I shot Auntie Soledad a look. Peter seemed amused. I continued to read the letter.

"He's looking to relocate to the East Coast. He is wondering if he can stay here for a few weeks! That's great!" I added excitedly. Esteban was one of my favorite cousins. We were inseparable until he left for America after college, petitioned by his brother Vicente, who was in the US Navy and now lived in Florida with his Filipina wife and two kids.

"Why didn't he just call?" Auntie Soledad asked. There was a hint of disapproval in her tone.

"He probably tried. Look, this has Ramoncito's address, forwarded here," I said, instantly feeling stupid. I put the letter back in the envelope and glared at Auntie. "Okay, Auntie Soledad, you seem to disapprove of Esteban being gay."

"*Aba, wala akong sinabi!*" Hey, I didn't say that! said a defensive Auntie Soledad.

I decided to drop the subject. "OK, then. I'll call him tonight and tell him he's welcome to stay here for as long as he wants, okay?"

Auntie Soledad just shrugged her shoulders. I'm not an expert on body language but even an amateur can detect censure in that.

I turned to Peter.

"Hey, I have nothing against gays!" he exclaimed, both hands raised in a gesture of surrender. *Pontious Pilate washing his hands*, I thought.

"Auntie Soledad used to think you were gay," I said, still fuming.

"What? When did I say that? I didn't say that! Hoy, Ligaya, watch your mouth, ha?" Auntie Soledad fumbled over her words.

"*Di ba*, you and Mother used to suspect that Peter, because he lived alone, was gay. *Di ba*?" Am I right? I felt giddily wicked that I hit a nerve.

"Okay, okay, let's put all this to rest. If Ligaya wants her cousin to stay here, that's her prerogative, right?" Peter addressed Auntie Soledad.

"Well, right," Auntie Soledad timidly answered.

"And I'm not gay, okay?" This he said to both of us. We said nothing.

"Just because a man my age is single and lives alone doesn't mean he likes guys. Maybe I'm just waiting for the right woman." He stole a glance at Auntie Soledad, who instantly reddened but managed to crinkle her eyes into a smile.

"Okay, now that that's settled, what do you say we celebrate? After all, it is New Year's Eve, isn't it? Where's the champagne?" Peter finished, all bubbly.

er

Auntie Soledad assisted me in the kitchen while Peter drove to Newark to buy firecrackers from a contact who sells them out of his home.

"Out of his home?" Auntie Soledad exclaimed earlier, wondering if the firecrackers were legal.

"You worry too much!" he said, frowning. "You said you want fireworks for New Year's Eve, just like in the Philippines. Well, you're getting your wish! Happy New Year!" He kissed her on the cheek and left.

"Hope we don't get into trouble for this," Auntie Soledad said, as she ladled fresh eggs into a pot of boiling water.

"It'll be okay, Auntie. Besides, we're gonna set them off in the backyard. It's safe there," I assured her, not really sure about the laws concerning firecrackers. We had set off quite a few in our backyard during our 4th of July barbecue without any incident.

"I suppose you're right," she agreed. "Oh, Ligaya, I just want us to have a good old Filipino New Year's Eve—firecrackers, round foods for good luck and *hoy*, don't forget to change into your polka dot dress before New Year, okay?"

I said "Okay" just to shut her up, but I wasn't really a big fan of polka dots.

"Hey, Auntie Soledad, so Peter *ha*?" I switched to a different topic. "*Serioso na yata 'yan, ha?*" Is the relationship serious? I asked as I started to cut and trim the flank steak for the *Morcon* dish, stuffed rolled steak. Our round-shaped piece de resistance.

"Well, we'll see. Oh, Ligaya, I do like him. Such a sweet man...for a *Kano*."

"What do you mean? White men can be sweet too. Auntie Soledad, Filipino men don't have the monopoly on sweetness, you know?"

"Yeah, I guess you're right. *Aray!*" Ouch! She burned her finger as she dropped another egg into the boiling water.

"Auntie Soledad, you okay?"

"Yeah, it's just a minor burn," she said, licking the burnt finger. "Didn't even see that my finger was too near the boiling water. *Naku Ligaya*. My eyesight is failing me. *Tumatanda na talaga ako*." I'm really getting too old.

In the Philippines, Auntie Soledad would be considered *Matandang Dalaga*. Old Maid. The Filipina spinster, unlike her western counterpart who may live alone, have a career, and basically have her own life, is not considered a liberated individual. Although she does not have her own family of procreation (husband and kids), she is still attached to her family of origination (parents, brothers, sisters, etc.). She usually lives with one of her sisters or brothers, helping them manage the household or with her parents, looking after them in their old age.

There is a social stigma attached to being a spinster. Because of the society's emphasis on getting married and raising children, most Filipinos do not understand how a woman can be over thirty and still unmarried. The only reason they can think of is that she never received a marriage proposal.

Some Filipinos even believe spinsterhood is a curse. If a woman does not marry by her early thirties, they believe she will never be married at all because she is cursed. They will point to two or three other spinster aunts in the woman's family as proof of the curse.

I didn't tell Auntie Soledad this, but I suspected the stigma of being a *Matandang Dalaga* had something to do with her hooking up with Peter. *Stop it! That is mean!* I immediately chastised myself for such a thought. I continued with my task at hand, pounding the flank steak with a mallet to flatten it.

"Hey, starting the noisemaker early, huh?" Auntie Soledad teased, pointing at the mallet with her lips.

I laughed, hitting the steak even harder. Over the loud pounding noise, I cried to Auntie Soledad: *"Manigong Bagong Taon!"* Happy New Year!

MORCON
(Stuffed Rolled Steak)

Ingredients
  2 lbs flank steak
  1 clove garlic, minced
  12 whole peppercorns
  2 tbsp soy sauce
  2 tbsp lemon juice
  1 medium carrot, peeled and cut into circles
  2 sweet pickles, cut into circles
  2 Spanish sausages, cut into circles
  3 hardboiled eggs, sliced into circles
  2 tbsp vegetable oil
  1/4 cup flour
  4 cups water
  1 onion, sliced into circles
  1 can stewed tomatoes
  3 bay leaves
  1 tsp ground pepper

1 tsp salt
1 tsp cornstarch, dissolved in 2 tsp water

Cut the flank steak thin, about 12 inches by 10 inches. Pound to flatten it. Pound the garlic and peppercorns. Add soy sauce and lemon juice. Pour the mixture over the meat and marinate for about an hour. Pour off and reserve the marinade.

To stuff the flank steak, place it on a cutting board and arrange the carrots, pickles, sausages and hardboiled eggs in alternate rows on top of the steak. Roll the steak carefully from one end to the other like a jellyroll and tie it with a string.

In a large oven-proof casserole, heat the oil over moderate heat. Coat the rolled steak in flour and brown it on all sides in the oil. Add the water, marinade, onions, tomatoes, bay leaves, pepper and salt. Cover and bake for 1-1/2 to 2 hours, turning the meat several times while cooking.

When the meat is tender, transfer to a warm serving dish and remove the strings.

Scrape the sides of the casserole dish and pour the liquid through a strainer into a saucepan. Bring this to a boil, thickening with the cornstarch and water mixture. Cook until it is the consistency of gravy.

To serve, slice the rolled *Morcon* crosswise, arrange on a platter and pour the gravy over the round pieces of *Morcon*.

Chapter Sixteen

ADOBO and LUMPIA, American-Style

I was pacing outside the freezing cold PATH Train station in Jersey City, waiting for Esteban. He had just flown in from San Francisco today, but refused my offer to meet him at the Newark Airport. He wanted to get used to the public commute, he said. I think he was just being considerate. Yesterday, on the phone when I called to inquire about his flight schedule, I mentioned a catering job this afternoon. Sweet guy, this Esteban, he just didn't want me to miss a money-making prospect.

I shivered. I tightened my winter coat and adjusted my wool scarf. I felt the need to pee but I looked across the street and saw the *Jersey Daily* and the urgency petered out. I knew Mr. Picardi Lancelloti no longer worked there, but I still felt nervous about going into the building. *Just go in there and say a quick hello to Stella and the other girls*, I said to myself, the need for relief coming back in full force. I made a tentative step towards the street and spotted Jim from the train ticket booth. I rushed to him instead.

"Hey Jim, hi! Remember me? I—"

"Oh, yes, I never forget the face of a damsel in distress," he said before I even finished my sentence. "How are you, girl?" he asked, grinning. I really loved his straight gleaming white teeth!

"Oh I'm fine, but I do need to-"

"Say no more. Just go right in and head for the ladies' room ahead. No charge."

"Oh, thank you, Jim. Thank—"

"And don't worry. It's not being cleaned so it's available."

I was grateful and also amazed at how he seemed to read my thoughts. While peeing, it dawned on me that he must get this kind of plea a hundred times a day. God bless Jim.

And God bless Esteban for coming to stay with me, to keep me company while Mother is away patching things up with Maria in the Philippines.

Esteban and I grew up together. We were playmates, though Maria would often tease him for playing with our dolls, especially

Skipper. She would call him *Batang Bading*, child homosexual. My mother would immediately shush Maria but the teasing never seemed to bother Esteban. At age ten, one of his interests was designing women's dresses. He sent some of his drawings to a local magazine and got them published. No one was angrier than his father, who smacked him so hard he lost a tooth and then grounded him for most of the summer. When Esteban was free again, the first thing he did was come to our house and draw fabulous dresses for Maria and me. Even early on in his gayness, Esteban is what you would consider a parlor-type gay in the Philippines.

Filipino homosexuals fall into three general categories. First, there is the parlor type. These are the ones associated with beauty parlors and other typically feminine businesses like cosmetics, couture and cuisine. They typically and simply want to look or dress like women.

The second type is the subdued type. They usually dress like ordinary men and are closeted, denying their sexuality for fear of ostracism. Many get married to hide their real personas and only seek out gay sex on the sly.

The third type is what I would refer to as the third kind. It comprises the straight-looking, straight-acting gays who prefer lovers like themselves. They often rationalize their status as, "I'm just a regular guy who happens to be gay."

Filipino society generally accepts and tolerates gays. Since the closeted and the straight-acting, straight-looking gays are already unknowingly assimilated into our society, we can only really chat about the parlor types.

There are various terms used to refer to them: *Bakla, Siyoke, Badaf, Bayot, Bading, Silahis, Sward, Mujerado* and "member of the Third Sex," which I personally think is demeaning because it implies inferiority, that homosexuals are mere subordinates of men.

The parlor types, though often made fun of in movies and TV shows, assume an important role in Philippine society, that of arbiter of taste. They are make-up artists, couturiers, interior decorators, cooks, hairdressers, and architects who set the trends in fashion and design. They are smart, fun-loving, witty, and entertaining. Many are considered a girl's best friend. Where else can a girl get a stylist and a confidante rolled into one fabulous package? Even straight men get along well with them. In extreme cases, during a typical *Binyag*—a pre-marital devirginization of men—when there is no prostitute to initiate a man sexually, the services of a *bakla* are engaged.

The Philippines have no laws against homosexuality among consenting adults. There are visible gay communities in metropolitan areas. There are gay bars, gay health clubs, and gay beauty contests. One of Esteban's last acts of rebellion against his family before leaving the Philippines was joining the Miss Gay Metropolitan contest. I acted as his wardrobe person, so I got access to the venue. It was just like a regular beauty contest. Contestants paraded in cocktail dresses, swimsuits and lavish evening gowns before an enthusiastic straight and gay crowd. In the interview portion of the contest, Esteban's question was, "What time is it when you see a tiger?" His award-winning response: "Time to kick off your high heels and run like hell!" He placed third and received the Miss Smiling Face Award as well.

Esteban did have a great smile. Much like this strange-looking guy standing in front of me, balancing two bags, foolishly grinning at me.

"*Hoy*, Esteban? Oh my god!" I said, my mouth dropping in astonishment. His hair was curly and had streaks of red and blond. He had hazel-colored contact lenses. His ears were pierced. He sported a nose ring. His frail-looking body was tightly wrapped in an all-leather outfit. But the smile was, without a doubt, Esteban's.

"*Dios ko*, you look different!" I exclaimed, still reeling from shock. I'd seen him in drag and dresses but this was like an almost completely different person. There was something else that I could not put my finger on.

"How are you, my fabulous cousin?" He greeted me with a hug and a kiss. He smelled of expensive cologne. "I'm so sorry about your loss. I wanted to come for the funeral but—"

"It's okay, really. The important thing is you're here now," I said, cutting him off.

"Are you okay? Really, really okay?" he asked, slipping into one of his odd speaking habits: repeating words for emphasis. Really, really? Truly, truly? Very, very.

"Yes, I am. Not really, really, but really. Thanks for asking, cousin Esteban," I answered, trying on a brave smile which didn't fit.

"Call. Me. Stefan."

"What?"

"Stefan. That's who I'm called now."

I gaped at him and broke into laughter.

"Watzza mattah with yah, girl?" he asked, showing mock irritation, nose out of joint.

Dios mio, my god, it's his nose! It's not sarat anymore! What did he do to it?

I laughed again. This time Esteban, AKA Stefan, joined in. I laughed until my eyes filled with tears. *It feels good to laugh again*, I thought to myself.

er

That night, Stefan and I shared *Lumpia* and *Adobo* prepared American-style.

I added potatoes, carrots, and hardboiled eggs to my *Adobo*. My *Lumpia* had mushrooms, carrots and bamboo shoots sauteed in white wine. Very American. Also, very gay.

ADOBO, AMERICAN-STYLE
(Chicken Adobo with Quail Eggs, Potatoes and Carrots)

Ingredients:
- 3 tbsp oil
- 3 cloves garlic
- 1 tsp ginger, grated
- 2-3 lbs chicken, cut up and skinned
- 1/2 cup distilled white vinegar
- 1 tsp salt
- 1 tbsp black pepper
- 1 cup water
- 1/2 cup soy sauce
- 2 bay leaves
- 2 carrots, sliced in small chunks
- 2 potatoes, sliced in small chunks

8 quail eggs, hardboiled, shelled

Heat the oil in a large pot and saute the garlic and ginger. Add the chicken pieces and lightly brown. Add the vinegar, salt, pepper, water, soy sauce and bay leaves and simmer for about 20 minutes. Add carrots and potatoes and simmer for an additional 20 minutes. Add the shelled quail eggs and continue to simmer until the liquid is reduced by half.

Serve with rice. Uncle Ben's Instant Rice is acceptable in this case.

LUMPIA, AMERICAN STYLE
(Fresh spring rolls with Mushrooms, Bamboo Shoots and Carrots)

Ingredients:
    2 tsp vegetable oil
    4 cloves garlic, crushed
    1 cup onions, finely chopped
    1 lb pork, sliced into short thin strips
    1 lb shrimp, peeled and chopped
    1/4 cup white wine
    1/3 cup chicken broth
    1 can bamboo shoots, drained
    1/2 cup portabello mushroom, chopped
    1 medium sized carrot, julienned
    salt and pepper to taste
    20-25 fresh lettuce leaves
    20-25 eggroll wrappers

In a skillet, heat the oil and saute the garlic and onions. Add the pork and cook for 5 minutes. Add the shrimp, the white wine, and the chicken broth and cook for another 3-5 minutes.

Add the bamboo shoots, mushrooms, and carrots to the mixture and simmer for 5-10 minutes. Season to taste with salt and pepper. Remove from heat. Drain and cool.

Place a lettuce leaf in the middle of an egg wrapper. On top, place 2 tbsp of the filling. Fold the bottom part of the wrapper over the filling and roll to the other side to make a neat package with the top part of the lettuce showing at the open end of the roll. Repeat for each egg wrapper.

Serve with sauce.

Eggroll Wrappers:
    3 large eggs
    ¾ cup cornstarch
    ½ cup water
    ½ cup vegetable oil

In a bowl, separate the egg yolks from the whites. Beat the whites until frothy. Add the yolks and beat until well blended.

In another bowl, add cornstarch to the water and mix well. Add this mixture to the beaten eggs. Mix well. Let stand for at least 5 minutes to allow bubbles to settle.

Brush a non-stick hotcake or crepe pan with the oil. Place over medium-low heat. Give the batter a quick stir, pour 2 tbsp of the mixture into the pan, and quickly tip the pan from side to side to spread batter into a thin wrapper. Cook until wrapper can be lifted easily from the pan.

Sauce:
    2-1/4 cups water
    1/2 cup brown sugar
    1/4 cup soy sauce
    3 tbsp cornstarch
    3 cloves garlic, minced
    Salt and pepper to taste

Heat 2 cups of water, brown sugar and soy sauce. Bring to a boil. Add cornstarch diluted in 1/4 cup water. Season to taste with salt and pepper and stir constantly until mixture thickens. Top with minced garlic.

Chapter Seventeen

RELLENONG TALONG

It is a Saturday afternoon, exactly three weeks since Stefan's arrival. After recovering from the initial shock, Auntie Soledad reluctantly hosted a *Bienvenida*, a welcome party, at her apartment in Stefan's honor. An assortment of friends and relatives showed up, mostly out of curiosity about Stefan's Westernized appearance. His nose job was the hot topic of *chismis*, gossip.

Filipinos have a predilection to gossip, to spread rumors, to frighten and titillate one another with dire warnings, salacious gossip, and preposterous allegations. Gossiping has practically been our national pastime for centuries. We gossip in beauty parlors. In restaurants. Restrooms. On buses. In supermarket lines. In bars. In funeral homes during wakes. On the phone. With our drivers. With our office mates. With our doctors. And sometimes, even with our priest confessors. A Filipino's day is jam-packed with these sometimes heartwarming, oftentimes heartbreaking, maybe true, maybe entirely false gossips. *Psssst! Did you hear about the movie star who had a collagen implant in her lips? She's now sick as a dog as a result of an infection. Hey, did you hear about the English actor who was caught with a prostitute? Heard he did that intentionally to hide his homosexuality. Hey, did you know that our town mayor is keeping a mistress on the side? She's that former beauty queen turned off-key recording artist. Hoy, I heard Juanita had a miscarriage. And no, it's not her husband's.*

But who doesn't gossip in this world, really? In a perfect world, there would be no gossip, no scandals, no rumors, no hearsay. There would simply be no reason for them to exist. But in a world of average, imperfect folks, we will always need to discuss our peers, our acquaintances, our neighbors, movie stars, government officials, and our heroes to evaluate their actions, their character, and their motives. And they will do the same to us. It's the human need to constantly compare ourselves to the world around us. In discovering other people's idiosyncrasies, peculiarities, and the inner threads of their relationships, we can gauge our own success (or failure) as a person. So we will always be inappropriately curious about others: *What's inside his closet? His medicine cabinet? His desk drawer? His safe and vault?*

Can you imagine a world without gossip? 70% of our daily conversation would not occur because that is probably how much of it is gossip. Gossip is like water in our bodies. Without it, we are just flesh and bones.

"Is there any gossip etiquette?" Stefan asked as we indulged in the pleasures of oral intercourse this lazy Saturday afternoon.

"Well, for one," I said, making up a rule on the fly, "I think it's alright to tell your spouse a confidence someone shared with you."

"Hey, that's a good one, really really!" Stefan remarked. "How about this?" he added, already getting into the game. "You may relate something derogatory about others as long as it's true!"

I didn't agree but I just thought of another so I ignored his remark and said, "It's alright to speak highly of someone to a third party. Highly, that's the operative word, okay?"

"That's lame," he commented, wryly.

"If you swear you won't repeat something that someone told you, but a third party persists, it is permissible to tell that third party a little!" I exclaimed, trying to make up for the lame one.

"Hey, now you're getting wicked, cousin Ligaya," he said about my latest contribution.

"Okay, maybe we should stop," I said, a bit red in the face.

"Okay, but before we do, let me tell you a funny story about *chismis.*"

"Okay," I said tentatively. Stefan's funny stories were always a bit naughty.

"So, it is the Miss Sphere beauty pageant and we're down to the five finalists. Miss France, Miss Sweden, Miss USA, Miss India and Miss Philippines. Miss France and Miss Sweden have been asked and have answered the same question and it is now Miss USA's turn. The interviewer asks her the all-important title-deciding question: 'Miss USA, how would you describe a male organ in your country?'"

"Stefan!" I exclaimed with feigned shock.

"It's just a joke, okay?" he said, trying to calm me down. "Anyway, she answers, 'Well I would say that male organs are like gentlemen.' 'Why do you say that?' asks the interviewer. 'Because it stands every time it sees a woman.' 'Good answer!', says the interviewer. Huge applause from the audience.

"Next, he asks Miss India the same question. She replies, 'I can say that a male organ in India is like a hard laborer.' 'Why?' asks the interviewer. 'Because it works day and night.' The audience roars at that answer.

"The interviewer then goes to a nervous Miss Philippines and asks the same question. Do you know what the *bruha*, witch, answered?" Stefan asked me with a wicked grin.

"No, and I bet it's something really gross," I said, resigned to letting him finish his joke.

"With a nervous giggle she answers that male organs in the Philippines are like *chismis*, gossip, because they pass from mouth to mouth."

"Stefan, *que bastos*!" How vulgar! Auntie Soledad was standing by the door. There was a fierce look of disgust on her face. Stefan and I immediately rose.

"Auntie Soledad, hello!" I said, stammering. Stefan tried to control a giggle in vain. Auntie Soledad shot him a look but he couldn't compose himself.

"I'm so sorry, Auntie Soledad," he finally said without conviction. Auntie Soledad shook her head.

"So how's the job hunting going?" she asked, going for the jugular. Stefan had been looking for a job as a graphic arts designer, but had not been lucky yet. In Aunt Soledad's eyes, he was a freeloader. I saw him as a godsend.

Stefan bowed his head. "I have some interviews lined up next week, so—" He didn't finish but showed us his crossed fingers.

"Hey, Auntie Soledad, are you staying for dinner? Stefan and I are making *Rellenong Talong*!" I blurted out, anxious to break the tension. Stefan giggled. Auntie Soledad reddened. I covered my mouth, horrified when I realized my foot-in-mouth gaffe.

Rellenong Talong is Philippine eggplant stuffed with meat filling. Unlike its Western counterpart, which is huge, round and squat, the Philippine eggplant is long, slender and royal purple in color— somewhat like an erect penis. Despite its shape, it is much tastier than the American aubergine, which tastes like cotton in comparison. The Philippine eggplant, like the tomato, is really a fruit that is eaten like a vegetable. *Talong* in the southeast Asian region is often referred to in English as the purple melon.

Much like Auntie Soledad's facial complexion at that moment, royal purple, because Stefan could not stop giggling. She huffed off, muttering, *"Ang kabataan ngayon, bastos, walang galang!"* The youth of today. Vulgar. No respect.

Once she was out of earshot, I told Stefan: *"Naku, Stefan, lagot ka."* Stefan, you're dead. "You've just worn out Auntie Soledad's welcome mat for you." I wielded a warning finger at him.

Stefan motioned with his finger to come nearer. I obliged. "Ligaya, just between you and me, I think Auntie Soledad's not getting it these days from Peter."

My mouth dropped. I gave Stefan a *kurot*, a friendly but still painful pinch, in his arm.

"Naku, Stefan, that is gossip! Didn't we just discuss etiquette about gossiping?"

Stefan just shrugged and said, "Alright, why don't we just go to the kitchen and prepare those *Talongs* for the *Relleno*?"

e7

I washed the penile-shaped eggplants in the sink. I blinked as I felt a familiar stirring in me. *Ramoncito,* I whispered.

"Hoy!" Stefan broke my stupor. "Those *talongs* are washed enough, okay? Mmm, what are you doing?" he asked, his frowning face trying to read my mind.

"Nothing, nothing!" I answered, face blushing.

"I know what you're thinking, Ligaya, you naughty girl," he said, taking the clean eggplants from me. "It's a natural feeling. Don't be ashamed! You're still young. You still have needs."

Over dinner, I thought about Stefan's comment for a long time. I was so deep in my thoughts I hadn't noticed he had snatched the last piece of the *Rellenong Talong* and stuffed it whole into his mouth.

RELLENONG TALONG

Ingredients:
 2 medium eggplants, halved lengthwise
 2 tbsp vegetable oil
 1 clove garlic, minced
 1 onion, finely chopped
 1 tomato, chopped
 1 lb. ground beef
 1 tsp salt
 1/2 tsp pepper
 1/4 tsp sugar
 2 eggs
 1/2 cup bread crumbs
 1/2 cup cooking oil for frying

Place eggplant halves on rack, skin up. Broil about 6 inches away from heat for about 15 minutes or until tender. Turn eggplants halfway through cooking to cook the other side. Let cool.

Heat the vegetable oil and saute garlic, onion and tomatoes in it. Add the ground beef and cook, stirring for 5 minutes or until meat is brown. Drain excess oil. Season with salt, pepper and sugar. Let cool slightly before adding 1 egg and blending the mixture thoroughly. Divide into 4 equal portions.

Peel eggplants. Split and spread like a fan. Top with one portion of the meat mixture and spread over surface. Beat remaining egg. Dip eggplant into egg, covering the entire eggplant and the filling. Coat eggplant with bread crumbs. Let stand for at least 10 minutes to set.

Heat oil in skillet. Fry eggplant until top is golden brown.

Chapter Eighteen

ARROZ CALDO

"You're doing what!?" Mother screamed in utter shock into the phone.

"It's called rhinoplasty, Mother. A nose re-shaping job," I repeated nervously.

"It's your *Mujerado* cousin, isn't it? He put that crazy idea in your brain! Ligaya, *naloloka ka na ba*?" Are you out of your mind? My mother had gone berserk on the phone.

I couldn't help thinking that a long distance operator was listening to this conversation and was either getting a cheap thrill or was preparing to cut us off.

It had been two months since Stefan first suggested I look into rhinoplasty. My initial reaction was identical to my mother's. My wide, indigenous nose turned red with indignation; my big nostrils flared even bigger. "How dare you!" I had shrieked at Stefan.

"Hey, Ligaya, please calm down. It's just a suggestion. I'm sorry. I didn't mean to offend you. You're the one who's always complaining about your *sarat*, pug, nose, remember?"

"What? What are you talking about?"

"I'm talking about those days when you would pinch your nose with a clothespin to make it narrower and higher."

"Stefan, we were kids then and that was torture," I said with a nervous laugh. "*Dios ko*, I did a lot of crazy things then," I added, remembering those days locked inside our bathroom, when I tried to will my 13-year old breasts into womanhood.

They did bloom naturally, though my nose remained the same. There are some things you can't hurry and there are some things you can't change. I learned to live with my wide nose. I accepted it as part of my Filipina look. When I looked at myself in the mirror, I saw straight black hair, yellow skin pigmentation, almond eyes, a broad flat nasal dorsum with thick lobular skin, and a somewhat flat face with high cheekbones. Though quite different from my sister Maria's Hispanic features, I was quite satisfied with what I saw. Honestly.

That's the beauty of being a Filipino. We encompass so many different physical features. Some of us have fair skin, some *kayumanggi*, brown skin, others yellow skin. Some have eyes that are a bit slanted, others have a *sarat* nose. Some of us have round faces, while others' faces are more chiseled. Some are slim, some are heavyset. Some are short, some are tall. There really is no single look that defines a Filipino.

History has influenced the evolution of the Filipino face. Some 30,000 years ago the earliest inhabitants of the Philippines arrived from the Asian mainland, perhaps over land bridges built during the ice ages. By the 10th century A.D., coastal villages welcomed Chinese commerce and settlers, followed by Muslim traders from neighboring islands. In 1521, Ferdinand Magellan claimed the land for Spain, whose imperial rule lasted until the United States of America gained possession after victories in the Spanish-American War in 1898 and the Philippine-American War from 1899 to 1901. United States authority, although interrupted by the Japanese occupation during World War II, led to independence for a republic founded on July 4, 1946. Through intercultural marriage, all of these races had mixed with the native Malaysians to create a mixed heritage population of Hispanic, Malay, Chinese, Japanese, and American ancestry. Thus, the Filipino face really represents a beautiful concoction of many Oriental and Western features.

Because our last occupation was by the United States, Western culture now dominates our Eastern ways. Young generations of Filipinos growing up today are exposed to many Western ideas and reject the old ways. Stefan and I grew up in this environment. Our daily lives were dominated by Western influences from Hollywood movies to fast food restaurants. We watched Robert Redford and Marilyn Monroe on the silver screen and saw blond, blue-eyed looks as the epitome of beauty. We saw our *morena* features, brown and ethnic, as unattractive and undesirable.

Stefan was especially influenced. When he arrived in America, he immediately searched for ways to adopt a more Westernized look. He dyed his black hair light brown, he bought hazel contact lenses to mask his dark brown irises, he used skin lightening chemicals and make-up to conceal his olive skin.

And in more radical moves, he underwent rhinoplasty to straighten and thin his nose and blepharoplasty to widen his eyes. The rhinoplasty entailed narrowing his nose through bone, cartilage, and nostril width reduction and elevating his nose through a dorsal graft. The blepharosplasty involved the surgical alteration of his eyes via a slit along the upper eyelid to create double eyelids and a rounder, larger, less "Asian" look.

"Believe me *Ate Ligaya*," Stefan began one day when the subject of his Westernized eyes and nose came up again. "My eyelids are the last place I would want touched by a scalpel. But as I did more research into the "Westernization of the eyes" procedure and looked at examples of before and after photos, I found myself noticing that those with eyelids do look better than those without. Besides, have you ever been called 'you slant-eyed dog eater' to your face?" Stefan reasoned, double-eyelid eyes flashing anger.

With all these changes, Stefan, as he colorfully described himself, had become the quintessential "Filipino-American bastard."

In the Philippines, cosmetic procedures are not always about vanity or assimilation. Many Filipinas are acutely conscious about the preservation of their figures and faces and the youthful elasticity of their skin. They spend much time in beauty parlors, beauty clinics and spas beautifying themselves. They do not see it as a luxury as Western women do, but as a necessity: the need to retain their beauty out of fear of losing their mates to rivals. While Western women may believe their mates will stay by their side through old age out of love, Filipino women know that though their mates may stay, they may also start getting some action on the side from some younger, prettier mistresses. The retention of beauty is a matter of pride too. Filipino women want their mates to be proud of their looks. Unlike Western women, they feel that if they let themselves "go to pot," then they can only blame themselves when their mates seek another mate. It is no coincidence that in the Philippines, the cosmetics market is one of the most thriving industries.

For many young Filipino people of both sexes today, Western clothing, makeup, and other adornments are not enough, so they dye and streak their hair blond or red, while many young women have their eyes surgically "Westernized" and their noses reshaped. The Philippines has some of the best beaches in the world, but you won't find many Filipinos there because they don't want dark skin. Many carry umbrellas on sunny days and whiteners are a popular cosmetic device.

"Ligaya, we are all conditioned to view things a certain way and anything that doesn't fit into that mold is condemned. I don't see fat people on the cover of fashion magazines, do you?" Stefan would rationalize to me whenever I teased him about his looks. Did it make sense? I don't know. Was it popular? Definitely.

Recent statistics released by the American Society for Aesthetic Plastic Surgery show that the number of ethnic minorities having cosmetic surgical and non-surgical procedures is increasing dramatically. Here are some typical complaints from those considering rhinoplasty: nose is too large, too flat, too humped, too fat, too long, too short, too crooked, too bulbous. More practically, some consider rhinoplasty to cure breathing problems, but they're far from the norm. Reasons for rhinoplasty, both silly and practical, range from: to have more dates or to attract a mate, to gain popularity, to improve self- esteem, and to advance a career.

The more we talked about this, the more I believed a nose-reshaping job wasn't such a bad idea for me. I couldn't lie and act like I didn't like the nose job that Stefan got. It was natural looking. Though he thought it made him look more Western, to me it just seemed to harmonize well with his other Asian features. And who was I kidding? I did envy Maria's aquiline nose at times. That is why I endured the torture of a clothespinned nose when I was younger. And, though I hated to admit it, I was sick and tired of Mother referring to my nose as *sarat*.

"You know that prayer, Serenity? 'God, please give me the strength to change the things I can?" Stefan said once, adding he knew of some people who told him that they wondered why they waited so long for the surgery. For some reason, I didn't think the writer of that prayer thought its purpose was to rationalize cosmetic surgery, but I wouldn't be surprised if I saw posters of this prayer displayed in cosmetic surgeon clinics' waiting rooms.

So one day, Stefan and I took the PATH train to downtown Manhattan to consult with a plastic surgeon who specialized in Asian rhinoplasty. I still had mixed feelings about the nose job because part of me still thought that altering my body was a violation against nature. At the same time, I had come to understand Stefan's perspective. He promised he'd keep his, uh, nose, out of it and let me decide for myself.

The doctor was thorough and wonderful. He went through the many possible surgical choices for changing the shape and characteristics of my nose. He interviewed me to ascertain whether I was emotionally ready for a new nose. He showed me a computer rendering of my post-surgery nose. He asked about my medical history, about allergies I might have had that could cause nasal stuffiness. He conducted an examination of my internal nasal structure. He studied and analyzed the size and shape of my nose in comparison to the rest of my face. And through it all, he kept telling me to have realistic expectations regarding the surgery, for that was the key to a happy outcome. What clinched it for me, though, was when he added that my nose would not become Westernized but more like subtly improved to "enhance the beauty that was already there but hidden." At the end of our long meeting, I felt comfortable, convinced that I could and should have a new nose.

A date was set for my nose reshaping surgery. The process would be quite simple. A hard silicone strip would be inserted to increase the bridge of my nose. Then my nose would be cut and narrowed. The whole procedure would cost a little more than $4,000, but the clinic had approved my credit application so I'd be getting the nose job on credit. "How very American!" Stefan mused.

Auntie Soledad made all sorts of pleas for me to reconsider. When I remained steadfast, she rolled her eyes, snorted loudly through her Filipino nose and made the sign of the cross. My mother threatened to fly back to America but somehow changed her mind. I suspected Maria had something to do with that.

et

It was the night before my surgery. As a pre-op procedure, the plastic surgeon had put me on a soft diet. Stefano and I were in the kitchen busy making *Arroz Caldo*, a soup with a rice and chicken base. It is a Filipino comfort food, much like the Western chicken soup, that we love to have during the rainy season or a period of convalescence.

"This is your goodbye-to-your-*sarat*-nose meal," Stefan wisecracked while stirring the pot simmering with chicken pieces, rice, garlic, onions and ginger. I smiled at Stefan, grateful for his keeping me company. I inhaled the aromatic smell. It brought back memories of a rainy day when Maria, Stefan and I were holed up in the *Bahay Kubo*, the Filipino equivalent of a tree house, eating *Arroz Caldo* and having not a care in the world. I suddenly longed for those simple days. I couldn't help but smile.

Filipinos are big on smiles. If there is any trait that aptly describes our character and personality as a people, it is the way we use smiles. We smile when we are happy, but we also smile when we are embarrassed. We praise and criticize with a smile. We extend condolences with a smile. We take life's trials with a smile. Confrontations are best avoided but when unavoidable, we meet them head-on with a smile. A smile is our response to almost everything from the funny to the catastrophic. *We smile to create the impression that all is going well.*

I was smiling again as we partook of the delicious *Arroz Caldo*. Stefan had a second helping. I declined, with a smile.

"Alright, why don't you go to bed early? You'll need all your energy for tomorrow's surgery. Don't worry, I'll take care of cleaning up here, okay?" Stefan said after supper. I thanked him, with a smile, natch.

eʒ

I was restless as I lay in bed. I tossed and turned, adjusting my pillow to this and that position to be comfortable. Near midnight, I finally managed to fall asleep.

I found myself in a strange hospital, sitting inside an ethereal white room. My face was heavily bandaged around the nose area. A surgeon entered, accompanied by three nurses. They were all Filipino, from their brown skins to their black hair to their wide, indigenous noses. In typical Filipino fashion, they all nodded upwards to greet me. Then the nurses all pointed at my nose bandage with their lips, a sign for the doctor to start removing my bandage. Without a word, he did, grinning at me for no apparent reason. After the bandages had been removed, one of the nurses handed me a mirror. I looked at my reflection. My nose was narrow and high but it was also so huge it occupied half of my face! I looked up at the doctor with an inquisitive frown. The doctor, the nurses, and somehow an audience of Filipinos that had magically appeared, were all looking down at me. They were all pointing with their lips and laughing at my gigantic Caucasian nose. I awakened with a start. *"Dios ko!"* I uttered to myself, touching my nose.

I got up, went to the bathroom, and turned on the light. I squinted at the sudden brightness. I found myself staring at my reflection in the mirror. I looked at my image for a long time. I saw the girl that, even with a pug nose, was having the time of her life. I saw the daughter my mother was proud of, wide nose and all. I saw the sister Maria loved so unconditionally, regardless of our different fathers and different faces. And I saw the woman Ramoncito fell in love with not so long ago, one starry night in Liberty Park. I burst into tears.

$\mathcal{O}$

A bleary eyed, pale-looking Stefan found me eating a bowl of heated *Arroz Caldo* in the kitchen. He noticed my moist eyes as I offered him a fresh bowl of the warm breakfast treat.

"What izzit, cousin?" he asked, though his eyes told me he already knew the answer. We began to eat in silence. After a while, Stefan stopped eating and brought his half-empty bowl to the sink.

"It's your nose, it's your life," he said as he poured the uneaten *Arroz Caldo* down the drain.

I smiled at him.

ARROZ CALDO

Ingredients:
   1 chicken, cut up into small pieces
   3 tbsp cooking oil

1 tbsp minced garlic
1 tbsp minced red onion
1 cup rice
1 can low-fat chicken stock
1 tsp grated ginger
pepper and soy sauce to taste
1 tbsp minced green onion
2 tbsp *patis* (fish sauce)
1 lemon, quartered

Clean and cut chicken. Heat oil in sauce pan. Saute chicken, garlic and onion. Add rice and stock to chicken. If needed, add water to cover rice. Season with ginger, pepper and soy sauce. Cook over medium heat 30 minutes or until rice is smooth and thick and chicken is tender.

To serve, place in a serving bowl; garnish with green onion, *patis* and fresh squeezed lemon juice.

Chapter Nineteen

PANCIT MALABON

The Filipino "yes" is a conundrum to most Westerners. A "yes" can mean "yes" but it can also mean "maybe," "I don't know," "if you say so," "if it will please you," or "I hope I've said it half-hearted enough for you to understand that I really mean no." In a Filipino's desire to please, he cannot bring himself to say "no" in a very frank Westernized manner.

An average Filipino will say "yes" when he does not know the answer, he wants to impress someone, he is annoyed, he wants to end a conversation, he only half-understands the instruction or what is being said, he is not sure of himself, or he thinks he knows better than the one speaking to him.

Instead of giving a flat refusal of "no," a Filipino will agree weakly with a "maybe," "perhaps," "not really," or "I'll try." To interpret the meaning of "I'll try" or similar vague responses, a little persuasion is required to change the vague answer to a reluctant "yes" or an apologetic "no."

Auntie Soledad paced the kitchen while nervously wringing an embroidered handkerchief in her hands. Stefan and I were uneasy as we watched her while sipping our breakfast coffee. I had never seen Auntie Soledad this agitated. Well, maybe once or twice.

"*Dios ko, napasubo yata ako!*" Auntie Soledad exclaimed. *Napasubo*, a statement that means a point of no return, or something that someone has publicly committed to and can no longer back out of it.

"Auntie Soledad, calm down. Why don't you sit down and tell us what's bothering you? What do you mean *napasubo* kayo?" Stefan said, offering her a chair.

Auntie Soledad sat. I motioned to pour her a glass of orange juice.

"No, no, just water, *iha*. Too acidic for my stomach."

"Okay tell us, Auntie Soledad," I said after giving her a glass of cold water, which she drank, bottoms up.

She let out a sigh. She smiled, which turned into a girlish giggle. Stefan and I looked at each other.

"Peter pro…proposed to me last night and I said—yes." She covered her face with the handkerchief.

"Oh Auntie, that's great!" I cried, rushing to her side to give her a hug.

"No, no, I think I made a mistake," she said but she couldn't stop smiling.

"No you didn't," Stefan countered. "Peter is a good guy. You two will be so happy together."

Auntie Soledad smiled at Stefan. I was touched. That's the first genuine smile that Stefan had gotten from her, I think!

"So you said yes, huh?" I teased. *But did she really mean "maybe" or "I'll think about it?"*

er

Auntie Soledad and Peter had set a date for their civil wedding after she'd called my mother and gotten her blessing (after much grumbling). Being way beyond a debutante, Auntie Soledad really didn't need Mother's approval (nor mine) but, in this case, she must have thought the symbolism of kin group acceptance could assuage worries of a disastrous union.

A sense of *Hiya* decided that Mother need not come back for the wedding and that the reception itself would be simple with just a few invited guests.

Hiya is shame: an emotional realization of having failed to live up to the standards of society. A clueless employee will not ask his supervisor for directions on how to do his job because of *Hiya*. A party host will spend more than he can afford because of *Hiya*. A woman who doesn't have a new dress to wear to a party will not attend because of *Hiya*. And Auntie Soledad wanted to keep her wedding party guests to a minimum because of *Hiya*. She thought she and Peter were both too old to celebrate their civil marriage with a lavish party.

So after the civil ceremony at the judge's office in the Jersey City City Hall, a few of us trekked back to Auntie Soledad's apartment for a wedding lunch which Stefan and I prepared. I was surprised to realize that none of Peter's relatives were invited. Is this the Western version of the sense of *Hiya*?

Stefan had been working as a part-time copywriter / art director for a boutique advertising agency in Manhattan. His latest work reminded me of that time when he and I spent a rainy afternoon gossiping. It was a poster for Listerine, a brand of mouthwash. The poster was very simply executed but, I think, very effective. The headline, which Stefan himself wrote said, "Psssst, it's healthy to gossip…with Listerine." No other text, no additional tagline, just the product shot at the end of the headline. Stefan thought his poster deserved a CLIO, the advertising industry's version of an OSCAR award.

"Pssst," I whispered to Stefan in the kitchen while we prepared the food for the wedding party. "Don't tell Auntie Soledad and Peter, but I took the liberty of announcing their wedding in the society page section of the *Jersey Daily*."

"You did what?" Stefan exclaimed. "*Naku Ligaya, lagot ka.*" You're so dead. "Did you not remember that Auntie Soledad and Peter don't want a lot of fuss over their wedding?"

"Hmmmph! *Pakitang tao lang iyon.*" Showing to others for the benefit of social approval. "I'm sure they're more proud of this union than they care to admit. You'll see. When that issue comes out on Monday, I'll show it to them and they'll thank me for doing it," I said with conviction.

"*Aray!*" Ouch. Stefan accidentally cut his finger while slicing the lime for the *Pancit Malabon*, our Philippine spaghetti. Some of the blood from the cut finger squirted on the noodles.

"Ewwww!" I said. I theatrically crinkled my face with disgust.

Stefan immediately took the whole plate of *Pancit Malabon* and dumped its contents into the garbage can.

"Esteban!?" I yelled, calling him by his Filipino name. I was incredulous at his overreaction. "You could have just scooped out the portion that is contaminated and kept the rest. So wasteful!"

"Don't worry, I'll make a new batch, okay?" he said, face crinkling with irritation. He was shaking and his face had turned white.

"Stefan, are you okay?" I asked, alarmed. "Look, why don't you take a break? You've been helping me here since last—"

"I said I'm okay. Okay?"

I nodded, biting my lip.

"Ligaya, I'm sorry. Just a bit warm here and—"

"Stefan, it's alright. We're all a bit excited over this wedding, you know?"

He nodded and smiled at me while washing his wound in the sink.

"So you think I made a mistake publishing their wedding in the paper?"

He shook his head. "I'm sure they'll be proud and happy with it, but I think you shouldn't tell them about it until they get back from their honeymoon in Atlantic City."

"Good idea, Stefan. Good idea," I said, lifting a tray of food to serve the wedding guests.

er

It was a cold Monday morning. Auntie Soledad and Peter were still honeymooning in Atlantic City, but I had work to do and so did Stefan who was still in his bedroom sleeping in.

"Hey cousin, time to get up. You'll be late!" I yelled, knocking on his door while perusing the society page of the *Jersey Daily*. I smiled at the small wedding announcement of Peter and Auntie Soledad's.

Stefan did not respond. I knocked again. "Stefan, hello?" I heard a groan. *What is Stefan up to?* I was not about to find out. I said, "Alright, cousin, if you wanna sleep in late, it's up to you, but don't you have work to do this morning?"

"Ligaya!" came a raspy voice from the room.

"Stefan?" I asked, already turning the doorknob. "Are you okay?"

Stefan was shivering in his bed.

"Stefan, *naku, my lagnat ka!*" Stefan, you're feverish! I said this after feeling his forehead. "Should I call a doctor?"

"No, no! It's just the flu, I think. I'll be alright, but can you do me a favor?"

"Yes?" I inquired.

"Please call my office and tell them that I'm sick and can't make it to work today. Please?"

"Okay, but maybe I should stay with you today? Look, I'm just going to bring Stella some of the *Pancit Malabon*. You know Stella? I used to work with her at the *Jersey Daily*."

Stefan nodded.

"I also wanna thank her for helping me with the publication of the wedding announcement. Look, it's here!" I said, showing him the society page.

Stefan managed a smile as he glanced at the announcement.

"Okay listen, I won't be long. Maybe an hour or two, then I'll have to make a stopover at the Oriental store to pick up some ingredients for that catering job this weekend. But I'll be back early afternoon. Promise," I said, feeling Stefan's forehead again. He was burning up!

I gave him a dose of Nyquil and rubbed his forehead and throat with Tiger Balm before I left for the *Jersey Daily.*

ℰ

"Ligaya, *kumusta*! You're looking good!" Stella warmly greeted me as if we hadn't seen each other for ages when barely a week ago, I was there to place the wedding announcement ad. I greeted her in exactly the same manner.

"*Uy ano ito?*" What is this? She asked when I handed her the Tupperware container filled to the rim with *Pancit Malabon*.

She opened the container. "*Uy Pancit Malabon*? Is this Por us?"

I nodded. "Lunch for you and the girls at classified."

"Thank you, Ligaya. You're so thoughtPul," she said, while sampling a piece of shrimp from the *Pancit*.

"*Naku, pasensiya na nga eh. Leftover lang ng kasal*" Sorry, it's just leftover from the wedding.

"Hey, talking about your Auntie's wedding, someone was just here to inquire about that."

I frowned. "Really, who was it?"

"Some woman. She was wondering iP she could get the address oP your Auntie. I told her I have no idea. Might be an old jilted girlPriend, you know?"

"Did she introduce herself to you?" I asked.

Stella shook her head. I thought to myself, "Her hair needs to be retouched, the black roots are showing." I was reminded of a black and orange Halloween motif.

"So do you wanna say hello to *da* girls? C'mon, they'll be happy to see you!" Stella said, replacing the cover on the Tupperware.

I shook my head. "Some other time maybe. I have to go to the Oriental store to pick up some ingredients and then go home. Stefan's sick!"

"*Ang iyong pinsan? Kawawa naman.*" Your poor cousin. "What is he sick oP?"

"Flu. I gave him Nyquil before I left."

"Oh yeah, two employees here called in sick with Plu this morning. Must be this stupid winter weather."

"Well, okay, I'll be going."

"*Salamat ulit, Ligaya ha? Pasyal ka uli,*" she said, waving her manicured hand. Thanks again, Ligaya. Come see us again sometimes.

I nodded and left, still thinking about that woman who was asking about Auntie Soledad and Peter's wedding. *Jilted ex-girlfriend?*

er

My heart jumped when I saw Aling Salvacion waiting by my mother's apartment door. I tightly clutched the two grocery bags I carried as I rushed to meet her.

"*Aling Salvacion, bakit po?*" What is the matter, Aling Salvacion? I asked. She had been crying.

"Ligaya, thank God you're here. I've been knocking on your door. No answer."

"Really? Stefan is in there. He called in sick with the flu," I said, rattling the house keys as I chose the right one.

"Why are you here, Aling Salvacion? What's the matter?" I asked as I pushed the door open.

"Stefan?!" I called out, rushing towards his room. Aling Salvacion touched me on the elbow.

"Ligaya, someone was at your Auntie Soledad's house this morning," she said, stammering.

"Who? Why? Oh God, something happened to them!" My hand flew to my mouth.

Aling Salvacion shook her head. "She introduced herself as Peter's wife!"

"What!? That's impossible! How—?" I stammered. I realized we had been walking towards Stefan's room. I was in front of his bedroom door. Aling Salvacion was right behind me, crying again.

I opened Stefan's door. "Stefan?"

He was sprawled on the floor, white as the sheet he clutched, looking lifeless.

One of us screamed. I wasn't sure if it was me or Aling Salvacion.

PANCIT MALABON
(Philippine Spaghetti)

Ingredients:

8 oz. rice noodles (substitutes: regular spaghetti or angel hair pasta)

1 tbsp annato seeds (achuete) - annatto seeds are used as natural food coloring to lend an orange tint to the dish. They are sold in packets or bottles at Asian and Latin American food markets.

1-1/2 tsp vegetable oil

3 cloves garlic, chopped and fried

1 cup shrimp juice

Soy sauce, salt and pepper to taste

2-1/2 tbsp cornstarch, mixed with 1/4 cup water

3/4 cup finely crushed chicharon (fried or sun-dried pork rinds)

1/2 lb. shrimp, shelled and fried

2 tbsp green onion, finely chopped

2 slices of hardboiled egg

2 tbsp fish sauce (patis)

Soak noodles in boiling water for 20 minutes or until softened. Drain well and set aside.

Soak and simmer the annato seeds over low heat in a pan with oil and garlic. Strain the oil free of seeds and burnt garlic.

Add the oil to the shrimp juice in a saucepan and season with soy sauce, salt and black pepper.

Stir in the cornstarch. Simmer until thick, stirring constantly. Put the noodles on a plate. Pour sauce over it, then sprinkle crushed pork rinds, shrimp, fried garlic and green onions. If desired, add patis.

Optionally, arrange sliced eggs on top and lemon wedges on the side of the presentation platter. Toss the *pancit* mixture and sprinkle with lemon juice to taste. Garnish with spring onions.

Serve hot.

Chapter Twenty

SANS RIVAL

When Peter and Auntie Soledad returned from their Atlantic City honeymoon, Peter was picked up by the New Jersey police for questioning, but within an hour, they let him go. The statute of limitations for bigamy was five years from the act of marriage, not from the discovery of the act. Since Peter married this woman more than five years ago, he had skirted the deadline. Peter's first wife had immediately filed an appeal.

Weird sex laws abound in America, I found out, after doing research on bigamy. For example, in a Minnesota city, no man is allowed to make love to his wife with the smell of garlic or sardines on his breath. If his wife so requests, law mandates he must brush his teeth. In a city in New Mexico, during lunch breaks, couples are not allowed to engage in a sexual act while parked in their vehicles, unless their car has curtains. In a town in Montana, a law bans all sexual activities in the front yard of a home after sundown if the sexual partners are naked. Apparently, if you wear gloves or socks, you're safe from the law! And in a Wisconsin city, no man shall shoot off a gun while his female partner is having a sexual orgasm.

Knowingly marrying a bigamist is considered a misdemeanor. When Auntie Soledad found out about this from her lawyer, she went ballistic, cursing Peter with the mouth of a dumpster. *Putang Ina Mo, Peter!* Your mother is a whore, Peter! *Walang bayag, walang hiya ka Peter!* No balls, no shame, Peter! A deluge of verbiage that even Noah's Ark wouldn't survive. My Auntie could be very colorful that way.

She told Peter she never wanted to see him again. Her sense of *Hiya* was tremendous!

To be ridiculed in public was the ultimate sense of *Hiya*. Though this was more imagined than real, Auntie Soledad thought that she had lost group support from her kin here. She felt that she had acted improperly, in a manner that resulted in the withdrawal of the community's acceptance. In her own chaotic world, she considered herself a social outcast, a very unhappy and angry person. She

143

refused to see any of us, especially me. She found out about the announcement I placed in the *Jersey Daily* and how it had led to this other woman finding out about Peter's second marriage.

Last time I checked, Peter's van was not in his garage. He probably left town. There was much talk in the neighborhood about his bigamy. I missed two Sunday masses to avoid questions about it. Catholics consider missing Sunday mass a mortal sin. I think maybe I damned myself two times over.

Or maybe not.

Most Filipinos have a penchant for what is known as Split-Level Christianity. We hold half-Catholic, half-pagan beliefs. The rational belief level of the indigenous convert was Christianized but the sub-rational level of consciousness remains decidedly pagan.

Many Filipinos are very religious but at the same time very superstitious. We have superstitious beliefs related to death, misfortune, illness and war such as: if a cock crows in the afternoon, it means somebody will die; if one cuts his fingernails at night, a member of his family will die; if a group of three have their picture taken, the one in the middle will incur misfortune; one should not decorate a dress with pearls because it means she will shed tears; sleeping with wet hair causes blindness; and the appearance of a comet foretells war, pestilence and calamity.

Some Filipinos believe in God but also revere *anitos*, minor deities who are esteemed as intermediaries to God. They believe in the gifts of quack doctors and faith healers to cure ailments that physicians cannot. They cower from the powers of witches to inflict illness on any individual who incurs their displeasure.

Some Filipinos believe in lucky and unlucky numbers. Number 13 is the worst bad luck number. The best good luck numbers are your birth date and the birth dates of loved ones. For this reason, Filipinos will bet on games of chance like the lottery, using the birth dates of their family members.

There are also unlucky dates. The second week of September is very unlucky because it is the week when Judas Iscariot was born.

I called on my split-level Christian beliefs in times like these. I missed mass to avoid the bad luck of encountering gossipy neighbors. I lighted candles in front of Mother's statues of saints to summon good luck, like the fat chance of Auntie Soledad returning my numerous calls.

I called Auntie several times but she never picked up her phone. I left several messages of apologies on her answering machine along with updates on Stefan. She didn't return any of my messages. I asked the saints to intervene.

I called my mother, who was still in the Philippines. She was dismayed at hearing about both Aunt Soledad and Stefan. She felt helpless, as we were divided by thousand of miles of sea. She offered that with Auntie Soledad, it was just a case of *Amor Propio*. "It will right itself, you'll see," she said with confidence. She was more concerned about Stefan's condition. She was worried on several levels: about his health, about me getting contaminated, about what our relatives would think.

I was incredulous. I told her to start reading up on the disease. She called me *Impertenente*, insolent. I called her *Ignorante*, uninformed. In our language, we have a lot of Spanish words that are almost similar in meaning to their English counterparts. We mostly use them to insult each other.

ᛒ

Yes, Stefan had AIDS.

He found out he was HIV positive two years before while still in San Francisco. He managed to hide it from practically everyone: his officemates, his friends, even his lover. And when he felt he couldn't hide it anymore, he left. He walked out on everyone, including his boyfriend of three years, who was puzzled and angry. My offer of bed and board in New Jersey was perfect for his escape.

AIDS. It was a relatively new thing for me when I left the Philippines. It was hardly news then, or perhaps news that was shoved under the rug, hidden out of *Hiya*. Reported cases represented only a fraction of the actual figures of Filipinos with AIDS. The stigma surrounding AIDS made it extremely difficult to talk openly about the disease. People with AIDS learned to survive by living a double life, unable to disclose their secret to most people for fear of rejection, discrimination, and abandonment.

I think AIDS is worse than cancer because cancer patients have family and friends who support them, while AIDS sufferers can be ostracized by those closest to them.

"It is a gay disease," I read in an article once, "because only gays are affected by it." Since the printing of that article, there have been cases of AIDS among heterosexuals, among women, among the young and the old. Yet the stigma has remained. In between visits to Stefan in the hospital, I managed to attend a few HIV awareness seminars. In one of them, I was horrified to see the attendees sitting at the farthest end of the room because two of the speakers had AIDS.

Whether we care to admit it or not, the stigma attached to AIDS is so deep it can kill the spirit of someone with AIDS faster than the virus itself. In the Philippines, there are a growing number of people who are working hard to educate the public about AIDS and HIV. One AIDS activist came under the harsh attack of the Catholic Church for his support of the use of condoms. He was publicly denounced as the agent of Satan at a Catholic rally. A high-ranking Catholic leader declared he should be thrown into the sea with a millstone around his neck.

Who can blame Stefan for hiding this horrible disease from his friends and from his lover?

Stefan was in the intensive care unit of the Jersey City Hospital. When Aling Salvacion and I found him unconscious in his bedroom, Stefan was suffering from pneumocystis pneumonia. He developed this opportunistic infection because of his weakened immune system.

After over a week in the hospital, he was assigned a new nurse. The first one was so rude that Stefan, even in his delirious state, had hit her with a folded magazine. She filed a complaint with the Health Department. I thought there was a need for sensitivity training for nurses and other hospital staff who attended to patients with AIDS.

"Cousin Ligaya," Stefan said weakly. His lips were dry and cracked. I offered him the glass of water with a bent straw. He sipped, clumsily. Water dribbled down his chin. I wiped it with a tissue.

"*Salamat,*" Thank you, he said hoarsely.

"How are you?" I asked.

Stefan snorted. "*Heto, mukhang kuago.*" Right here, looking like an awful owl.

I inhaled deeply. I had to admit, without his hazel contact lens, his eye make-up, his earrings and nose ring, and the expensive gel on his dyed and frosted hair, Stefan looked awful.

"No, you do not. You still look fabulous, cousin." I lied. I swallowed hard. *I must not cry in front of him*, I ordered myself.

"Hey, look what I brought you!" I said, showing him a box wrapped in cellophane.

He squinted at the contents of the box. *Was he wearing prescription colored contacts?*

"*Sans Rival*!" I exclaimed. He grinned, then reached for them.

"I don't know if you're allowed to eat them. Maybe we should ask your doctor?" I said, but I was already helping him open one.

"Are you kidding me? *Sans Rival* is like my ultimate favorite decadent dessert," he said, grabbing the half-opened *Sans Rival*. He took a bite.

"Mmmm, this is like a...foot massage!" he said dreamily.

"What? Oh, I see—" I stopped myself. I took a piece of the *Sans Rival* and started to eat too. How did one measure decadence? It was eating this heavenly *Sans Rival* knowing you should feel guilty because it's laden with fat and calories and other bad-but-yummy stuff but doing it anyway, and not feeling a tinge of guilt.

"Like sleeping till 2 in the afternoon," I said, telling my own decadent analogy of eating *Sans Rival*.

"A leisurely bath while sipping champagne!" he said.

"A movie marathon of classic love films!" I added, totally getting into it.

"Like a kiss or...or good sex!" he exclaimed, reaching out for another piece of heaven. I giggled. He did too, but his giggles quickly changed to coughing fits. I was alarmed.

"Stefan?" I asked, as he continued to cough. "Nurse!" I screamed. "Nurse!" Stefan crumpled to one side of the bed, clutching his chest as he coughed forcefully.

A nurse rushed in just as Stefan vomited mucus, blood, and *Sans Rival* onto the cold, linoleum floor.

SANS RIVAL
(Meringue-crusted, cashew nut cake)

Ingredients:

Filling
    6 egg yolks
    1/2 cup light corn syrup
    1/4 cup sugar
    2 tbsp water
    1/2 lb softened butter

Meringue
    10 egg whites
    1 cup sugar
    2 cups finely chopped, roasted cashew nuts

Garnishing:
    1/2 cup coarsely chopped cashew nuts

Beat egg yolks until well mixed. Heat corn syrup, sugar and water over low heat. Stir to dissolve sugar. Slow boil for at least two minutes.

Add hot syrup in a thin stream to egg yolks, beating continuously. Chill to cool.

Beat cooled yolk mixture into the softened butter. Set aside.

Preheat oven to 350 degrees F. Line 8x12" cookie sheet with butter and flour. Set aside.

Beat egg whites until soft peaks are formed when beater is raised. Blend in sugar slowly, beating well. Beat until stiff. Fold chopped cashew nuts into the mixture.

Spread evenly on prepared cookie sheets, about 1/4" think. Bake for about 30 minutes or until golden brown. Cut each meringue in two equal parts as it comes out of the oven. Loosen bottom with spatula and place baked meringue on waxed, paper-lined, flat surface.

Assembling Procedure

Spread 1/6 of cooked meringue along the bottom. Spread 1/6 of icing mixture (cold not warm) on top. Sprinkle with 1/6 of cashew nuts. Repeat process to make 6 layers. Place in the refrigerator or freezer to harden.

Chapter Twenty-One

PANCIT MOLO

After that incident, Stefan's nurse made me promise not to bring food of any kind to him. I was crushed but I promised I wouldn't. She also told me she and the other nurses in the hospital loved the rest of the *Sans Rival* and hinted she wouldn't mind enjoying some more of that "unrivaled" dessert. But a promise is a promise.

Most cases of pneumocystis pneumonia (or PCP) in America are in children and adults who have problems that affect the immune system. This disease is marked by fever and rapid or difficult breathing. Left unchecked, it is usually fatal among people with AIDS; however, it is now preventable and treatable if caught soon enough.

Stefan was released from the hospital after three weeks of taking strong antibiotics with strange names such as bactrim, pentamidine, and atovaquone. The names of these drugs roll off my tongue easily now that someone I loved had been threatened with PCP.

The doctor placed Stefan on an antiviral therapy to prevent recurrence of the disease. I was grateful that his part-time employment at the advertising agency provided him with full major medical insurance. In the Philippines, this was unheard of. I felt a great degree of *utang na loob* towards Stefan's employers.

Literally a "debt of the inner self," *utang na loob* is what the phrase "I owe you one" to a Westerner means. It is the sense of gratitude a Filipino feels when he or a loved one becomes the beneficiary of a favor or significant assistance. Although the benefactor is not obliged to demand reciprocity, the beneficiary nevertheless feels a strong need to repay the kindness. Taken too far, this trait can compel a recipient to feel eternally indebted to the benefactor. For example, I felt I owed Stefan's employers a lifetime supply of *Sans Rival*.

We were both surprised to find Auntie Soledad waiting for us by the door of Mother's apartment.

"Auntie Soledad!" I exclaimed as I assisted Stefan out of the car.

"Hello, Ligaya. Stefan. *Naku, ang payat mo iho*." She greeted both of us and added: Stefan, you've lost a lot of weight.

"Auntie Soledad, *kumusta po*," Stefan greeted her, using the word *po*, a politeness marker used to address elders with respect.

Auntie Soledad blinked when she heard this. It was seldom used nowadays. In their trying so hard to be Westernized, Filipino-Americans have conveniently forgotten this very Filipino polite way of treating elders.

Stefan reached out for Auntie Soledad's hand. She stiffened for a second, then slowly raised it and offered it to him. Stefan took it and placed it on his forehead, the ultimate show of respect to an elder. Auntie Soledad broke into tears. *"Iho, iho..."* Son, son. It was all she could say as she sobbed uncontrollably. The tightness in the air that had seemed to strangle all of us the past few weeks was gone. I sniffed deeply. There was a lightness in my chest now.

e7

Auntie Soledad told us Peter had called from his brother's place in upstate New York. They had quite a civilized talk, she said, making quotation marks in the air as she said civilized. Although the State couldn't hold Peter for any crime because of the statute of limitations clause, there were still complications. The first wife had filed an appeal in the New Jersey court asking to nullify Peter's second marriage and Peter had filed for divorce from his first wife. "Peter, the bigamist," she told us, scolding Peter. But she couldn't hide the hopeful smile.

While Stefan and I made some calls, Auntie Soledad busied herself in the kitchen preparing our meal for tonight: *Pancit Molo,* a Filipino adaptation of Chinese wonton soup. It is a specialty of the town of Molo in Iloilo, a southern province in the Philippines with rich Hispanic and Chinese history. In the past, *Pancit Molo* actually contributed to the building of a church in the town of Molo. The egg whites, which were discarded in making *Pancit Molo* wrappers because the recipe requires only the yolks, were used in forming the concrete walls of the church.

It was storming outside. Every few seconds, lightning illuminated the corridor followed by a tumultuous thunderclap that shook the rafters of Mother's old apartment. A short while ago, Stefan had excused himself to call his lover in San Francisco. He used the extension phone in his room so I was not privy to the emotional *tsunami* that occurred during the conversation, but judging from his red puffy eyes, it must have been a tidal wave of gigantic proportions.

"Stefan, are you okay?" I asked, concerned about his emotional and physical health. "Is it time to take your anti-virals?"

He shook his head. "In two hours. After dinner, I guess."

I did not pursue what I really wanted to know. I figured when he was ready to talk about it, he would.

Stefan rubbed his eyes, blinked at the brightness of the three-tiered *Capiz shell* chandelier in Mother's living room. It had a dimmer switch so I diffused it to a soft haze.

"Wow, look at that. The unique marriage of American technology with Philippine ingenuity," he joked, though there's a lot of truth to it. The floor of the Pacific Ocean near the Philippine islands is seeded with millions of beautiful, iridescent, naturally transparent *Capiz* shells. The use of *Capiz* as decorative accents dates back to the Spanish era when the Hispanic churches were established. The church builders of the time were fascinated by the possibility of using *Capiz* seashells that had washed up on the shore following a particularly violent storm. They cut them into shape and formed them into magnificent window shutters. The splendid combination of natural wood and *Capiz* in church windows beautifully replicated the stained glass windows of the European churches. Today, the traditional *Capiz* seashells are used extensively for making such arts and craft items as sun catchers, candleholders, food trays, wind chimes, and of course, the world-famous *Capiz* chandeliers. I heard Liberace had two of these chandeliers installed in his Las Vegas mansion.

"Those are called *Capiz* shells, right?" Stefan asked, pointing at the exquisite glimmering seashells.

"*Oo, iho.*" Yes son. "Those are called *Capiz*, from the Visayan province of *Capiz*," Auntie Soledad answered as she entered the living room carrying a tray topped with three huge steaming bowls of *Pancit Molo*.

"Auntie, are we eating here?" I asked, rising to help her with the tray.

"*Bakit hindi?*" Why not? Auntie Soledad answered. "There's a slight draft coming from the dining room window, not good for Stefan." Stefan and I exchanged a smile.

I cleared the coffee table to make room for the tray.

"And the lighting here is just perfect for this dish," Stefan added, gesturing expansively at the dramatically lit room.

"I know, look at our complexions!" I chimed in. The diffused light from the shiny *Capiz* shells made our complexions radiant, ethereal, especially pale-looking Stefan's. I swallowed hard, instantly regretting what I had just said. Auntie Soledad gave me the eye.

"*Loca-loca,*" Stefan said to me, feigning being put out. It was his way of diffusing the tension that was threatening to build. *Loca-Loca,* crazy girl.

"Auntie Soledad, this is super delicious!" Stefan had switched from being turned off by my comment to being turned on by Auntie Soledad's *Pancit Molo*.

"Hey, isn't *Capiz* province also known for its *Aswangs?*" Stefan asked. I almost choked on my *Molo*.

Aswangs are some of the known creatures of the lower Philippine mythology. *Aswang* is a collective term for witches, werewolves, demons, ghouls and vampires.

"Well, it is, but that's completely ridiculous," Auntie Soledad reluctantly answered. She continued to eat her *Molo* as we stared at her. She looked up.

"What? What!?" she asked, *Molo* dribbling down her chain. She wiped it off with her hand.

"Auntie, tell us all about the *Aswangs* of *Capiz?*" Stefan pleaded. "Pretty please?" he added, giving Auntie a pleading puppy-dog look.

Auntie shook her head and grinned. "Oh, I suppose, but I'm warning you kids, this story is not for the faint of heart."

"Please, Auntie Soledad?" Stefan and I chorused. Nothing like a scary story on a night like this in an eerily lit room.

Auntie put down her bowl of *Pancit Molo*. "I call this story the Two Sisters of *Capiz*," she began in her perfect *Tagalog*.

Not so long ago, a spinster lived on the island of Capiz. *One afternoon, she was visited by her rich younger sister who used to live in* Capiz *as well, but now lived and worked in the cosmopolitan city of Manila. The whole town was elated! The small island village hardly saw outsiders anymore. A fiesta in her honor was planned for the next night, which was the first full moon of autumn.*

Banners and buntings and multi-colored Christmas bulbs were hung in the spinster's courtyard to give the banquet area an exceptionally festive atmosphere.

The sister brought with her many gifts from the big city. Clothes, costume jewelry and make-up for the sister and the other ladies of the town, transistor radios and imported cigarettes and wines for the men, toys and games for the children. She also brought with her some electronic appliances she no longer needed: a second-hand stereo set, a second-hand refrigerator and a used washer and dryer. Such conveniences were warmly appreciated by the spinster and the whole town who, no doubt, would make good use of the appliances as well.

"So good of you to come visit, my dear sister," the spinster said while trying on a pair of jade earrings before a beautiful antique mirror. Side by side, the images of the two sisters were identical— square face, deep-set eyes, aquiline nose, heart-shaped lips and long, deep black shiny hair. The spinster looked as young as her sister!

"You wouldn't come visit despite my many invitations, so here I am. My, those earrings look really good on you," the sister said, admiring the presents she had brought her spinster sister.

"Yes, they're beautiful, thank you. I shall always wear them," the spinster said as she moved closer to the mirror to examine the earrings.

"Well, why don't we get some sleep, my sister? Then we can be well-rested for tomorrow's fiesta."

That night they slept in the same huge bed together, a lambing, *childish request, from the sister who longed for a bonding moment with her spinster kin.*

At midnight, the sister felt the bed move. She opened her eyes and saw the spinster's shadow as she silently crept out of the room. The spinster momentarily looked back, but the younger sister quickly shut her eyes feigning sleep. The sister could hear the bamboo floor creak under the spinster's footsteps as she walked out the door. "Where is she going?" the sister thought to herself. Her curiosity got the better of her. Once the footsteps were out of earshot, the sister got up to follow.

What she eventually saw made her skin crawl and her blood curdle. The spinster was standing in the dark kitchen, naked. She was rubbing something greasy around her waist. In the pale moonlight, the sister was horrified to see that the spinster's facial features were transforming. Her teeth were growing into fangs, her nails into sharp talons, her eyes bulging and bloodshot. There was a crunching sound, like that of bones being broken, as two protrusions shot through the skin covering her vertebrae and suddenly, magically sprouted into bat-like leathery wings. Then, paralyzed with horror, the sister witnessed the final transformation: the lower portion of the spinster's body violently detached itself from the upper torso. Exposed intestines dangled as the horrible split completed.

The Aswang spinster scooped up her lower body and hid it inside the broom closet. With a loud flapping sound, she took flight and disappeared into the night.

A long time passed before the younger sister felt brave enough to leave her hiding place. "Dios ko, dios ko!" My God! My God! she cried. Her whole body was trembling. As a child, their deceased mother had regaled them with stories of Aswangs and other lower mythological creatures but to her, they were silly figments of her mother's rich imagination. Until now. She gave a nervous laugh. Soon, she was laughing and crying. "I went to Manila to get away from all this rural, backward thinking, these archaic beliefs, and now, and now—"

She stopped. She heard the familiar flapping sound again. Without looking for its source, she ran to the bedroom, jumped back into the bed, and threw the blankets over her head.

Soon after, she heard the bedroom door creak open. In a couple of seconds, the spinster was lying next to her in bed, sound asleep. The sister's fearful eyes remained open the rest of the night as her paralyzed body twitched within. Before long, the rooster crowed outside to announce the beginning of a new day.

The sister feigned more sleepiness as the spinster got up to prepare for the feast.

"*Sleep as long as you want. You are our guest,*" *she said before walking out the door.*

The sister was grateful for the time alone. She tried to remember the endings of their mother's tales. How were the Aswangs *destroyed? She remembered that salt sprinkled over the lower torso would prevent the* Aswangs *from returning to their human shapes. When hit by sunlight, the* Aswang *would crumble to dust if still in that ghoulish form. She also remembered laughing at this silly ending. Regular table salt? A vampire killer? She was not laughing now.*

She awakened to festive music. "Oh, God! I must have fallen asleep! The fiesta!" She immediately got up to prepare herself for the feast in her honor. She thought she must have dreamt it all. A nightmare. She clung to that comforting thought as she dressed.

The spinster's courtyard shimmered in the twinkling Christmas lights and other festive decorations. A huge ornate wooden table stood proudly in the middle. A huge Capiz *shell chandelier glittered in one corner. Gracing the table were plates and trays of* Lechon, Adobo, Pancit Molo, Bibingka, Kutsinta, *mangoes, and papaya. People helped themselves to* Lumpia *and* Empanadas. *Wine flowed freely. The sister was greeted, hugged and kissed by everyone. She tasted many exotic, wondrous foods that she couldn't get in Manila. The pork* Lechon *was wonderful. The* Chicken Relleno, *divine. The onion and liver steak, to die for. She was swooning and shaking with happiness. It was a great party and it felt so good to be back, she told herself, grinning. She looked around. Her eyesight seemed clearer than before. Her sense of smell sharper. She felt great!*

"*Oh sister, thank you for giving me this unforgettable feast!*" *she exclaimed to the spinster when she found her among the revelers. "Thank you! Thank—" She saw her reflection in the spinster's eyes. It was inverted! She remembered her mother's words, "To identify an* Aswang *in her human form, one must look at one's reflection in the suspected* Aswang's *eyes. If the reflection is inverted, then that person is one of them." One of them. Dios ko po! She jerked her head back and stumbled against some surprised revelers.*

"*Sister, are you okay?*" *the spinster asked with concerned eyes.*

"*Yes, yes! It must be the wine,*" *she answered hastily, averting her eyes.*

The spinster studied her and finally said, "Alright, no more wine for you, city girl. Perhaps you'd like to go up to the bedroom and rest?"

"But won't they miss me?" the sister asked, gesturing at the revelers in the courtyard. Everyone was having a good time.

The spinster shook her head. "I'll see you later?" she said as a question, kissing her goodnight on the cheek.

Some time past midnight, the sister awakened with a start. It was quiet. The party had ended long ago. She glanced at the spinster's side of the bed. She bolted upright. The spinster was gone!

The sister slowly got up and tiptoed into the kitchen. With a quick prayer, she opened the broom closet. She let out a snicker. There was no half-torso in the closet. She shook her head. What a nightmare, she told herself. She moved toward the bedroom, but stopped when she spotted the washer and dryer unit. They were unpacked and shoved into one corner of the laundry room next to the kitchen. Something caught her eye in the dark. She frowned as she approached the washer-dryer. The lid of the washer was raised slightly. Her eyes widened. Hairs on the back of her neck stood on end. She opened the washer. There, squeezed into the small space, was the spinster's lower torso. Staring up at her was the ragged cut area. There were bloody entrails showing, like a bad piece of steak. She vomited violently into the adjoining kitchen sink.

Long moments later, the sister was still staring into the darkness in the laundry room. Outside, the sky started to turn light, dawning a new morning. She rose, walked towards the washer-dryer unit. She lifted the lid and whimpered when she saw the lower torso again. She raised her hand. She was carrying a can of salt. Morton Iodized Salt, it said, beneath the familiar "girl with the umbrella" logo. With unsteady, trembling hands, she began shaking salt on top of the torso. Afterwards, she crouched in the semi-darkness and prepared herself for her spinster sister's return, while holding a long dagger in her hand.

A little while later, she heard a flapping sound approaching. She straightened up to see the spinster soar in, not noticing her. The spinster opened the lid of the washer-dryer unit and lowered her upper torso onto her lower half. She let loose a stunned scream when *she felt the salt. She turned around and spotted her sister crouched in the corner, holding a dagger pointed toward her.*

"My sister, my sister! What have you done?" the spinster asked in a voice that was a spooky imitation of her human one. The spinster looked outside to see the light slowly creeping over the horizon.

The Aswang *hovered over the sister. Beneath her horrible* Aswang *features was the face of her spinster sister pleading, begging for her own life. The sister was confused.*

"Please, sister, please. Don't you know you are one of us now? Please, before it is too late!" the Aswang *said in that a shrill voice.*

"What do you mean one of us now? What do you mean!?"

"Last night, you ate the liver of a human. You are one of us now!"

The sister's mind reeled back to something from her mother's Aswang *stories. "Someone can turn into* Aswang *from eating the liver of a human, probably sacrificed to some vile* anito, deity. *He may not even know that he has been fed the organ, such are the ways of these creatures. The liver will begin to affect the victim's mind. His eyesight will become clearer. His sense of smell sharper. Very soon, he will have a perverse fascination with butchery, blood and death. It is at this point that he has turned into an* Aswang *himself.*

"NO!!!" the sister screamed, remembering the onion and liver steak that she ate last night. "Nooo!!!"

Slowly, the sister got up, still holding the dagger. Without looking at it, she wiped the salt off the torso with her free hand. She then used a kitchen towel to finish wiping it clean.

The Aswang appeared grateful. She flew towards the washer and magically connected with her lower torso as the sister watched, still badly shaken.

The bat-like wings disappeared, the spinster's facial features softened, becoming human again. She was naked except for the pair of jade earrings she wore.

"Sister, I have to wash off, then we talk, okay?"

The sister nodded, then walked out of the room to give the spinster some privacy.

A few months later, the spinster's house was remodeled. It became the biggest, most expensive house in the island town. It was now a Spanish mansion. The two sisters continued living there and gave extravagant parties every time the moon was full. Also, every time there was a new visitor in town.

"End of story," Auntie Soledad finally said in a raspy, tired voice.

Stefan and I sat motionlessly, wondering if we would be able to sleep that night.

"Perhaps another helping of *Pancit Molo* will help," Auntie Soledad suggested, malevolent eyes twinkling under the shimmering *Capiz* light.

PANCIT MOLO
(Filipino Dumpling Soup)

Filling:

    1/2 lb. ground pork
    1/2 cup cooked and shredded chicken meat
    1 egg
    3 tbsp green onions, chopped
    1/2 lb. shrimp, peeled, de-veined and chopped
    3 tbsp garlic, minced
    1/2 cup onions, diced
    1/4 cup water chestnuts (jicama), diced
    1/2 cup sesame oil
    1 tsp salt
    1 tsp black pepper
    1 tbsp soy sauce

Wrapper: Two dozen wonton wrappers. Available in Oriental stores.

Broth:

    2 tbsp garlic, crushed
    1/2 cup onions, chopped
    3 tbsp vegetable oil
    12 cups chicken broth
    4 tbsp patis (fish sauce)
    1 tsp salt
    1 tsp black pepper
    1/3 cup green onions, finely chopped

Combine and mix well all the filling ingredients. Divide into 2 parts: one part will go into the broth, the other part will fill the wonton wrappers.

Place 1 tbsp of filling in the center of each wonton wrapper. Fold over one corner of the wrapper until it meets the opposite corner. Seal edges with water. Set aside until ready to add to the soup.

Saute garlic and onions in vegetable oil. Add the remaining mixture and cook for about 5 minutes. Add in the chicken broth and *patis*. Bring to a boil. Add the stuffed wontons. Boil for about 10 to 15 minutes, stirring occasionally. Add salt and pepper. Ladle into individual bowls and garnish with green onions. Serve hot.

Chapter Twenty-Two

CALDERETA

Auntie Soledad's *Aswang* story had nothing to do with the liver-based dish I was cooking today. It is called *Caldereta*. It is a dish of Spanish origin, but the name comes from a Tagalog word, *caldero,* which means cooking pot. I was preparing this dish because a Filipino family had asked me to cater their daughter's sixteenth birthday party and *Caldereta* is one of their favored dishes.

My Filipino food catering business had provided me with a decent income in America, though what I had wasn't exactly what you would call a full-blown catering business. I did my research on owning and running a catering business and I can honestly say it would cause too many headaches for me.

By definition, catering is the act of providing food and services for a fee. It involves so many things: the food, the table and chair set-up, napkins and eating utensils, complete clean-up and, of course, billing. Then there are the legalities involved. You need a business license. Sometimes you have to look into zoning laws. And because your business involves food, you have to make sure you carry out your work safely and hygienically.

The catering equipment alone can cost over $5,000. Warming cabinets, convection ovens, deep fryers, small appliances like mixers and rice cookers. These and a hundred and one more things you need to know, rent, buy or do to establish a full-scale catering business. As my mother put it, "Not my bowl of rice." But someone out there, someone with enough business savvy might want to pursue this lucrative business. That someone should just make sure he really loves to cook!

Stefan's birthday was coming up and I was thinking of treating him to one of the latest Broadway musicals that he absolutely adored. "Proceeds from this latest catering job will take care of that," I said while opening a can of liver spread for the *Caldereta* dish.

Against my wishes, Stefan went back to work after just a few days of recuperating at home. "I needed to earn some bread, Ate," he said, using a modern slang term for money. The first time I heard this in

America was from a homeless man. He said, "Hey, can you spare some bread?" I almost shared with him the loaf of *Pan Americano*, white bread, I had in my grocery bag. It's a very practical thing for new immigrants here to learn as much American slang, idioms, and colloquial expressions as possible. They come in handy and they're necessary to fully acculturate yourself to American thought processes. Most likely, you'll add many such expressions to your vocabulary subconsciously, but it doesn't hurt to pick up a book or two on slang. Nothing screams "outsider" more than a confused look in response to something said in the local vernacular.

I know why Stefan needed bread. He wanted to go back to California. A very sad thing happened as a result of Stefan not telling his lover he had AIDS: His lover also got infected. Stefan sobbed over this, but as they say in America, though perhaps a little insensitively in this context, there's no use crying over spilled milk. Stefan decided the best thing was for them to go through this crisis together. So in a few weeks, it was back to California for my dear cousin.

California is the state with the largest foreign-born population. It is home to about one-third of America's immigrants, a sizeable number of which are Filipinos who came here in search of better educational and economic opportunities. As immigrants, Filipinos have an obvious advantage over other Asian settlers like the Vietnamese, Chinese or Koreans. Because of the U.S. military presence in the Philippines until recently, Filipino immigrants are more likely than other Asian immigrants to be acculturated to American ways and to speak English. Filipinos are so well integrated in California that there is no Filipino counterpart to Koreatown or Chinatown. Though, according to Stefan, there are malls that make public announcements in *Tagalog* and sometimes, in other major Philippine dialects. And there are cities that are heavily populated with Filipinos. He should know. Before moving to San Francisco, he used to live in a nearby California city where the mayor is Filipino-American and some of the streets are named after Philippine heroes and flowers.

The Filipinos in San Francisco have come in several waves. The first wave arrived during the 1920s and 1930s when San Francisco was a stop between agricultural plantations in Hawaii and those in the

San Joaquin Valley. Since the Philippines was a possession of the U.S. at the time, Filipinos weren't affected by restrictive immigration laws; however, the U.S. did tightly control their passage to and from the mainland. This first wave of Filipinos, much like the Chinese community at the time, were a "bachelor society" since the U.S. restricted the passage of Filipina women and anti-miscegenation laws prohibited the men from marrying non-Filipinas.

The second wave of Filipino immigration came after World War II. Naturalized Filipino war veterans brought their wives and children to San Francisco, creating the first community of Filipino families here.

The third wave had been the largest. Poverty in the Philippines and declaration of the Marcos martial law in the 1970s fueled this wave and the enactment of an Immigration Act that puts priority to family reunification opened U.S. doors.

Stefan joked that the fourth wave was the members of the Philippines' third sex, the *baklas*, homosexuals. And that, he said, was how San Francisco became truly the gay and lesbian capital of America. *"Loca-loca,"* I told him when he made this declaration.

I had grown terribly fond of Stefan and there would be a sad void when he left. Even Auntie Soledad had learned to accept his flamboyant ways and his sickness, though I still occasionally caught her dousing our utensils, plates and glasses with boiling water. *"Mabuti na ang maingat, iha."* Better to be careful, she rationalized.

There was no denying Stefan's health was poor and his energy level was low, so I was hoping there wouldn't be any major opportunistic infections in store for him. The PCP seemed under control with his antiviral therapy, but his T-cell count continued to be low, so I continued to worry. I considered calling Vicente, his brother in Florida, but Stefan made me promise to keep his brother out of this unless he was really dying. "My dear, dear cousin," Stefan said when I brought the subject up one day, "I still have a long way to go so keep my heterosexual brother and his narrow-minded ways out of this."

I didn't know his brother very well but I knew enough to realize Stefan and his brother were both fiercely independent individuals who lived their own lives, not pushing their problems on each other, and they kept to themselves. For example, Stefan had not given Vicente a call since he arrived in New Jersey. I doubt if Vicente even knew of Stefan's whereabouts. I was deeply saddened by this, but that was their personal lives, and it was just that, personal. Stefan mentioned one night that "It's none of your/my business" was their unspoken rule. I suspected Stefan's homosexuality had a lot to do with that rule.

The Filipino term *Pagsasarili* comes to mind. *Pagsasarili* means to be a person in his own right. In spite of being dependent people because of our close-knit families, we also have an innate desire to strike out on our own. A true Filipino aims to achieve the principle of *Pagsasarili*, self-reliance, in order to overcome dependency, and therefore be responsible for himself. It is a vital goal of every Filipino to be himself, to be his own man, to make up his own mind, and to do his own thing. He may not say so in so many words. Sometimes he may not even be conscious of it, but it's always there, *Pagsasarili*. Perhaps we put so much value on this principle because it has been denied us for so long due to centuries of foreign domination.

A famous Filipino statesman said it all: "Only when we rise from the knees we have bent in beggary and stand beside the other nations of the world, not on crutches but on our own feet, thinking and speaking and acting as free men and as free citizens of a true republic in name and in fact...[only then] can we rightly claim to have achieved and deserved our independence."

Stefan and Vicente were great fans of this principle, but I was thinking that they were still missing the whole point of *Pagsasarili*. We try to develop in us this value of self-reliance so we can get along with others, *Pakikisama*. I would have very much liked to bring this up with Stefan but I felt a sense of *Takot*, fear of losing Stefan's trust and friendship.

er

The catered party was a success. I guessed correctly that the *Caldereta* would be a hit, so I had put aside a generous serving for Stefan and me to enjoy after the Broadway show. It was Stefan's birthday and after a sumptuous birthday brunch that Auntie Soledad prepared, Stefan and I took the PATH train to midtown Manhattan to see a matinee Broadway musical.

Stefan really looked pale. I was vacillating between going and canceling, but Stefan insisted we go, since the musical was one of his all-time favorites. Of course, most musicals fall in the category of "Stefan's favorite musicals." My golden boy was a walking encyclopedia of show tunes. So, in our vagabond shoes, we strayed towards New York, New York, all bundled up to brave the chilly weather.

I was a bit alarmed when we reached the theater, a good eight blocks from the PATH train station. Stefan was shivering.

"Are you sure about this? Maybe we should go back home?" I asked Stefan, giving him a very concerned look.

"No way, no fucking way," he answered in a tired but firm voice. When he resorted to using the F-word, there was no stopping him, so we continued into the theater. My worried eyes studied his pale profile as we took our expensive orchestra seats. The sky was the limit for my cousin's birthday.

Soon, the theater dimmed and Stefan whispered to me, "Thank you, Ligaya, for this wonderful birthday present." He held my hands as he added, "I love you, sister."

I felt something catch in my throat and tears in my eyes. I squinted at Stefan in the darkness and saw that he was crying too.

On stage, a funny revue was being performed. We both giggled through our tears as we quickly became absorbed in the show.

A few minutes before the end of Act One, Stefan leaned over and whispered, "I want to be cremated." I gasped loudly, which elicited a "Sssssh!" from someone behind me.

"What are you saying?" I whispered to Stefan.

"Ligaya, promise me, when I die, that you'll have my body cremated."

"Stefan…"

"Promise me, Ligaya. I hate the thought of my body being buried, decaying, being feasted on by worms. Uggh!"

"Sssssssh!" Hisses again from someone behind us. We both looked back and gave her the eye.

"Alright, I promise, dear cousin, but please, let's not talk about that, okay? So morbid! Hey, it's your birthday!" I whispered, giving him a playful *kurot*, pinch.

"*Aray! Masakit!*" he whispered, feigning hurt. I barely touched his skin when I did that.

"*Loca-loca*" I whispered back.

We watched the rest of Act One in silence. It was a phenomenal show. Act One ended with the cast doing a musical number that brought down the house.

The houselights came up to much applause. I turned to Stefan, who was slumped in his chair. My heart slammed into my throat. "Stefan! Oh no! Stefan!" I felt the eyes of the entire orchestra section on us. I dropped to my knees, cradling Stefan. *"Dios ko. Dios ko!"* My God, my God. I screamed.

"Ambulance. Someone call an ambulance!" the woman who had shushed us earlier yelled on top of her lungs. For a brief moment, I thought she sounded like Ethel Merman in "Gypsy", another favorite Broadway musical of Stefan.

The theater audience was being ushered back inside the theater for the second act when the ambulance finally arrived to take an unconscious Stefan to the hospital. *The show must go on*, I thought bitterly.

Stefan was taken to a New York hospital. While the doctors were looking in on him, I remembered to call home. Auntie Soledad picked up the phone on the second ring.

"Ligaya? Are you guys on your way home? Good, I'll heat up the *Caldereta* so it'll be ready when you get here," she babbled right away.

"Auntie Soledad!" I screamed into the phone.

CALDERETA
(Beef with Liver Sauce)

Ingredients:
    1 lb stewing beef, cut in serving pieces
    1/2 cup vinegar
    6 whole peppercorns, crushed

3 cloves garlic, crushed
3 tsp cooking oil
1 onion, minced
1 can tomato sauce
2 bay leaves
1 tsp sugar
2 tsp salt
1/2 cup hot water
1 red pepper, cut into strips
1 green pepper, cut into strips
1 tsp Tabasco sauce
1 can liver spread
1 can green peas
Garnishes
3 hardboiled eggs, sliced
1/4 cup stuffed olives

Marinate beef in a mixture of vinegar, peppercorn, and garlic for 1 to 2 hours. Drain. Brown in hot oil. Set aside.

Saute onions. Add the beef. Add tomato sauce, bay leaf, salt, sugar, and hot water. Cover and simmer for 1 to 2 hours or until beef is tender.

Add red and green pepper slices and tabasco sauce. Cover and simmer for additional 10 to 15 minutes. Add liver spread and green peas. Stir and cook another 5 to 10 minutes.

Garnish with sliced hardboiled eggs and stuffed olives.

Variations: Use lamb, goat meat, pork, or chicken in place of beef making sure you adjust cooking time accordingly.

Chapter Twenty-Three

SALABAT

Stefan had a seizure and went into a coma for three days. On the fourth day, he peacefully slipped out of his AIDS-ravaged body. The doctor told us later he could not determine the cause of the coma and, had Stefan lived, he would probably have had brain damage or paralysis. I stared at him in a discomfiting silence. He cleared his throat and excused himself, mumbling something about seeing another patient.

Glen, Stefan's Caucasian lover, flew in from California. Stefan had shown me some pictures of him so I recognized him right away when I met him in the hospital lobby. I noticed he had lost some weight. The photos showed a more filled-out Glen.

"He never lost his sense of humor," I told Glen as we waited in the reception area for the hospital to release Stefan's body. Glen started crying immediately. I laid my hand on his shaking back as he sobbed uncontrollably. The hospital receptionist gave me a nod. She too was misty eyed.

Stefan's body was cremated. I was under the impression the Catholic Church did not sanction this practice, but Auntie Soledad, who consulted our parish priest about this, had some startling news. In the late 1960s, The Vatican's Holy Office had lifted the prohibition forbidding Catholics from choosing cremation, although I'm sure a lot of bible-thumping Catholics still frown on it. The prohibition must have originally arisen from Catholics' belief in the Resurrection, the idea being that a cremated body cannot recompose itself to change into an eternal being come Resurrection time. That line of reasoning knitted my brow. After the body died it decomposed anyway, so what's the harm in speeding the process? And what about people who have died in fires? If cremation interferes with the Resurrection, then all those poor reformed "heretics" that were burned at the stake during the Inquisition must now be body-less in the kingdom above. Poor Joan of Arc must have died in vain.

I argued this point with Auntie Soledad. She glared at me and mumbled, "Atheist!" when my back was turned. I took no offense. I was sure she meant no harm.

The standard crematory practice, according to our priest, is to celebrate the funeral liturgies with the body and then take the body to the crematorium. Glen snorted at this when told but he conceded, respecting our Catholic traditions.

For the funeral liturgy, we rented a regular casket from the funeral home/crematorium, which was a shock to me. I assumed that a body undergoing cremation would not need a casket. After the funeral, Stefan was cremated and his ashes were placed in an urn paid for by Glen.

er

We were all gathered at my mother's apartment holding a simple memorial service for Stefan. The topic of discussion had shifted to what we were going to do with the urn. Glen said he wanted to scatter Stefan's remains into the Pacific Ocean from the Golden Gate Bridge. Some mourners had difficulty with this because the practice of scattering cremated remains into the sea or from the air onto the ground did not qualify as "reverent disposition" as the Catholic Church requires. Vicente, Stefan's brother from Florida, who showed up after the cremation rites, said he wanted to bury the urn just as one would bury a casket, in a cemetery. He explained this would offer a permanent place for loved ones to visit him.

"May I remind you, I am family!" he screamed at Glen. "Not some, some person he used to live with." Vicente could not bring himself to say lover, boyfriend, mate or companion. Glen glared back in silence.

As I listened to this, I thought, *Where were you, Stefan's brother, when he was sick?* But I kept this thought to myself. No matter how much this angered me, it didn't seem appropriate to attack a grieving sibling.

The purpose of this memorial service was for us to release our bottled-up feelings and share our grief with other loved ones, to begin the healing process. Well, we had been there only 20 minutes and we were already getting in each other's faces. *It's going to be a long night,* I said to myself as I excused myself to help Auntie Soledad with the food and drinks.

I left the living room, nodding at Aling Salvacion and some other mourner friends and neighbors. Glen and Vicente continued to glare at each other.

I found Auntie Soledad in the kitchen pouring *Salabat* into several coffee mugs. *Salabat* is tea made out of ginger, one of the world's oldest spices. Centuries ago, this spice was considered so valuable it was traded for gold and other precious metals. Today, it is cheap and readily available all over the world as fresh ginger root, powdered ginger, and minced ginger.

Depending on the recipe, ginger may be smashed, sliced into rounds, cut into strips, grated or pulverized. Mature ginger root has a robust flavor that can be used to reduce fish and gamey tastes. Young ginger adds a subtler flavor to a dish.

Salabat is a favorite Filipino beverage taken along with *bibingka* or *puto bumbong* on cold December mornings after *Simbang Gabi*, a series of early morning masses held each day of the week before Christmas. It is believed that drinking *Salabat* regularly improves and strengthens one's voice and vocal chords. It has thus become a favorite drink of opera singers and cabaret warblers in the Philippines.

That night, it served its purpose as a hot calming drink to keep the mourners warm and soothed.

Auntie Soledad grunted a hello when I entered the kitchen.

"So, how are those two doing?" she asked, referring to the conflict between Vicente and Glen. I rolled my eyes and shrugged my shoulders. Auntie Soledad shook her head as she placed rows of *Kutsinta*, rice cakes, onto a platter. "I wish your mother were here," she said.

e

Two hours later, I was sitting in the living room again, noticing the lack of conversation. This memorial service had been the quietest service I'd ever been to. At Ramoncito's, people talked to each other, exulting Ramoncito's good traits, regretting his early demise, expressing anger for the way he had died. Here people examined their hangnails, feigned watching TV, or explored mother's knick-knack collection for the third time.

"What is the matter with you people?" I finally shouted, shocking everyone into attention. "What difference does it make if Stefan died of...of AIDS. He's dead! A good human being died, someone we love very dearly, I'm sure. We need to talk about this! It's not something we can just sweep under the rug, you know?"

I looked around. Everyone had busied himself slurping the warm Salabat. I shook my head.

"*Ay,* excuse me, Ligaya." It was Aling Salvacion. "I don't know much about AIDS. How can I prevent myself from getting infected?"

Bless your heart, Aling Salvacion, I said silently. I told the crowd about the ways to prevent AIDS infection that I'd learned from the research I'd done since Stefan told me of his disease. Glen, who was an AIDS activist in San Francisco, chimed in often to expand and clarify what I'd said.

"...and you definitely cannot get AIDS from handshakes, hugs or just being around an infected person," he concluded.

"Is there a cure for AIDS?" a neighbor asked.

"No, so far there is no cure for AIDS nor is there a vaccine for HIV," Glen answered.

"What is HIV?" someone else asked.

"HIV is the virus that causes AIDS. When someone becomes infected with HIV, the virus attacks that person's immune system. A person develops AIDS when his immune system becomes so damaged it can no longer fight off disease and opportunistic infections."

"Do you have AIDS?" Vicente asked Glen, hesitantly.

Glen shook his head. "No, but I am HIV positive. I have what is called Category 1 HIV disease. I am asymptomatic, meaning symptom-free. I am not suffering from any opportunistic diseases like pneumonia or Kaposi's sarcoma and my blood count is still in the healthy range. I consider myself a healthy person and, with God's help and the anti-viral drugs I am taking, I may just outlive a lot of you folks."

This drew a weak chuckle from the listening crowd. Weak but good enough to melt the ice.

"Isn't AIDS a gay disease?" Auntie Soledad chimed in. I smiled at her. She knew that AIDS affected heterosexuals too, but she asked it for the benefit of the others in the room.

"No, no," Glen answered, shaking his head. "AIDS can infect anyone - white, brown, straight, gay, old, young. If you think your family members need not worry about AIDS, you are gravely mistaken."

And through the night this went on until the last mourner left, until the last question about AIDS was answered, until only Vicente, Glen and I were left in the living room lit by the three-tiered *Capiz* chandelier. Auntie Soledad had excused herself earlier, yawning. I told her I'd take care of cleaning up for which she nodded gratefully. My eyes focused on Stefan's remains in the urn on the table.

"Excuse me, Ligaya, but believe it or not, I loved my brother very much. He was my kid brother, for God's sake!" I lifted my face. Vicente was staring directly at me. *Had he been staring at me for a long time?*

"But we didn't know. I didn't know. I am so heartbroken. Our mother and father and my sisters are, too. I spoke with them this morning and they are totally devastated. But, you know, they're also angry with Stefan for keeping this disease to himself, for not sharing this with us. As his family, we had a right to know. We should have been allowed to help him!"

I blinked. I hadn't seen this coming.

"I guess this is what happens when you take privacy to extremes. We both did, I guess. Even intelligent people can be incredibly, stupidly pig-headed at times. Stefan and I are both guilty of that. I knew of his homosexuality a long time ago, but I never told him. I figured his business is his business. I worried when this AIDS epidemic hit America. But what could I do? He had his own life, which he guarded with such fierceness, such fierceness. Yes, I hate to admit, but a part of me is mad as hell at Stefan for keeping this from us. But at the same time, I can understand his fear of telling us."

He looked at Glen. "I'm sorry for what I said earlier. I guess with Stefan the way that he was, being family just wasn't enough anymore."

Glen nodded but stayed in his seat across from him.

"And oh, Glen, you have my permission—my family's permission—to bring Stefan's remains to San Francisco. I'm sure he would like that a lot." Glen smiled at him.

There was respectful silence after that. It was broken only by the noisy slurping of the warm, soothing *Salabat*.

SALABAT
(Ginger Tea)

Ingredients:
1 inch slice (about 1-1/2 inch thick) fresh ginger root, peeled and crushed.
4 cups water
4 tbsp brown sugar

Bring all ingredients to a boil. Lower heat and simmer for about 10 minutes. The longer it cooks, the stronger the ginger flavor.

Remove ginger slice before serving. Serve hot.

Variations: Do not add sugar. Serve ginger tea with honey or your preferred sweetener.

Chapter Twenty-Four

RELLENONG ALIMANGO

For sheer aerial awe, I recommend flying into the San Francisco airport on a sunny, fog-free day. As I approached the city, I became mesmerized by the spectacular view of the Golden Gate Bridge connecting San Francisco to the mainland. We flew almost to the end of the bay, which afforded me a bird's-eye view of the entire city. We turned, descended, and right at the moment I thought we would surely make an emergency water landing, I felt the satisfying connection of pavement to airplane wheels. As the plane slowed to a stop, I realized I had landed in perhaps the world's most romantic city. Of course, I had been told that a clear San Francisco day is an extreme rarity. I was terribly lucky, I guess.

Walking through the busy airport terminal, I noticed there were many Filipino employees in the airport. Some of them acknowledged me by shouting out, *"Hoy Kumusta?"*, Hey how are you? Others greeted me with the "eyebrow talk." It is a unique Filipino way of greeting others using the eyebrows. Eye contact is established and instantly both eyebrows are raised up and brought down. It is a signal of recognition. A smile usually accompanies it, becoming a warm friendly "hello" without words.

I told Glen of this unique Filipino greeting and the next thing I knew, he was raising his brows at a Filipina baggage checker and smiling. The Filipina covered her mouth as she giggled. A Westerner who makes an effort to 'get into' the Filipino culture is much appreciated.

Glen had invited me to spend a few days in San Francisco to participate in a memorial service he had planned for Stefan. A young Filipina traveling alone with a Caucasian man? Auntie Soledad would have normally had a fit, but since she knew Glen was gay, she relented.

"I will be in safe hands, Auntie Soledad. Don't worry," I told her. She nodded in agreement, ludicrously limping her wrist. I glared at her. Auntie Soledad was not really homophobic, she's just a plain, well-meaning lunatic. I hope she's not taphephobic because sometimes, I felt like burying her alive. Oops! My spelling bee slip is showing again!

I had always dreamed of visiting San Francisco. Everything about the city fascinated me: the Golden Gate Bridge, the cable cars, Fisherman's Wharf, its very diverse and colorful denizens. On our taxi ride to Glen's apartment in the Twin Peaks area, I got a preview of these attractions. For a moment I forgot why I was there until the taxicab made a precarious turn and a clanking sound inside my hand-carry bag reminded me I was transporting Stefan's urn. I held the bag tightly. The interior of a cab was not exactly where we wanted to scatter his ashes.

Glen and his friends chartered a yacht for the ash-scattering ceremony. "Party" was a more fitting word to describe it actually. There was a disc jockey on board playing dance music throughout the sail to the Golden Gate Bridge where Stefan's ashes would be scattered.

"Where we went to on our first date," Glen told me. "It was one of those magical full moon evenings. Stefan and I crossed the Golden Gate Bridge on foot. We had an amazing view of the whole San Francisco Bay Area, sparkling like multi-colored jewels."

Glen introduced me to his friends as Stefan's Filipina cousin. *Like Stefan's not a Filipino*, I wanted to interject but decided they might not know. With his altered eyes and nose, hazel contact lenses, and dyed light brown hair, Stefan had managed to Westernize his appearance enough that some people might not even know he was Filipino. I felt neither sad nor revolted. It was more like, more power to you, Stefan! He went for and got what he wanted. Not many people, dead or alive, had done that.

Glen and Stefan's friends were a mixed lot. For my benefit, Glen referred to each of them as gay, lesbian, transsexual, transgendered, or intersexed. I really couldn't tell nor differentiate, especially the transsexuals and the transgendered ones. They all looked like super models if you ask me. For a brief moment, I regretted not getting the rhinoplasty.

There was an assortment of food aboard the yacht: sandwiches, cheeses, fruits, crackers and toasts, and black caviar. One serving plate had roasted eggplant hummus while another featured chicken and salmon pates. There was a bar where guests could choose from vodka, whisky, brandy, wine, cocktails, or soft drinks. But no Filipino food, I noticed sadly.

I should have prepared something! I thought with a pang of guilt. *Stefan would have liked that.* I reflected as I bit into a cracker smothered with liver pate.

"Hello," said someone from behind me. I turned around. *Oh, one of the male model types. Gorgeous but not available,* my naughty mind proclaimed.

"Hello," I said back while wiping my mouth with a napkin.

"You must be Ligaya. I'm Paul," he said, offering a hand.

"Yes, I am. Hi, Paul." Paul had gorgeous blue eyes. I felt guilty just admiring them. Technically, I was still in mourning. *And Ramoncito still owned my heart,* I reminded myself. *And he was gay, anyway,* I consoled myself.

"I'm Glen's cousin." *Oh, another gay cousin,* I thought to myself as I smiled back.

"Are you—"

"Here we are, boys and girls! Here we are!" A booming, shrieking voice interrupted Paul. We had arrived beneath the Golden Gate Bridge, Stefan's final destination.

Paul stood by my side. I chewed the rest of the cracker as daintily as I could. *Why am I acting like an idiot?* I asked myself. The answer smiled at me: *Boy, what a nice set of teeth, too. Sayang.* Too bad.

Glen and a friend dressed like a nun stood at the rail at a right angle to the wind to prevent the ashes they were about to scatter from flying straight back at them and us. Glen raised the urn for everyone to see. I felt a lump in my throat and a block of lead in my chest. My hands tightened into fists. *Oh Stefan!*

"Are you okay?" Paul whispered in my ear.

I nodded but I knew tears were already springing in my eyes. He put his arms around me. I didn't budge; it felt good, comforting.

Glen tipped the urn into the wind, launching a long stream of gray particles.

"*Adios,* our dear, dear, Stefan," said the gay in a nun's outfit. "And don't you dare come back! Don't you dare!" he added, screaming. But of course, Stefan did. A back-wind forced bits of him to spray onto the mourners, causing pandemonium. There was much crying, giggling, and screaming as the boat sailed back to the San Francisco shore.

"So you've already met my straight cousin," Glen said as he approached us after the ceremony.

Straight? my face asked.

"Ligaya, don't look so surprised," Glen said, reading my face. "There is a smattering of straight allies in this boat, too. One of which is my cousin here, Paul."

Paul, Glen filled me in, was new to the Bay Area. He held a master's degree in electrical engineering from the University of Michigan and had recently accepted a teaching post at UC Berkeley. Both Glen and Paul came from a small town in Michigan which was, as Glen put it, seriously lacking in flavor—a homogeneous sea of blond, blue-eyed, light-complexioned Christians for as far as your eyes could see, he joked. I think I heard Stefan laugh but realized it was just the wind.

Lights were springing to life as we approached the San Francisco shore. The city glowed red, gold, and silver through its sinuous layers of fog. The yacht met the landing noisily but everyone on the boat was quiet. There was an immense sadness in the air as if we all had just realized that the lights were turned on signaling the end of a great party. The fun was over. A feeling of panic seized me. *What do I do now?* With Stefan's ashes gone, I suddenly felt no connection with these people anymore. It was a foolish feeling of course. These people knew and loved Stefan. That made me one of them, that made me part of this family. I glanced at Glen, who was standing beside me, and smiled gratefully. He smiled back and pressed his hand in mine. Paul, who was pressed against the rail watching the glorious city skyline, looked back and waved at us. Or maybe, waved just at me. I didn't know for sure.

et

That night, I learned a new American expression. To repay Glen's hospitality and to make-up for my horrible error in judgment about Paul, I offered to cook dinner for them. On our way back to Glen's apartment, we passed by Fisherman's Wharf where I bought four Dungeness crabs. They were the perfect main ingredient for the dish I planned to make: *Rellenong Alimango*, stuffed crab.

When I presented them with the cooked dish a few hours later, Paul took one look and asked me if I really made them. I nodded, face still pink from my previous gaffe at the yacht.

"Get out of here!" he exclaimed. *Huh?!*

My pink hue deepened as I retreated to the kitchen with the tray. Glen jumped up to follow me. He told me in the kitchen what the expression means. By the time I sat down to dinner with them, my complexion had turned to lobster-red.

Please Lord, no more embarrassing gaffes tonight, I prayed as I showed them how to tear into the luscious crab shell dish.

The night went perfectly without a further gaffe. But I should have expected it. After all, how can one go really wrong with *Rellenong Alimango* served with a side dish of Rice-A-Roni, the San Francisco treat?

RELLENONG ALIMANGO
(Stuffed Crabs)

Ingredients:
    4 medium sized Dungeness crabs
    6-8 cups water
    3 tbsp salt
    2 cloves garlic, minced
    1 medium onion, minced
    1/2 cup green bell pepper, chopped
    1 cup tomato, chopped
    2 cups plus 2 tbsp vegetable oil
    1 tbsp patis (fish sauce)
    1 tsp sugar
    1/2 tsp black pepper
    1 small box raisins
    2 green onions, chopped
    2 eggs
    1-1/2 cups dried breadcrumbs
    frozen crabmeat (if meat from crabs is not enough)

Wash the crabs. Put them in a large pot and add water and 2-1/2 tbsp of salt. Cover and bring to a boil. Lower the heat and simmer for 15 minutes or until shells turn red. Drain and let cool.

When cool enough to handle, remove the crabmeat from the shells. Clean and save the body shell for stuffing later.

In a skillet, sautee the garlic, onions, bell peppers and tomatoes in 2 tsp of oil. Add the crabmeat, rest of salt, fish sauce, sugar, pepper, raisins and green onions. Add frozen crabmeat if needed. Sautee for 3 to 5 minutes. Remove from heat and allow to cool.

Fill the crab shells with the crab mixture, mounding it slightly in the center. Beat the eggs. Add the breadcrumbs. Sprinkle the mixture over the top, spreading to fully cover the top.

Heat the remaining 2 cups of oil in a deep fryer pan or wok. Fry the stuffed shells, shell side down. Occasionally spoon the hot oil over the exposed stuffing. Cook until golden brown. Drain on paper towels and serve.

Chapter Twenty Five

EMBUTIDO

On my last day in San Francisco, Glen and Paul showed me more of the city's attractions: the Coit Tower, Golden Gate Park, the Palace of Fine Arts, Japantown. The whirlwind tour was capped with a dinner at a Filipino restaurant.

"How on earth did you find this place?" I asked Glen.

"Stefan, he would take me here sometimes—" he began.

"Of course. Of course! I'm sorry!" I interrupted, immediately reddening. I had reddened so many times recently that I had become an expert on how to acquire a perfect blush in one easy step: not thinking before opening my big mouth! Of course, it didn't help that I could feel Paul's eyes on me all the time. Well, not ALL the time. Right now, his eyes were squinting at the restaurant's name, trying to read it correctly: *Tomasita's Turo-Turo*.

"*Too-roh - too-roh,*" I told him. "In English, literally point-point," I added, demonstrating the way to do it, to make my point.

Turo-Turo is the generic term in the Philippines for any eatery where the entire menu for the day is spread out in pots and pans or bowls and platters behind a glass-paneled counter for customers to look at and choose what they want to eat. The important part is that choosing is always done by pointing to the desired dish. You don't need to speak the *Tagalog* language to order. Just point-point at the food you want to order. The Filipino *Turo-Turo* is considered to be the forerunner of today's modern fast food stalls.

We entered the *Turo-Turo* and all eyes were on us. It must have seemed strange, a Filipina walking in with two blond, blue-eyed Caucasians. I nodded hello as we passed by diners, all Asians, mostly Filipinos. They nodded back, smiling mouths filled with food. *Dios mio, ang tsismis!* Oh dear, the gossip! I thought to myself, remembering our predilection for that favorite Filipino pastime. I shrugged and thought, *It's not like I'm dating either of them.*

Is there any dating etiquette for Western men dating Filipinas? There isn't a "Dating 101 Handbook" or anything but yes, there are some unspoken rules:

- Filipinas expect that the man will always pay, even when the date was at the girl's invitation. In a group date, she expects the boys to split the bill among themselves.
- Some Filipinas bring a chaperon on a date. The chaperon is usually a sister, a girl friend, a cousin, or even an aunt. The chaperon is almost always a girl, though in some cases, a male chaperon materializes. However, Filipinas as a whole are more and more aware that uninvited guests or chaperons catch Americans off guard.
- If the woman still lives with her parents, a curfew is set for her. It is wise to ask the woman her curfew time to make sure she is home on time.
- Again, if the woman is still living with her parents, the woman must usually ask for permission from them to go out. The permission is usually granted after much detailed questioning: where she is going, with whom, what time will she be brought back? For first dates, the parents need to know a bit of the man's background: name of his parents, what he does for a living, how old he is.
- Do not call your Filipina date's parents by their first names. It shows a lack of respect. Refer to them as Mr. and Mrs. So-and-so. This is actually a blessing in disguise because many Filipino first names are hard to pronounce for Westerners. It's much easier to say "Mr. And Mrs. Cruz" then to say "Policarpio and Bonifacio."
- If the man has a gift for the woman, he shouldn't expect the woman to open the gift in front of him. It is considered bad form to open gifts in public. Opening presents in front of the giver implies that the recipient is avaricious, concerned with the material value of the gift rather than the act of giving. The woman will usually put the gift aside. Do not be offended by this. The next time you meet, "Miss Non-Material Girl" will verbally thank you again. This time she will identify the item.
- If the date progresses to a higher level of bonding, please remember her birthday and Valentine's Day. These are very important dates to Filipinas.

- If it is a dinner date, don't act surprised if the woman leaves some food on her plate. This is done to indicate she's been amply fed and is satiated.
- Kissing on the first date is considered taboo, though everyone seems to ignore this except on bad blind dates.

Why should Westerners date Filipinas anyway? Here are some reasons. I prepared them ala David Letterman's Top 10. Take them with a grain of salt, or a bowl of rice.

10. Filipinas are affectionate, romantic, and thoughtful.
9. Filipinas are less materialistic than Western women. Well, at least they put family first before money.
8. Filipinas are religious. A bit of spirituality in a relationship always helps.
7. Filipinas are sympathetic, tolerant and supportive. You can be sure there will always be an ear to listen to your grievances during those trying days of whine and (bad) bosses.
6. Filipinas have flexible personalities. They can adapt to situations as quickly as a chameleon can change colors.
5. Filipinas are excellent homekeepers. They are all Martha Stewarts in their own right.
4. Filipinas believe in a one-man, one-woman relationship. This monogamous attitude is a result of their usually conservative nature.
3. Filipinas are generally educated. A high percentage have college degrees. Most speak and write English.
2. Filipinas hold their partners or providers in the family in high esteem. There is great respect and gratitude for the other half, the better half.

And the number one reason? We could wax eloquent here on the best and finest traits of Filipinas but I think this borrowed quote says it best:

"They're beautiful…that's why I married one"
—a Western guy

To be fair, I want to include some reasons why a Filipina might want to date a Westerner. Consider this co-authored by Stefan because we did beat this subject to a pulp one rainy, gossipy afternoon.

10. There are more Western men in America than Filipino men. That is a fact, a practical one.

9. The white skin of the Western man is relatively attractive. It just is, consider that a compliment.

8. The opportunity to become equal in all aspects of life. This contrasts with the machismo and patriarchal style of most Filipino men. To a Filipina who wants social fairness, this is a very attractive reason to date the more liberal Western man.

7. It is a means of access to a more advanced, less tough life. Filipinas who want a more sophisticated, less bumpy ride should heed this reason.

6. Dating a Western man enables a Filipina to exercise freedom of choice. Divorce? You're more likely to get one from a Western man than a Filipino man.

5. To find a less jealous man. Filipino men can get green-eyed over the slightest things. They are typically possessive by nature.

4. To expand your economic status. This, of course, is conditional on the relationship having developed from dating to marriage or cohabitation. Owning a second home, for example, is one way a Filipina can inflate her financial status. And it is common knowledge that more Westerners have a preference for a second home.

3. To find someone who is a more open-minded and liberal thinker. There is nothing more exhilarating to a Filipina than a conversation that is balanced and unbiased.

2. The possibility of multi-racial, mixed complexion babies. Nancy Kwan. France Nguyen. Enough said.

And the number one reason? To find happiness and bliss through L-O-V-E, of course! Hey, as Stefan once said, diversity sometimes makes the heart grow fonder.

et

Without even consulting each other, we took a *Turo-Turo* table farthest from most of the diners. Still, a lot of eyes followed us as we placed our coats on the backs of the chairs and proceeded to the glass-paneled counter to make our Point-Point choices. I could hardly breathe. Paul was so close I could smell his pleasant mild cologne.

There were many Filipino dishes to choose from. There was pork *adobo*, chicken *adobo*, two kinds of *pancit*, two kinds of *lumpia*, *arroz caldo*, and a variety of Philippine desserts like *sans rival* and *kutsinta*.

I told Glen and Paul what each one was called, what each dish's main ingredients were, what each food's taste might be like. It was exhilarating. I found myself remembering my mother's cooking lessons many, many summers ago in the Philippines as I expounded on the unique vinegary-garlicky-peppery flavor of our *adobos*, on the long-life aspect of our *pancit*, on the crunchiness of the fried *lumpia*, on the decadent sweetness of the *sans rival*. I was unstoppable until we reached the end of the glass-paneled counter. I licked my dry lips. I was trembling. My throat hurt. The Filipina behind the counter had an amused and admiring look. Glen and Paul were grinning. Paul uttered, "Wow!" I blushed once more. Paul, he of the dreamer's blue eyes and astonishing freshness of lips, had had quite an effect on me already. *Ramoncito, please forgive me.*

We ended up ordering most of the dishes. After that terribly compelling discourse on Filipino food, how could we not?

In the middle of our dinner, one of the Filipina clerks approached with a tray. She softly said, "Here, compliments of the house." She placed the tray in the only space that wasn't already taken by our Point-Point orders. *"Bagong luto,"* she shyly explained to me. Fresh off the stove, so it wasn't on display yet.

"Wow, what is that?" Paul asked.

"This is called *Embutido*, the Philippine version of the American meatloaf," I answered while quickly reviewing in my mind, step-by-step, how this dish was prepared.

"Oh, that I can relate to," Paul said, nodding his head.

"Yeah, we both grew up on meatloaf!" Glen added.

"I remember Mother serving meatloaf every Thursday. It always came with a side of lime jello with suspended fruit."

"That's right! Meatloaf is such a comfort food now. Makes me think of home."

Paul bit in and said, "Wow! I think I'm in love with meatloaf!" He looked at me with those big, blue eyes and gave me that boyish grin.

EMBUTIDO
Beef or Pork Meatloaf

Ingredients:
 2 lbs ground pork or beef
 1 cup breadcrumbs, soaked in 1/2 cup milk
 1 chorizo Bilbao, Spanish sausage
 1-1/2 tbsp sweet pickle relish
 1 small onion, finely minced
 1/4 cup raisins
 salt and pepper to taste
 2 eggs, hardboiled and quartered
 2 tbsp softened butter

Sauce:
 1 cup chicken broth
 1 small can of liver spread
 1 small can of tomato sauce
 3 tbsp catsup
 1 tbsp cornstarch dissolved in 2 tbsp water

Combine all ingredients except eggs and butter.

Butter the center of a piece of heavy-duty aluminum foil, about 15 inches long. Spread mixture on the foil making a rectangle abut 6" x 10" or bigger. Arrange eggs in a row at the center, lengthwise. Roll meat around eggs and wrap with the foil sealing the edges securely.

Bake in a pan for 1 to 1-1/2 hours. Let cool for 15 to 20 minutes before unwrapping. Slice crosswise.

To make the sauce:

Mix together all ingredients except for the cornstarch and water mixture in a sauce pan and simmer for 5 to 10 minutes. Thicken with the cornstarch and water mixture.

To serve *Embutido*:

Arrange the slices on a serving platter. Pour sauce on top.

EPILOGUE

It is summer again. It is hard to believe that I've been in America for six years. I am in my bathroom in New Jersey, freshly bathed, freshly lotioned. It feels good. Even at this ungodly hour of six in the morning, the promise of a sweltering day is already making me sweat.

I look at myself in the mirror. I remember a summer of long ago spent in a bathroom not quite as comfortable as this, flexing and squeezing my tiny 13-year-old breasts, forcing them into full womanhood. I also remember that same summer, in an aromatic kitchen learning to cook one Filipino dish after another under my mother's sharp-eyed, sharp-tongued tutelage. I can't help a smile when I reflect on the valuable lessons I learned that summer. There are some things in life you can't hurry. There are some things in life that take time to grow, take time to master.

Some things in life we must wait for, simply because waiting makes it more worthwhile. And as I say goodbye to you, faithful readers, who have been following my adventures here in America and hopefully have been trying out some of the recipes as well, I want to tell you about two more of those just-can't-hurry-in-life instances.

Today I am becoming a naturalized American citizen. Naturalization is one of those processes you can't hurry. To become a citizen or to be naturalized, a person must meet certain requirements. I am proud to say I have met them all.

I am over 18 years old. I have lived in America as a legal resident for at least 5 years. I am of good moral character (you can ask my mother, Auntie Soledad, my relatives, my friends and my food-catering customers). I am able to speak, read, write and understand basic English (you're reading this aren't you?). I have a basic knowledge and understanding of American history, government, and the Constitution of the United States (I'm prepared to take a pop quiz anytime!). And I am willing to take an oath of allegiance to the United States of America.

The latter I'm doing symbolically this morning in a mass swearing-in ceremony; that is why I am up so early. The ceremony takes place in Newark, New Jersey at nine this morning. I heard that close to a thousand new citizens will be sworn in.

I chose a simple, light blue dress with a matching jacket for the occasion. Earlier, Mother suggested I wear a *terno*, our Filipina national costume. I rolled my eyes and let her idiotic idea go in one ear and out the other. As I have matured, I have learned to handle my mother that way. I give her the benefit of the doubt and always the unconditional love she should expect from her daughter. Since her return from the Philippines, we have related much better. I realize she is like a bee, who merely wants to smell my skin but usually ends up buzzing and stinging me instead. A bee, but a well-meaning bee.

Bzzzzzz, buzzes Mother now as she rushes all of us to get ready. Uncle Peter, who came back and re-married Auntie Soledad (isn't that wonderful?), is driving all of us to Newark in his newly purchased SUV.

"Congratulations, Ligaya. You are now a *gringa!*" he says when I finally emerge from my room. "Here," he adds, handling me a wrapped gift.

"Oh, Uncle Peter, you shouldn't have!" I say, calling him by the name that makes Auntie Soledad brim with tears.

"Open it," he says. I hesitate, remembering our belief about opening gifts in front of the giver.

"*Uy, American ka na,* so it's okay!" Auntie Soledad teases, reminding me that I will be a full-fledged American citizen in a few hours.

I shrug and start tearing at the wrapper. It's an American flag!

"Oh, Uncle Peter, this is so wonderful! Thank you," I exclaim. I am truly touched by the gift. I look around. Everyone else is misty-eyed. There's a lot of hugging and re-touching of smudged eye make-up (among the ladies). Then mother, the loving queen bee, buzzes us off to the waiting van.

er

The Newark, New Jersey auditorium is packed. Those who are to be sworn in occupy the orchestra section and their guests, relatives and friends, are seated in the balcony. I crane my neck, look out into the crowd, and see that my relatives and friends have managed to get front row balcony seats. *Good*, I say, as I wave at them. They all wave back.

I sit beside an Asian woman who must be in her sixties. I smile at her. She returns a nervous, toothless grin. She points at me and asks, "Filipino?"

I nod. "You?" I ask back.

"Korean," she says proudly. "But American soon!" she adds.

"Yes, yes!" I grin.

"Congratulations," she says, tapping my hand. She wears a bracelet adorned with an American flag charm.

"Same to you," I say back, putting another hand on top of her hand.

We both sit back, thinking the same thing, I'm sure: the long road to getting here. The many steps we took to get to the end of that road.

First was the submission of the naturalization application form with all its necessary requirements and attachments such as police reports, passport photos, and a check for the filing fee.

Second was the multiple-choice examination, which included questions about US history, government, and English proficiency. In the packet I received from the immigration office when I requested the naturalization form was a study guide with a list of possible test questions. I spent so many nights going through that list that I started dreaming about it: What do the stripes on the U.S. flag represent? What is the name of the form of government used in the U.S.? What are the three branches of the U.S. government and the function of each? What special name is given to the first ten amendments to the U.S. Constitution and what are some of the special rights granted by these amendments? How many members are there in the U.S. House of Representatives and in the U.S. Senate? How long is each of their terms of office? Who are the U.S. senators from your state? Who is the Secretary of State? Where is the capital of your state? Who is the governor of your state? I often woke up from these dreams in a cold sweat but with a better knowledge of American history and government.

Step three was the actual citizenship interview with an immigration officer. The experience was akin to that of someone in the waiting room of a hospital's emergency room: you see a lot of anxious-looking patients waiting to be examined, which makes you sweaty with worry as well. You get called, you stand and nervously follow the rigid-looking nurse to a cold examination room where you're asked to strip and put on a thin piece of paper gown. You sit on the cold, metallic bed and wait for the doctor. He comes in, sticks a thermometer in your mouth, and presses a stethoscope to your chest. He hits your knee with a hammer and, with a cheesy grin, pronounces you in perfect health.

It's okay to be nervous about taking this test. I read the study guide, answered the sample questions, and took several practice exams with a relative or a friend to prepare myself. I hoped to pass it the first time. I heard horror stories about impatient INS officials who are quick to fail someone who doesn't understand a question the first time it's asked, but I know of no one who has actually experienced this, so…

Step four was awaiting immigration approval and the date for the naturalization ceremony. I knew it could be a long wait or a mere week's wait. I tried to not constantly think about it and get on with my American life. That official-looking brown envelope came in the mail eventually. I knew the moment that I opened the letter I had won the prize.

The fifth and final step is the swearing-in ceremony. This involves taking an oath of allegiance to the United States, an oath to uphold the U.S. constitution and an oath to renounce citizenship of all other countries.

er

The Korean woman and I and hundreds of other new citizens around us are crying as we recite the Pledge of Allegiance. I choke on my pledge to renounce the country of my birth, yet after the certificate of naturalization is given to me, I feel the weight lifted. The cheers that fill the auditorium when all of us become US citizens reverberate throughout the building. When I look at the flag, it seems much more red, white, and blue than before.

I turn around and look up at the balcony section. I wave wildly at my relatives and friends who wave wildly back.

There's my mother, who is instrumental in my being here in the first place. My mother who gave me things that don't often happen in human experience: grief, unconditional love, and the power to create endless wondrous dishes.

There's Auntie Soledad, a pillar of strength for everyone. She has showed a lot of courage and grace and, may I add, open-mindedness under pressure. With Stefan's health and death, with her ill-fated marriage to Peter, with whatever life throws at her.

Then there's Peter, uncle to me now, a familiar kind face in our family. Living proof that a Western partner is as wonderful as any partner.

Aling Salvacion, simply the best neighbor in the world. Less nosy now than before, but still a lousy mahjong player.

And Maria! Yes, my dear sister who at this very moment is throwing me a kiss! Yes, she's here on a tourist visa to be with me on this special day. Her plane ticket cost my mother the equivalent of a *Jeepney* driver's annual salary, but that's not an issue between adoring mothers and daughters. Not anymore.

There is an empty seat between Maria and Mother. I imagine Stefan sitting on it, waving a sequined American flag as he celebrates my special red, white and blue day. I miss Stefan so.

And there at the end of this line is someone who is now a great part of my life as well. Paul! He is grinning as he excitedly waves at me a bouquet of red roses artfully tied with white and blue ribbons.

I wave back with my certificate of naturalization. He mouths, "I. Love. You."

There are some things in life you can't hurry. Another one of them is the process of falling in love…again.

Yes, I am in love again but it took some time. Paul and I have a long-distance relationship. He lives in San Francisco and teaches at UC Berkeley. I live in Jersey City and do my food catering business all over the New York-New Jersey area. We are together whenever possible: long holiday weekends, vacations, and summertime because his classes are out. Oh, it is a far from perfect arrangement. There are so many hurdles, so many differences: cultural, religious, social, ideological. But through all this, Paul and I somehow manage. Love manages to triumph.

I have also managed to teach Paul a thing or two about Filipino foods. I am not as good a teacher as my mother, but I think I did well with Paul. One evening while visiting him in San Francisco, he surprised me when he prepared an all-Filipino dinner, all by himself! *Lumpia* for starters, rice and *Rellenong Manok* for the main course, and *sans rival* for dessert. After dinner, over coffee, he proposed. How could I say no to someone who single-handedly managed to prepare an entire Filipino meal from appetizer to dessert?

We have set a wedding date, January 7, Paul's birthday. It is only a few months from now and a few years from when I fell in love with Ramoncito, who still holds, and will always hold, a special place in my heart. Paul and I visited his grave at the Bayonne cemetery. I say the meeting went well between these two men in my life. Oh yes, the third man, Pedring, is now married with kids. He sent me a card congratulating me on my citizenship. He also asked me if I could be the godparent to one of his kids. I will say yes to that, of course, even if it will be done by proxy.

My family, friends, and I manage to hedge and elbow our way out of the crowded auditorium with just one minor incident: a new American steps on my right shoe as he rushes out of the hall. He doesn't even bother to look back and apologize despite my loud *Aray!* Ouch. I glare at his retreating behind. *From green card holder to Yankee Doodle asshole,* I mumble to myself.

Outside, the late morning air is still clear and there is a surprisingly cool breeze. I take in a breath of air. It is good. It smells of scented summer trees, of mesquite charcoals being lit for barbecue. It smells of the land I now love.

Today, after the swearing in ceremony, Paul, the rest of my friends and family, and I are heading back to my mother's apartment for a good old American barbecue. My mother initially frowned at the idea. "Not really my bowl of rice," she said but, after much cajoling, she relented. It is my special red, white, and blue day after all. An American-style barbecue seems fitting. Paul and Peter are taking over the barbecue grill to make barbecued baby back ribs, chicken on spits, and grilled hamburgers.

Pardon?

You want the recipe for hamburgers?

Get outta here!

F
ESC

DATE DUE

GAYLORD   PRINTED IN U.S.A.

Lake Washington High School
Library
12033 NE 80th Street
Kirkland, WA 98033

Printed in the United States
108406LV00003B/315/A

9 781403 388834